This book is dedicated to every person who has the guts to be a dealer. I respect your courage, your faith, and the tremendous commitment you've made.

I also want to thank everyone at Joe Verde Sales and Management Training, Inc., for making our company the best training organization in the world.

A Dealer's Guide To Recovery And Growth In Today's Market

A step-by-step guide
for every dealer and management team
that guarantees a fast recovery today and
continued growth, year after year.

For Dealers and Managers

Joe Verde

Books by Joe Verde

- Top 7 Revenue & Profit Sources In Your Dealership
- How To Sell A Car & Close The Sale Today
- Earn Over $100,000 Selling Cars – Every Year
- 38 Hot Tips On Selling More Cars In Today's Market
- 4 Secrets Separate You From Your Competition In Sales!
- 10 Critical Skills Every Automotive Sales Manager Needs
- Manage Your Career In Sales – Goal Setting For Salespeople
- A Dealer's Guide To Recovery And Growth In Today's Market

A Dealer's Guide To Recovery And Growth In Today's Market

Joe Verde

Copyright © 2016 by Joe Verde – 9th Edition

ISBN 978-1-60530-842-5

Inquiries should be addressed to Permissions Department, Joe Verde Sales & Management Training, Inc., 27125 Calle Arroyo, San Juan Capistrano, California 92675-2753.

JoeVerde.com – JVTN.com

Toll Free: (800) 445-6217 • International: (949) 489-3780

Update

The car business didn't end when the recession hit and we didn't lose any manufacturers. If you're reading this, congratulations, you also survived the worst recession in decades and you did it by adapting and adjusting to the emergencies you had to deal with.

Now it's time to start growing.

You and your dealership have survived, started back on the road to recovery, or you've recovered completely, and now it's time to focus on growth. However, too many people confuse the word 'growth' with having a good year. Sure, you want to have a good year every year, but a good year is just that, a good year in which you probably sold a bunch of cars and made good money.

But there's only one definition of growth:
Having a record year, every year.

For that to happen, you have to learn how to improve the processes that generate growth, and improve the skills of the people responsible to follow your processes. That old saying is correct, "You can't keep doing what you've always done and grow." Growth requires continuous improvement in the key areas I cover in this book.

Can you really grow in today's new economy?

Absolutely, because growth is a process, and that's what this book is about. Follow these directions step-by-step, and you'll fully recover to your previous levels in units, gross and net profit. As soon as that happens, you can start to grow again or start to grow for the very first time.

Read this book today and get ready to...

Have Your Best Year Ever!

"Be courageous. I have seen many depressions in business.
America has always emerged from these stronger and more prosperous.
Be brave as your fathers before you. Have faith! Go forward!"
– Thomas A. Edison

CONTENTS

FOREWORD

"One way or the other..."

One of life's greatest options is the ability to choose what we do, and it's also one of life's greatest burdens.

As the general manager for the Joe Verde Group for 30+ years, I've watched hundreds of our customers make the decision to change, grow and improve. I've also watched some dealerships make bad decisions, while others made no choice at all, rode the market wave and hoped for the best.

Well, the wave crashed, and today every dealer is faced with critical choices. How will you play it, now that we're in the toughest climate in the car business in years?

The clock is ticking and you can't just sit on the fence anymore, you have to make a choice. Are you going to just hope you'll get back to 'business as usual' and wait for the market to improve? Or will you go to the effort to change, create a turnaround in sales, and have your best years ever? What will you decide; to do nothing or do as little as possible and hope it all works out OK, or really dig in, give it your best and set new goals to succeed?

If your goal is to succeed and grow in this new market, what's your plan – how are you going to improve sales and raise gross? Do your managers and salespeople have all of the tools and training they'll need to help you pull this off? All of the choices you make today will affect you and everyone at your dealership, for years to come.

The great news is whether your goal is survival, recovery or growth, Joe wrote this book to help you through the maze of tough choices you have to make today, so you can improve and grow tomorrow. He'll walk you through a step-by-step process so you can stabilize your dealership, improve sales and start growing again right away.

Get your managers together and use Joe's book as your foundation to create a new, improved sales process and a new, improved sales team – and take your dealership to the next level.

All the best,
Kathleen Rittmaster, General Manager

INTRODUCTION

Which best describes your dealership?

❑ We're doing good and we want to do even better.

❑ We're doing OK for now, but we need to improve.

❑ We're struggling, and have to get back to making money.

❑ If we don't make it happen right away, we're done.

Whichever you picked, this book is for you.

We're in the worst market in decades and we're facing so many challenges that are unprecedented, especially for most salespeople, managers and dealers in our business today.

For dealerships who are doing OK or doing good and want to do better – you just need to stabilize everything in the dealership, track all of your sales opportunities, activities and results to find out exactly what you're doing, and start training, coaching and managing your salespeople to improve in each area.

If your dealership is struggling, there's more urgency in what you have to do, and your first step is to recover, stabilize and then start growing. The recovery steps I'll give you will take your dealership to a stable state, so we can start the growth process right away. The growth steps are the same steps as in the previous paragraph; stabilize, track and then improve in each area.

If your dealership is in a critical stage right now, with the red alert alarms blaring – it is *urgent* that we get you started on a survival process immediately. You have to take immediate action in the steps we'll cover, so we can move you from survival, into recovery and onto growth again in your dealership.

No matter which stage you're in, we'll cover exactly what you need to do to survive, recover and grow in today's challenging market.

I know you're anxious to *get it done* quickly – so I need you to slow down and read this book chapter by chapter, instead of jumping a few chapters ahead. Each chapter builds on the last one to become the steps you have to take in your recovery and growth.

If you're ready, let's get started.

MY GOALS WITH THIS BOOK

A lot of the problems in dealerships today are obvious without even reading this book. Once you start peeling back the onion though, you find dozens of hidden core problems that control everything you want and need to happen. If you don't address your core problems, nothing will change – it can't. So one of my goals in this book is to help you pinpoint exactly what you need to work on at your dealership to grow and improve.

Whether you're a dealer, manager (or even a salesperson), and whether you're struggling or having a great year – everything in this book will apply to you and benefit you, across the board. It's time to stop relying on the market to drive your growth and it's time to focus on goals, education, and effective management (execution).

If you're right on the brink, follow my directions and you'll pull yourself and your store back to profits, almost overnight. If you're doing well in this market, that's great, and now is the perfect time to put the pedal to the metal to steal market share from the dealerships who are asleep behind the wheel.

Whether your dealership sells 50 or 350 units a month, I will show you how to double your sales within 3 to 6 months. We'll use a 100 unit store in our examples and I'll show you several (easy) ways to pick up another 100 deliveries per month, and how to raise your gross profit 40%–50% today. Your return may not be that dramatic, but you can easily improve sales and gross if you're ready to work *smarter,* and with more focus, than you've ever worked in the past.

My three specific goals to help you improve...

- I want to remind you of the incredible potential you have today, even in this market. (When you can see it, you can get it.)

- I'll cover exactly what you, your managers and salespeople have to do to sell more units and hold more gross right now.

- My biggest goal and challenge will be to talk you into making a total commitment to improving your unit production and income.

    If you're ready to grow, I'll show you how to sell more units, have more fun, and start making more money – today.

HOW TO MAKE THIS A 'WORKING' BOOK

This book is filled with information you can use to sell more today, and to continue to grow throughout the rest of your career. Your goal? To take as much away from reading this as possible.

Here Are 8 Tips For Success...

1. Make A Commitment To Improve Sales, Starting Today!

2. Take Notes: Open a new Word® document, or get a new spiral 'subject' notebook or three ring binder with tabs. Everywhere you take this book, take your notebook with you. The good ideas you think of as you read this will come and go faster than you can remember, so write down every important point you discover.

3. Wear It Out: Treat this book like your personal workbook. I have two kinds of books on my shelf, the good ones that are marked up and falling apart from use, and those pretty ones that are hardly used. *Use this book.*

4. Get A Highlighter And Pen: Highlight every key point in this book you want to work on. Jot short notes in the margins and fill that document or notebook with your notes and ideas.

   Tip: Write the page number to the left of every note in your workbook for easier reference back to that page in the book.

5. Complete The Homework: At the end of each chapter or section, utilize the short summary and 'list of things to do' that could help you improve in the areas we cover.

6. Get A Book For Every Manager: You need every manager in your dealership to understand the problems and see the same potential, so you all work together toward a common goal.

7. Meet Twice A Week: Schedule management meetings on a chapter or section and get everyone in management in your dealership involved in improving sales today, and every day.

8. Don't Take 'No' For An Answer: Stop asking your managers and salespeople if they want to sell more and stop waiting for them to take action. Require every manager to read this book and get involved, or let them go lose sales somewhere else.

A QUICK SHORT STORY

If you've read my book, "How To Sell A Car And Close The Sale Today", you pretty much know my background. I went to school in Early, Texas, population 916 back then. My family didn't live in town, we lived in the suburbs of Early, about 8 miles out of town. While there were a lot of things I kinda liked about growing up on a farm, I couldn't wait to escape. So the day I turned 18, I joined the Army in search of new adventures.

For my first few hours in the Army (while we were still on the bus to Fort Polk), I was still that cocky kid who was thinking I had it made. I had escaped the farm, I was on my own and I felt like I was ready to start having some serious fun. *And then the bus stopped.*

When that drill sergeant came through the front door of our bus screaming at the top of his lungs – it scared the cocky right out of me. Worse, my new home (barracks) just happened to be right across the street from the stockade (prison) and my new sergeant assured all of us that if we screwed up, we'd end up in there forever.

So much for my new 'fun' adventure.

I'm sometimes slow to catch onto things, but I caught on real quick to the fact that if I didn't do what these guys were telling me to do, there would be serious consequences. In fact, they had me so scared I honestly thought if I didn't do what I was told, that I would either be shot or spend the rest of my life across the street where they had the sharp curly wire on top of the fence.

I became a model soldier...

I was still kinda lazy, though, so I figured out how to get out of KP (working in the kitchen) and guard duty by volunteering for extra training, and I decided to volunteer for a short 'leadership' class. It was only for 3 days, but it was 3 days of not washing pots and pans or having to walk around an empty building all night to guard it.

After Basic, next came 6 weeks of Advanced Training. I was supposed to become a Radar Operator, because that's what I signed up for, and I got to my next school a week early. So while I was waiting for Radar

Recovery and Growth

School, to avoid more KP and guard duty, I volunteered for another one-week leadership school. *Saved again by more education.*

But when my Radar Training was over, they made me a clerk, because I could type. I protested, "What about the Radar job I was promised?" ... and they reminded me that I did get the Radar Operator *Training* as promised, and now here was my new *job* – a clerk.

From milking cows, feeding chickens, to now typing all day – somehow it all seemed the same and no fun at all. So what's a bored kid to do? Of course, volunteer for another school. This time it was a 6-week leadership course, called the NCO Academy. The best part, I would only be an hour's drive from home (and my girlfriend). *I was really starting to appreciate getting an education.*

One thing I had learned in my first 3-day school on leadership was that if you don't do well in these courses, they won't let you take any other courses. Since I liked being in class more than washing dishes or typing, I always tried hard enough and studied at least *some* to usually end up being very close to the top in my classes. Plus, after attending all these courses, they started handing me promotions, which meant more money – all because I was learning more than the average Joe. Wow, get out of work and earn extra money. Such a deal!

When that course ended though, it was back to typing, and I really didn't like that job. So I looked for a way to get out of that, too, and the only way out was to go to school again (imagine that). The only catch was that this school was on helicopter maintenance, and after school, there was only one place to go; Viet Nam. But what the heck, flying around getting shot at had to be better than sitting in an office in the middle of the desert typing all day.

I finished that 6-week course on maintenance, and then as luck would have it, I just happened to find another 6-week *advanced* course on helicopter maintenance. I finished that one too, did good and got promoted again. And can you believe it, I found one more 2-week course I could attend before I was sent to Viet Nam.

This one was a 2-week train-the-trainer course. I liked it because I figured that after I became a trainer, I wouldn't have to *work* on helicopters, I could just teach other people how to do it.

That didn't exactly work out as planned, either.

I had managed to go through 8 different schools up to this point for close to 40 weeks total, and my number was up. I got my new orders and then I spent my next 809 days in Viet Nam fixing my helicopter at night and then flying around all day, and I just kept repeating that daily routine for 2 years, 2 months and 19 days.

With all of my (accidental) education and experience, by the time I was 20, I was promoted to E-6 and put in charge of a maintenance platoon. My guys did good – we broke every maintenance record they had recorded on keeping the most helicopters flying in a combat zone.

Even though my motives for attending those schools wasn't what it should have been, the fact is, I learned a lot of stuff in the Army for a 20 year old kid. I understood how to do the job and I knew how to get other people to help me do the job. I really think the most important thing I ever learned about being a good Leader, is that I had learned how to follow directions – I was a good soldier.

After 7 years in the Army, I got out here in Southern California. I didn't know how to do anything except plow fields, milk cows, feed chickens and train on, or fix helicopters. Unfortunately there just weren't any of those jobs around, so I had to find a new profession.

Instead of going over all of the great challenges I faced trying to get hired in the car business, let's keep it short and just say, *I was able to answer all three questions correctly in the interview.* Technically, it took me longer to find a parking spot to apply for my first job in sales, than it did for me to be interviewed, hired and trained as a 'professional' in automobile sales.

I became a real superstar in sales my first five years. By working only 10-12 hours a day, 7 days a week, I was able to average 8 units per month. But after 5 years, some quick math and one of those "duh" moments, I realized I wasn't even an 8-car guy, I was just a 4-car guy working two jobs. So I quit and opened my own pin-striping business.

That worked out well and I ended up with a retail store and 3 trucks on the road. Two years later though, after going through about 100 books, tapes, and seminars on how to sell, how to manage, how to close, follow up, prospect, get organized, set goals and how to become successful, I started selling cars again.

Recovery and Growth

*In just 7 months with my new skills, I sold more units
and earned more money than I did my first five years combined.*

I can guide you step-by-step through the process of recovery and growth, because I've been the 8 car guy and I learned how to become the 38 car guy. I've been the manager with the top team and highest gross, I've been a dealer and for 30+ years at the Joe Verde Group, we've worked with half a million dealers, managers and salespeople showing them how to improve and grow in any market condition.

If you're willing to make changes in how you sell and manage, I can show you how to improve and grow immediately, too. You can't succeed in *sales* today with what we were taught out in the huddle or by some below average salesperson or manager.

You can't succeed in *management* today either, if you rely on the input you got from managers, who I'm sure worked very hard, but also had no training. But you can improve yourself and your salespeople right now by learning and applying the "core principles" of selling, closing, negotiating and managing people we'll cover in this book.

Selling more isn't easy – but it isn't rocket science, either. Selling more or managing your salespeople more effectively to sell more does require a disciplined and repeatable approach, though. I've developed that process for both sales and management, and I can teach this to you, your managers and your salespeople.

*For 30+ years, our average growth rate at the Joe Verde Group has
been 60.4% per year, and I can show you how to do the same thing.*

If you're ready, I'll teach you how to *assess* your situation, I'll help you determine the skills or *changes* you need to make, I'll help you establish a *plan* you can follow and I'll squeeze as much of the *"how to"* as possible into this short book.

What's important for you to realize is that as a dealer or manager, you can't wait for everyone else to jump on board. No matter what management position you hold in the dealership, ultimately, *you* are in charge of your own success and the success of everyone who reports to you. How far you get in sales, management or in life, *is not* up to the market, the weather, the economy or your competition down the street, it's only up to you. Write this down and read it often...

If it is to be – it's up to me!

"The Joe Verde sales training is the single most important thing we do here.

Our entire sales staff from BDC reps to General Managers go thru this training program a few times a year. In addition we are all required to complete the Joe Verde on line training that is offered. The results speak for themselves.

We have received a 14% increase in new car volume vs. 2013, while at the same time having a nice lift in gross profit. We consider it the cornerstone to our success. It's one thing we refuse to do without."

– Michael Brown, Atlantic Auto Group

SECTION 1

A Few Quick Questions About Your Dealership And Today's New Market

1

How would you like to sell more cars, have more fun and make more money?

And what if that wasn't a highball?

What if in just this short book, you could pick up enough new ideas and reminders of the potential you really have in today's market to put your dealership back on track quickly, and then continue to grow month after month and year after year?

If you're serious, this is the book for you, because I will guarantee you're sitting on more lost sales and profit today, than many dealers were earning in those good times we've been enjoying.

Logic: Changes and improvements have to start at the top.

People don't really like change, that's why I wrote this book for *dealers*. This is your dealership on the line here, and if *only a few* of your managers and salespeople try to improve, not much will happen, it can't. You need a groundswell of enthusiasm, motivation and training to get you all back on track fast. That means you have to personally get behind whatever changes and improvements *you decide* you need, and then *you're in charge to make it happen.*

We've made a lot of friends over the years, and I know some of you are struggling. So your first copy of this book is *on the house* from me, for any dealer who wants one. Check the back page and get a free copy for any other dealer you know, too. (Free is for a limited time only.)

*Let's get ready to learn how to sell more cars,
have more fun and make more money – even in this market!*

2

Are you finding that it's tougher to do business as usual?

90% of the dealers today say 'yes' – what about you?

Over the past few years as sales have been slowly dropping from our 17 million high (before the nose dive), we've started every workshop by asking dealers this question. And in every class, almost every hand in the room goes up.

Business didn't get bad *yesterday.* Like an approaching storm, we've seen this coming for the last few years. Sales hit the 17 million mark and have been tapering off ever since. Nobody, though, predicted that everything bad that *could* happen, *would* happen to our economy and our industry *all at once.*

The good times lulled us into careless selling and business practices...

In the last couple of decades, businesses across America and around the world have had it made. Sure, we had to put in lots of hours, but in real life, we've been able to 'wing it' at work and still succeed – because the market was great.

Dealerships have been running strong and making money, because the market was there to support them. Most dealerships have had minimal policies or procedures, little or no training, few requirements and virtually no accountability in sales or management. Lots of dealers, managers and salespeople were making a lot of money in spite of all the things they should have been doing, but weren't.

Wasn't life in sales in those record years fun!

Recovery and Growth

Uncharted Waters

We just did several meetings in the Los Angeles and San Francisco areas for Lexus dealers and managers, and their salespeople. One of the key points, and one of the most common problems all dealerships face today, came out in one of our management sessions while we were still doing the introductions.

Because these last dozen or so years have been so great, almost every product and dealership has seen consistent growth:

Great Products + Great Times = Consistent Growth

The catch: Almost all of the salespeople and managers today, have only been in the car business for 5 or 10 or 15 years, which means they've only been selling or managing during these great times.

Most managers, salespeople and even some dealers today have never been in any kind of extended downturn in our business. They've all worked hard and have been very successful in these great times. But if you're suddenly thrown into the middle of combat, and you haven't had any combat training, there are definitely going to be casualties while you try to figure out what you should be doing.

What's the biggest challenge today? Most salespeople and managers have never had any formal sales, management or leadership training. They're very hard workers with great intentions and a ton of product knowledge, who have focused on providing a great customer experience.

In great times, it's easy to just learn all about your product and focus on CSI. *Selling skills* aren't much of an issue because people are *buying*. So it's been work hard, smile, know your product and get those 'Perfect 10' letters in the mail to guarantee great CSI.

In these great times, dealers sold cars, made money and earned great CSI because of their friendly people and great products. Now their floor traffic is way down and those same dealers don't have enough prospects for their salespeople to talk to. When someone does show up, they're tougher shoppers, and they're more careful and more cautious than ever. That means good selling skills are more critical right now than at any time in the last decade.

Dealers have practically ignored three critical areas;
management training, selling skills and customer retention.
Today, these three areas are more important than anything else.

3

Do you have less floor traffic now than you've had in the last few years?

Of course, and that makes selling more even tougher!

One of the biggest challenges in this recovery is that there are fewer people in the market. Logically, if you can't put prospects on your lot, you can't make many sales. It's also unlikely you're going to drag many people who *aren't* in the market right now, into the market, with another big event or more advertising. *That's the bad news.*

The good news: The people who are in the market right now are more serious when they come onto the lot than they've ever been. While the statistics on the 'prospects who buy' haven't changed, what has changed is how informed and how well prepared today's prospects are to do business today.

More good news: Even in today's market, with less floor traffic, you can increase your sales 30-to-50-to-100% quickly. I'll show you how in this book, I'll prove you can do it, and you'll agree.

More good news: Your 'Market Driven' competitors are going to be sending you prospects by the bus loads. They don't get it. They're treating this new, more concerned, more cautious buyer the same way they've been treating prospects in the past – very badly.

Trust this common sense thought: The untrained, poorly managed, demotivated 6-car guy down the street is not a serious competitor *today*, even if he offers the lowest price on the planet.

In this book, we'll talk about how to improve sales with your current floor traffic and steal high gross deals from your competition!

4

What's different about today's new buyers, in today's new market?

They're Cautious – Fearful – Concerned...

It changes daily, but today in the paper, 8.5% are unemployed and another 29% are in fear of losing their jobs. Some areas have double digit unemployment. I've changed this paragraph 5 times since I started writing this because the news changes *daily*. But we all know things are still very uncertain with banking, housing, manufacturing, and where the dust will settle in our business.

Chrysler and GM have both now filed bankruptcy and both are announcing their dealership closures, which creates even more uncertainties. Foreclosures are still higher than ever (but hopefully tapering off), unemployment may still hit over 10% in the next few months, that 29% 'fear factor' is lingering and retail sales are stalled everywhere.

Almost every family in America has felt the impact and whether they're in trouble or not, almost everyone is taking a much more cautious approach to buying expensive products.

UPDATE: Chrysler and GM have both made it through the worst of it, but everything else above is still about the same. Unemployment is still too high, people are still losing their homes, and people are still more fearful and cautious than ever.

It's 'good news' and 'bad news'...

As today's news focuses on a bright spot in the economy and recovery, the next segment is still about something that isn't going as well. It's good news – caution – good news – caution – more good news.

Even people who are doing OK right now are being more thrifty. For instance, more people are clipping coupons than ever before. Online services let you search by the product, download the coupons and head to the store. On the news the other day, one family said they bought $175 worth of groceries for just $73.

No question about it – people are more concerned than at any time in decades. Because buyers are more concerned, that makes *selling on a professional level* more important than it's been in years.

Value Is More Critical Now Than Ever

Even the people who are not in fear of losing their jobs and are on your lot today, are more cautious and careful about the money they spend. They're making calculated choices, and cutting back on the extras in their lives. While they are definitely concerned about *getting a good deal* – it's *the value you create* that they'll use as a measure of the *deal* they get ... not how cheap you'll sell it.

If You Lower The Price – You Lower The Value

Too many salespeople, managers and dealers misunderstand the relationship between price and value and they assume *low price* is what it takes to sell to today's buyer. But when you drop the price, you aren't raising the value – just the opposite happens; *as you lower price, you also lower value.* As you say, "I can save you $5,000 on this $26,000 vehicle," what they hear is, "It never was worth $26,000 to begin with, so let's start at $21,000 and work our way down." When you lower the price, you lower the value.

Worse, as you drop the price, you actually create a more wary prospect, who is now more likely to question you, shop and compare your prices. Why? Because if you're dropping the price, what will the dealership down the street do for them?

We'll talk more about how to handle price and sell more cars to today's prospects. Just keep in mind you're under a microscope now, more than ever. You and your salespeople have to make your prospects feel comfortable and see value in your product.

5

On Your Market:

You know your market best,
so what's the real deal on potential?

With everything that's going on, is there the possibility or the potential to sell more in your market today? Some markets are harder hit than others, some have double digit unemployment and some seem to be humming right along, almost as usual.

How about your market – is there opportunity for growth?

To help you get back to seeing the potential in selling cars in your own market – take a few minutes to do an honest evaluation about your prospects and the potential you really have to sell more.

Whether you're a dealer, manager or salesperson, this is *your own personal evaluation* of what you think about selling cars in your market. Just check your answer to the next 18 true or false questions. At the end, your conclusions about your potential will be based on your own analysis – not mine.

Analyzing your real potential in the car business is critical to your recovery and growth, so slow down and talk about this in your management and sales meetings.

About Your Market

Are there buyers in our community right now?

1. Even in today's market, except for the people who are too young to drive or too old to drive, 95% of the people in our community either own a vehicle now or they'll eventually purchase their first vehicle. ❑ **True** ❑ **False**

2. If #1 is true, since practically everyone in our community owns a vehicle now or will get one soon, that makes almost everyone in our community a *buyer*. ❑ **True** ❑ **False**

3. If #2 is true, since almost everyone in our community is a buyer, the only two questions there really are when someone walks on the lot, with anyone we meet on the street, with every existing customer in our database and with everyone in our Service drive are…

    1) *When* they'll buy their next vehicle and …

    2) *Which dealership* will make the sale? ❑ **True** ❑ **False**

    (If you're unsure on 1–3, for a limited time, we're providing a free Market Share report by R.L. Polk at www.joeverde.com/polk)

What about the competition we face in our market?

4. With prospects in the market today, if we do a better job of building value and closing the sale than the salesperson our prospect may meet down the street, we'll sell some of the people he or she would have sold. ❑ **True** ❑ **False**

5. If #4 is true, if we just do a better job of presenting, demonstrating and closing than every other salesperson in town, and if we continue to learn more about selling to today's new buyer, we can improve our sales right now and continue to improve them, every year. ❑ **True** ❑ **False**

About those price questions and objections our prospects have…

6. Whether it's a question or an objection, most of our prospects bring up *price* in some form out on the lot, before they actually find a vehicle they're willing to take home today. ❑ **True** ❑ **False**

7. Price is important to almost everyone, but in the end, people make their *decision to purchase* based on the *value* they feel they'll receive for the price they have to pay, and that's based on how well we do in #5. ❑ **True** ❑ **False**

8. If #7 is true and buying is based on *value*, after our presentation and during our attempts to close the sale, if we have a prospect who honestly objects to the price – the real objection is that we didn't create enough value *to justify the price* we're asking them to pay. ❑ **True** ❑ **False**

What about our work habits and skills in sales...

9. Even if we get better at closing and handling objections, it will still be tough to close more sales and sell more cars today, and it will be hard to earn the big bucks if we pre-qualify people, talk price on the lot, take shortcuts and skip the basic steps of selling. ❑ **True** ❑ **False**

10. If we do our best, but still don't close the sale and a prospect leaves without buying – *if we follow-up effectively,* there's a *pretty good chance* they'll come back in and buy the vehicle from us. ❑ **True** ❑ **False**

11. If we didn't close the sale today and if we don't follow-up effectively, unfortunately statistics prove the prospect will buy their new vehicle from a salesperson at the dealership down the street. ❑ **True** ❑ **False**

12. If we *don't* follow-up, when our prospects do buy their vehicle down the street, those other dealers, managers and salespeople we're sending deals to every month will not spiff us for the referrals. ❑ **True** ❑ **False**

13. Even if our salespeople *never* become lean, mean, closing machines, *if we follow up* all of our working prospects and sold customers, we'll still sell more vehicles each year. ❑ **True** ❑ **False**

About experience and training…

14. If all it took was experience (not training) to get better at selling and closing, then someone who started selling 10 cars a month 10 years ago, should be selling 30 cars a month now, but they usually aren't. ❑ **True** ❑ **False**

15. A well-trained salesperson will almost always sell more units and earn more money than a salesperson with no real training or education in sales, so if we continually teach our salespeople more about selling and make sure they apply what they learn, we'll sell more and earn more. ❑ **True** ❑ **False**

16. Most dealers, managers and salespeople are only taught, or only bother to learn enough about selling or managing to produce average sales results, but they all seem to learn how to explain why being average as a dealership, manager or salesperson is never their fault. ❑ **True** ❑ **False**

What do I think is the potential in our market, at our dealership?

17. Based on my answers to these first 16 questions – whether our salespeople sell and earn just average wages or whether they sell more and earn professional wages; it really isn't up to the weather, the economy or our local market. Whether they sell more and earn more depends on their selling skills, their work habits, their attitude and whether they do their follow-up and prospect in our community to create their own floor traffic. ❑ **True** ❑ **False**

18. Using what we already know, if in sales and management, we all really applied ourselves and if we just did our very best job with every opportunity on our lot today, in real life, *we could deliver an extra* _____ *units per month.*

   If we delivered those extra _____ units, since our average gross is $ _____ per unit, we would increase our gross profit by $ ____,_____ per month even in today's tougher market.

Be careful – you're already getting off track!
If you're serious about recovery and growth, go back and actually
✓ *your answer in each box, and do the math on #18. There's a reason.*

6

Can you sell more in today's tougher market?

The question isn't...
"Can you sell more in today's market?"

The only real question we have to figure out is...
"What do you have to do <u>differently</u> in today's market to sell more units and earn more money?"

Take a minute to ✓ the statements on
the next page that you agree with.

"Nothing can stop the man with the right mental attitude
from achieving his goal; and nothing on earth can help the man
with the wrong mental attitude." — *Thomas Jefferson*

Recovery and Growth

What can we do differently (improve) to sell more in today's market?

Please ✓ the statements you agree with...

❏ If every salesperson just came to work *to work*, had a plan for the day and was more organized, we'd sell more.

❏ If every salesperson just treated every prospect on the lot as a buyer (like they do the last day of the month), we'd sell more.

❏ If every salesperson gave better, and more effective presentations and demonstrations to build more value, we'd sell more.

❏ If every salesperson knew more ways to close and overcome objections so they could get a firm commitment, we'd sell more.

❏ If every salesperson did the paperwork the way we ask, and if they set up the negotiation properly each time, we'd sell more.

❏ If every salesperson worked the customer to *buy* on every deal as hard as they work the desk to *take* the deal, we'd sell more.

❏ If every salesperson contacted every person who didn't buy, we'd get more people back in, and we'd sell more.

❏ If every salesperson knew how to prospect, and then met at least a couple of service customers each day, we'd sell more.

❏ If every salesperson made just five, 5-minute prospecting calls per day, we'd sell more.

❏ If every salesperson focused on nailing down the appointment on incoming calls, more of them would show and we'd sell more.

❏ If every salesperson avoided talking about the price on the lot and focused on value, our gross would go up.

About sales management...

❏ I am aware that nothing above will improve until management takes responsibility for our sales force and until management creates more effective sales processes, trains everyone initially and then daily, tracks what they do, gives them clear goals, keeps them motivated, and holds them accountable.

❏ Selling more units and holding more gross isn't up to our salespeople – selling more is a management responsibility.

If we just did a better job in each area I checked above, I think we could deliver at least _____ more units each month.

I can vs. I can't

Most people are just a ... " 't " ... away from more success.

Want to sell more? Just change your mind!

One of the biggest challenges in getting back on track is to regain and then maintain a constant belief *every day* in the potential this business offers any dealer, manager or salesperson who is serious.

When I first started selling cars, I thought everybody was a buyer. Since that's what I believed, I gave everybody I talked to my best presentation and demonstration. Even though I didn't know much about the product or selling, my enthusiasm carried me through and I sold cars in spite of what I didn't know.

In fact, one of the most common questions from new salespeople is, *"I started out good, then my sales dropped – what happened?"*

The answer is easy. After a couple of months' experience, we think we have the system pegged. We start pre-qualifying every prospect to make sure they can and want to buy today. Why go to the trouble to give them a great presentation and demonstration, if we don't think they're serious or can't qualify? Plus, the most negative people in the dealership have worked hard to steal our enthusiasm.

It really isn't rocket science; within weeks salespeople stop getting excited about every opportunity to sell and they head for the shortcuts. They start demanding that prospects prove they're interested and can buy before they do their best to get them to want to buy. They stop building value and start focusing on price.

To deliver more units in any market, you and your managers (and your salespeople) have to make several *positive assumptions* about every prospect who walks on your lot:
- They can buy.
- They came to buy.
- You will deliver them a vehicle if your salespeople do their job.

In a tough market like we're in today, if you aren't careful, you and your salespeople start questioning and disbelieving these three critical assumptions, and that's when everything starts falling apart. That's why learning more every day is critical.

Learning more helps you keep "<u>can't</u>" out of your vocabulary.

7

Have you started cheap-selling your product instead of focusing on value?

Value is usually the first thing to go on a busy weekend with a lot of traffic, or in a tough market when salespeople, managers and dealers get scared.

Today's prospects are more fearful, more cautious and more careful than they've ever been. The prospects you're seeing on the lot today *are also more serious about buying*. Why? Because when people are struggling with money, they don't usually go out and do 'wish list' window shopping – it's too depressing.

Your customers are *also more concerned than ever* about the *value* they feel they'll receive for the *price* they'll end up paying you.

This is not the time to cheap sell your product. This is the time to do just the opposite and learn how to follow the process I'll cover to give a great value building presentation and demonstration that leads straight into a closing sequence and a delivery.

Your managers and salespeople need to develop their skills to meet today's buyers' tougher standards. Then with an effective warm-up process, followed by a great value building and closing process, you'll end up delivering more units without focusing on price, trade, rebates, special interest rates, or discounts.

You need to get back to selling cars. That's the one thing you can quickly learn to do better than your competition. Just keep a positive focus on the value in owning your product (and learn to close).

Value ... "*The worth of something compared to the price paid for it.*"

Read the definition again to understand the real decision your customers today have to make. They aren't making price decisions, they're making *very calculated value decisions based on their budget.*

Aren't prospects today saying, "Is it worth it?"

Aren't most of their common objections price related?

"I don't think it's worth $22,000."

"It's too much money."

Since *value* determines *worth,* if the price is too high, then that means we're short on value. The good news; building value on an expensive item like a car, comes from several things we can control:

- Does 'liking' the salesperson they talk to add *value?*

- Does a salesperson finding out *why* they specifically want this vehicle, and then focusing on that in their presentation add *value?*

- Would introducing the prospect to a manager, the receptionist or the Service Manager as part of a salesperson's presentation, make them more comfortable, and add *value* to buying from your dealership?

- How about when salespeople take shortcuts on the lot (like no demo) and ask those pre-qualifying questions like: what kind of payments are you looking for, how much down do you have, what do you owe on your trade, what do we have to do on the price to earn your business today? Do those questions add *value* or focus prospects even more on pricing, trade, down, discounts and payments?

- Do those shortcuts and those pricing questions take the focus away from value and change it to how cheap you can sell a car? In a cautious consumer's mind, does *cheap* affect whether it's *worth what you're asking for it?*

Good selling means building great value and closing properly. In every course we teach, we've always talked about how important building value is to selling more of your product, to holding higher gross profit and to making your customers happier.

This is especially critical today, because value affects everything. And the more value you start building in your product, the faster and more likely you are to recover and grow.

8

Did you develop some bad habits in the last few great years?

A great market sure made us all look good, didn't it?

Hasn't it been great! Everybody was working hard and making good money. Credit was flowing freely, and banks would loan just about anybody enough money to buy a vehicle, and to make us a profit. And that 120% to 150% financing sure made it easier to keep rolling all that negative equity into the next vehicle, plus home equity lines just kept getting bigger, as home prices kept rising.

We were lulled into apathy when it came to focusing on improving our sales skills. We didn't have to, so we didn't.

Buyers were in a frenzy to trade *out and up* at the drop of a hat, which helped average salespeople, managers and dealerships float to the top or stay above average these last few years.

Not because *they* were great – because *the market* was great.

They weren't actually *running* their stores with clear processes, or *managing* their people or *selling* their products – most of their success was *market driven* and buyers were everywhere.

Too often, we weren't *selling* – people were *buying.* You couldn't tell though, because our total volume was great and grosses were good. To make a good living they had to work hard, but nobody in sales or management actually had to do the job they were hired to do.

That was then – and this is now!

Traps: Some Of The Bad Habits
We Developed In Those Great Times

These aren't in any order. Just ✓ any bad habits you, your managers or any of your salespeople have developed over the last few years in your dealership *that are costing you sales today.*

❑ Business was so good, salespeople have gotten into the habit of just coming to work to *wait* (for a prospect to show up).

❑ Management has gotten into the habit of just watching salespeople *wait* instead of taking action to train, coach and manage them and their daily activities to generate traffic.

❑ Managers got into the habit of expecting salespeople to manage themselves and kept repeating, "I'm a manager, not a baby-sitter."

❑ We expected prospects to just show up, instead of working hard every day on the phones to get more people on the lot.

❑ We don't track sales activities or source our advertising, we didn't need to the last few years – we had plenty of traffic.

❑ In the good times, when we had 500 people on the lot and only closed 20% (100), even though 78% of those 400 (312) were still going to buy *somewhere*, we were making money, so we didn't train or require our salespeople to follow up our own hottest prospects.

❑ We even stopped having our 'save a deal meetings' – we didn't worry about a few lost sales – besides, we were too busy.

❑ Because we didn't train them, manage them or hold salespeople accountable for selling more units, now we've developed too many low achievers in sales with no goals and a list of excuses.

❑ We didn't teach our new or experienced managers to recruit, interview and hire the best salespeople – so we don't have many 'best salespeople' right now when we need them the most.

❑ We got into the habit of hiring whoever showed up for a job, even when we knew they probably wouldn't work out.

❑ Because times were good, we held on to too many salespeople who should have never been hired in the first place.

Slow down and actually ✓ the bad habits you've developed.

Recovery and Growth

❏ For the last 5 or 10 years, we've never made training our new managers and salespeople a priority – and now we're paying for it every month in lost sales and revenue.

❏ When times were good, we kept changing the pay plan because our highest achievers were making 'too much money'.

❏ After we cut their pay and our highest achievers blew out, we got so cocky we just shrugged it off as though we could replace a 15 to 20 car guy anytime we wanted to.

❏ We've been relying on advertising to drive business into the dealership, knowing that only half of it works, at best.

❏ When we made money in spite of ourselves, we even laughed about how we knew that only half of our advertising worked, and that we just weren't sure which half.

❏ For years, we've been rewarding underachievers (under a 10 unit average) with bonuses and spiffs. This got so bad, we'd even pay a 3-car guy a hat-trick bonus of $300 if he managed to sell all three of his units for the month in one day.

❏ When we were selling more, it was easy to justify seeing if new salespeople would work out before we trained them. Even if they did work out, we still didn't train them – why bother, they worked out well enough and were selling some cars.

❏ We've been hoping and expecting our new salespeople would succeed without training – and blaming *them* if they didn't.

❏ Business was so good, we'd promote a salesperson to management and just put them in charge of generating $30-50 million in revenue each year, <u>with no training</u> – and somehow it all worked out.

❏ We haven't really been holding anybody accountable for much, in either sales or in management, including upper management.

❏ We got away from having management meetings to set clear goals for the year – breaking them down to monthly goals and then meeting regularly to make them happen. Why bother?

❏ We've never focused on follow up to retain more customers, certainly not when business was at 17,000,000 units per year.

❑ We never bothered to focus on making sure every delivery became a service customer, and as a result, 80% didn't.

❑ We've had so much traffic over the last 5 to 10 years, we haven't had hardly any focus on real selling skills or building value, we've been focusing on the 'deal'.

❑ Even though it's *the most critical step* in the buying and selling process, we haven't been requiring our salespeople to give a demonstration to every prospect, and now only 40% get one.

❑ We tell them 'they should', but in real life, we've stopped making salespeople turn every prospect or even touch the desk before they let a prospect leave without buying.

On Training Your Salespeople

Business was so good, we didn't train our salespeople to:

❑ Greet each prospect correctly.

❑ Avoid price, trade and terms on the lot, to focus on value.

❑ Quickly build rapport and investigate for the prospect's wants and needs, so they could build value.

❑ Give great presentations that focus on the prospect's wants and needs and the benefits of having those features.

❑ Give great demonstrations – to everyone.

❑ Start the closing sequence at the end of the demo, which is the highest emotional point in the selling process.

❑ Close the sale on the value, not the price.

❑ Get solid commitments to own, before the write up.

❑ Set up the negotiation effectively, for maximum gross.

❑ Complete *all* of the paperwork and effectively transition the customer to Finance, if we sold it.

❑ Follow up if we didn't sell it – for another chance tomorrow.

❑ Follow up if we did sell it, to retain that customer and their family who will purchase a total of 36 vehicles, lifetime.

❑ Prospect for new business by phone and/or in person.

❑ Turn incoming calls into appointments that actually show up.

❑ Turn internet leads into appointments that actually show up.

Recovery and Growth

How about the processes in your dealership?

Which of these haven't been consistent or were never initiated to begin with? *Our dealership has no clear, written processes or training on:*

- ❑ How to dress in sales.
- ❑ How management wants every prospect treated, what steps of the sale to follow and how to follow the Basics.
- ❑ *How* they should, *if* they should, and *when* in the sales process salespeople should talk 'price' – if at all.
- ❑ How and when to close the sale and get a commitment.
- ❑ How to set up the negotiation.
- ❑ How to negotiate for maximum gross.
- ❑ How to transition each buyer into Finance.
- ❑ How to turn every delivery over to Service before they leave in their new vehicle.
- ❑ What to do with every prospect who doesn't buy, before they leave.
- ❑ How and when to contact each prospect who didn't buy, and what to say so that we can get them back in.
- ❑ How to answer incoming calls to generate appointments.
- ❑ What to do and what to say to every sold customer to turn them into a loyal 'customer family' for life.
- ❑ We certainly have clear processes in our business office, in our Finance department, in Parts, in Service – just not in the Sales department where we can increase revenue overnight.

Do you honestly want to sell more?

1. It's so much easier to just read this book than to use it correctly to help you grow. In just 21 pages, we've hit dozens of ways you're losing sales today and most readers just 'nod' in awareness of each error they make, instead of making plans to improve in each area.

2. Everything I'll ask you to do is for a reason. So go back through these first 8 chapters, highlight every area that rings a bell, answer every question, and check everything on this list that applies in your dealership.

You can tell this is going to make sense, so slow down and start following the tips on page XI, so I can help you recover and grow faster.

9

How important is discipline to your dealership's recovery and growth?

'discipline' ... noun

"Ensuring people obey rules by teaching them
and by punishing them if they do not."

As a teenager, I definitely lacked *discipline*.
One of the first things I learned in the Army was *discipline*.
The very first thing to go once I started selling cars was *discipline*.

Of 3,355 salespeople we've surveyed online, the average person got 7.3 hours of initial training when they started selling cars and rated their training a 4.4 on a 1–10 point scale.

That's almost 2 weeks *less training* than the counter people get at McDonald's. They get weeks of training on how to make and serve a $2 burger. The people who sweep dirt in a bucket at Disneyland and give directions around the park, get 2 weeks of initial training plus ongoing training the rest of the time they work there.

We're selling $30,000 products in one of the toughest times we've seen in our business, and we're doing even less training now than we were in the best of times. Do you really expect your salespeople to be disciplined, high achievers and sell $30,000 products to cautious, concerned strangers with virtually no training, non-existent coaching, no 1-1s and no daily 'sales management' by the managers?

Recovery and Growth

The ad I responded to when I first started selling cars...

"No experience necessary, we train.
Highest commissions in town, flexible hours, demo."

The only thing I got that was promised in the ad was a demo. We didn't even get our 7.3 hours of training, we got a sheet of paper with my manager's version of the '10 Steps To Selling'. Not only were the steps wrong, they were just 10 short bullet points. His training was, "That's the new car lot, that's the used car lot, here's how you sell, memorize these 10 steps, and get out there and make me proud."

Not only are almost all salespeople poorly trained, they're given no clear sales process or coaching from managers (the supposed experts), and there definitely are no consequences for not doing their job.

In fact, as a below average, negative salesperson, if you work at most dealerships long enough, *soon upper management calls you loyal.* Once that happens, they protect you, feed you house deals and other spiffs, and they won't allow anyone to punish you for not doing your job.

I went from being very disciplined after 7 years in the Army, to becoming completely undisciplined in the car business within 30 days. I learned you don't have to do *anything* your manager says to do, as long as you give them a good excuse why you didn't do it, like:

MGR: You're late.

SP: Traffic was bad.

MGR: Don't do it again, blah, blah, blah.

SP: Yes Sir, Boss.

Or...

MGR: How come you didn't demo that guy?

SP: He was in a hurry / stuck in his trade / no money, etc.

MGR: You should, you need to, you ought to, blah, blah, blah.

SP: Yes Sir, Boss.

Most dealers and managers reading this have failed to develop a disciplined selling staff. If you want to recover, you'll have to become a disciplined dealer and manager first or it just can't happen.

"He who has never learned to obey, cannot command." – Aristotle

10

Is your dealership Market Driven or Management Driven?

In good times we develop bad habits because we can.
In bad times we develop good habits because we have to.

In all of our classes, we talk about the differences between a market driven dealership (or salesperson) and a management driven dealership (or salesperson). If you'll look close, especially at dealerships today, this distinction is very likely to be the difference between shutting the doors and having your best year ever.

The difference is pretty simple:
Market Driven dealerships hope and wait for it to happen.
Management Driven dealerships make it happen!

Recovery and Growth

The 'Market Driven' Dealership

Market driven dealerships ride the waves. When times are good, they do pretty well. When times are bad, they follow the market trend right down the drain. We aren't just talking about small dealerships, either. A lot of big dealerships and dealer groups are also market driven. They aren't training and managing their people to bring their sales averages up – instead, they've focused on advertising, acquisitions and expense controls. When the market changed, their sales also went south, some as far, or farther than most average dealers.

Because market driven dealerships don't focus on developing their own floor traffic, they have to rely on a great economy, easy credit and even on good weather to make their month. Their staff is always weak in their core management and sales skills, but nobody notices when times are good.

When times get tougher, though, their sales and revenue start dropping right along with, or even faster than the market. So they, along with the manufacturers, open up their checkbooks and then beef up their advertising even more. They start scheduling weekend events and giving away prizes if people will just show up.

Since the staff didn't develop or improve their selling skills or their work habits though, putting more people on the lot doesn't help much. In fact, with more traffic, their salespeople take more shortcuts than ever. Their salespeople and managers focus more on price, and less on the value of their products than they did before.

In the end, sales decline, attitudes go south and those market driven dealerships start losing some of their best salespeople, while dealers and managers start making lists of reasons why none of it is their fault.

Add a tough economy like we're in now, with unemployment rising every month and with even less floor traffic – then toss in more careful and more cautious buyers, and market driven dealerships are in serious jeopardy. Highly leveraged dealerships and dealer groups can't spend money fast enough on advertising to buy enough business to turn a profit.

Today, you're seeing the devastating effects on those market driven dealerships, dealer groups, salespeople and managers who have never developed their leadership, management and selling skills and who don't know how to develop (and retain) their own customers.

The 'Management Driven' Dealership

Management driven dealerships also enjoy the benefits of a great economy. They're already good – and in good times, they're great.

Even in the best times, management driven dealerships work hard to develop their leadership and management skills. They develop effective processes, they develop their salespeople and they focus on employee and customer satisfaction. Most important, so they can guarantee their independence from the constant swings of the market, they focus on total customer retention.

Management driven dealerships understand it's 5 times less expensive to keep a customer than to try to buy a new one. They don't just follow up their sold customers to get better CSI scores. They walk every sold customer to their Service department before delivery, so they remain a customer of the dealership until it's time to become a customer in the Sales department again, for that next purchase.

Management driven dealerships have effective management and sales *processes and procedures* to ensure that everything that's supposed to happen in sales every day – does happen every day.

Trained managers would never just leave giving presentations and demonstrations up to salespeople. Salespeople's activities are *monitored* and *measured,* with the focus on continued improvement. They don't hope salespeople follow up the unsold prospects, there's a process in place to make sure it happens. They don't just hope a sold customer makes it back to Service, the process guarantees it.

Management driven dealerships don't settle for *warm bodies* in sales and they don't stick an unqualified, or under-qualified person in a management position. They hold out for the people who can help them grow, because they know for every *wrong* salesperson they hire and for every wrong manager they put into a position, they'll lose unrecoverable sales, profits, prospects and customers.

When they hire a new salesperson, they don't hope they figure out how to sell. They train them initially and then daily, the rest of the time they work there. Same with promotions – no matter how smart someone is, or how hard they work or how much potential they have, they don't just stick a new manager in a job and say, "Make me proud." They explain, train and teach them how to do the job and they monitor their management activities.

*Effective managers don't call this baby-sitting, they
understand these are critical management responsibilities.*

All teams in sports have coaches and players. Management driven
dealerships understand the importance of daily coaching so the
team can improve. Bossing isn't coaching and leadership isn't saying,
"Get out there and do your job like I told you to."

Management driven dealerships have a clear vision of where they're
headed, they have clear goals to get them there and they develop a
plan of action that will lead them directly to their goals.

Becoming management driven isn't rocket science, but you won't pick
it all up on a day-by-day basis, and you won't learn the critical skills
of the job through experience. That's especially true since most of us
didn't have a great leader, great trainer or great coach as a mentor. Most
of us just learned by example to duplicate what the hard working
manager beside us did – who was also untrained.

It isn't like you need 4 years of college or a master's degree to become
a great manager who knows how to and can control sales in your
dealership. We have a total of 3 courses on sales to attend, so you know
what you're managing. Then we have 3 leadership and management
courses so you know *how* to train and manage effectively.

We'll cover more in detail later, but the critical skills you need boil
down to *leadership, training, coaching and daily management*. The
salespeople you need to manage have to know how to *get, sell and keep*
customers for life. That means you have to develop all of those skills,
too. Sound like a lot? Actually we're talking about just 13 days of
classroom time in 3 to 6 months, to change your life in management.

Can you imagine the advantage you'd have over the market driven
dealerships who just keep looking to their financial statements for
answers? They're making critical mistakes right now because they're
only focused on controlling expenses, not on growth.

Management driven dealerships will win hands down, because they've
already cut the fat (like everyone should). Now they're working to
develop everyone's skills, giving them clear guidelines on what they
expect, and they're holding everyone accountable to do their job.

*You can do this – because growing, even in a tough market
like today's, is simply a step-by-step process that anyone can learn.*

The Market Driven Dealership Snapshot

Their Traffic Generation...

❏ *Big ad budgets – high cost per sale – no source tracking – low ROI*

❏ *Little or no internal business development / follow up / prospecting*

Their Marketing & Selling Focus...

❏ *Marketing: (ads, signs, stickers): $$$ – rebates – discounts*

❏ *Selling: pre-qualifying – $ focused Pres. – $ closing – $ negotiation*

Their Breakdown Of Sales By Type Of Prospect...

❏ *30% to repeat, referrals, dealership customers, outside prospects*

❏ *70% of monthly sales dependent upon $$$ focused walk-in traffic*

Their Sales Staff ...

❏ *Ineffective hiring – training – daily management*

❏ *Below average (less than 10 units) performance – low gross*

❏ *High turnover - and / or - protected 'Loyal Underachievers'*

Their Management Staff ...

❏ *Receives less 'management' training than salespeople get for 'sales'*

❏ *Poor, or anti-teamwork attitudes, in both sales and management*

❏ *No real tracking – no clear goals – no clear processes*

❏ *Common excuse: "too busy" to hire, train, manage effectively*

❏ *Old school processes – systems – pay – schedules – management*

Their Production & Growth...

❏ *Low Production – No Growth (below average sales / profits)*

❏ *Losing sales, gross, customers, and now best salespeople*

❏ *Losing more market share, every quarter*

Their Basic Reasons For Lack of Growth...

❏ *They leave almost everything to chance, and just hope for the best*

❏ *Management blames the market, the weather, their salespeople, their manufacturer, their competition and even their customers*

Recovery and Growth

The Management Driven Dealership Snapshot

Their Traffic Generation...
- ❏ *Low ad budget – low cost per sale – effective sourcing – high ROI*
- ❏ *Internal business development – prospecting – follow up – retention*

Their Marketing & Selling Focus...
- ❏ *Marketing: Product – Value – Location – Service – Budget*
- ❏ *Selling: Value Selling – Value Closing – Value Negotiations*

Their Breakdown Of Sales By Type Of Prospect...
- ❏ *70% to repeat, referrals, service, employees, outside prospecting*
- ❏ *30% to price focused Walk-Ins from advertising*

Their Sales Staff ...
- ❏ *Effective Hiring – Initial Training – Daily Coaching & Management*
- ❏ *Above average units per salesperson and above average gross*
- ❏ *Virtually no turnover of good salespeople*

Their Management Staff ...
- ❏ *Good initial training, daily coaching, ongoing education*
- ❏ *Develop effective teamwork with all salespeople and managers*
- ❏ *Track – Average – Chart ... use for effective goals and coaching*
- ❏ *No excuses because they adapt, adjust and grow in any market*
- ❏ *Common sense sales and management processes and procedures*

Their Production & Growth...
- ❏ *High Production – Continuous Improvement in all areas*
- ❏ *Consistent growth annually: Units, Gross, CSI, Retention*
- ❏ *Gain market share, every year*

Their Reason For Continued Growth...
- ❏ *They leave nothing to chance – and have clear processes and procedures*
- ❏ *Management completely understands: "If it is to be, it's up to me!" so they train, coach and manage their salespeople daily*

11

How do you spell the secret to success in every position?

S – H – A – C

Dealers – Managers – Salespeople

In the two years I wasn't selling cars, I was learning more about how to sell, manage and run a business. The most important thing I learned is there really are just four areas that determine your success in every position in any company, including your dealership.

The specific duties and responsibilities of each position are different, but the four areas to focus on for success are the same for dealers, managers and salespeople:

S .... Your Skills and abilities

H.... Your work Habits and organizational skills

A .... Your Attitude in everything you do

C .... Your Choice of Customers

We'll take a look at the big picture on skills, work habits, attitude and choice of customers on the next few pages, and spend the rest of this book breaking down your four secrets to success.

S – H – A – C

Your <u>S</u>kills …

No matter what profession you're in, and no matter what position you have, your skill level at your job controls your level of success. This is more common sense than rocket science; the more skilled you are, the more you can do, and the more money you can earn.

Skills are different for every job and that's exactly why being good in sales *should not* be the only qualifier for promotion to management. The skills it takes to build value, close the sale or to become a phone prospecting ninja, are much different than the skills a manager needs to hire, train and manage salespeople and their activities.

No matter what position you hold in any company,
the more skills you develop, the more successful you'll become.

Work <u>H</u>abits …

This business typically requires a lot of hours, but there's a huge difference between being *at work* in the dealership for 10 to 12 hours every day and *effectively working* while you're there.

Like skills, effective work habits also control your level of success in every position. *Effective* is the key word here, though, or you'll end up being there 14 hours instead, yet accomplishing very little.

Waiting around <u>isn't</u> working.
The definition of "Work" for a salesperson means...

"Doing something every minute of your shift that has to do with selling a vehicle right now, or that will help you sell a vehicle in the future." (That means they're either with a customer, prospecting by phone or in person, doing their follow up, working internet leads, training, or getting a vehicle ready for delivery.)

'Work' for the manager in the sales department means doing something every minute of the day to make sure each salesperson knows *what* to do, *how* to do it and to make sure they *are* doing something that will end in a sale today, or at some point in the future.

"The ability to concentrate and to use your time well
is everything, if you want to succeed in business." – Lee Iacocca

Because they aren't trained, when they aren't with a customer, most salespeople really don't know what to do or how to do it.

Problem: Salespeople weren't taught the core selling skills (Basics, Closing, Objections) they need to succeed in sales, much less how to follow up, how to prospect or how to manage their customer base.

Not knowing *what* to do, or *how* to do it, and not having a coach to work with every day, sure makes it difficult for your salespeople to figure out what they're supposed to be doing all day when they aren't with a prospect on the lot or in their office.

Problem: As managers, we weren't taught those skills, either. Nor were we taught the skills as sales managers that we need so we can train, coach and manage our salespeople's daily activities.

From a lack of training, too many managers only learn through experience to bark out orders (that no one follows, because they don't know how and because they won't be held accountable). Orders like...

- Go work the Service drive.
- Go make some calls.
- Call that guy on the blue truck and get him back in tonight.
- You need to sell something today.
- Go find somebody to talk to.
- Get out of this office and go do something.
- Go call all of your customers from the weekend.
- You need to do some follow up.
- Why don't you prospect?
- I want you to make 10 calls, every day.
- #?@#X!## – GO SELL SOMETHING!

Tip: In sales management, your job is to manage 'sales', and that means you need great skills in both *selling* and *managing*.

In upcoming chapters we'll cover both skill sets. As we go through those chapters, highlight all of the skills in sales and management that you know you score below an 8 or 9, then start improving in your weakest areas, so you can become a great manager and pull your dealership back to the top fast.

Recovery and Growth

Attitude …

Smiling all day doesn't mean you have the right attitude in sales or management. You can smile, be friendly and still lack skills and confidence. You can be positive and still not see hitting your next level. You can be a happy person and not like being in management.

Our attitude is so important though, because it controls our short and long term success; and that means our 'attitude' really does control *everything* we do. That's why one of the first chapters in every sales or 'self help' book is about our attitude.

All of the wisest people have left us memorable sayings about how important attitude is...

> *"Confidence is contagious, so is lack of confidence."* – Vince Lombardi
>
> *"Whether you think you can, or can't, you'll be right."* – Henry Ford
>
> *"I will prepare, and some day my time will come."* – Abraham Lincoln

Check the *attitude* areas below that affect your ability to manage your salespeople and help your dealership recover quickly...

- ❑ Whether I think there is potential in my market or not.
- ❑ Whether I think training and managing them to sell more is my responsibility, or their responsibility to learn and sell on their own.
- ❑ Whether I think *they* should take on the responsibility to give everybody a demo, or whether I should be involved.
- ❑ Whether I feel more *sorry* for our salespeople for not selling, or more *responsible* to make them learn and work to improve.
- ❑ Whether I think *how long* they've worked for us should be a 'get out of jail free' card for requiring them to produce.
- ❑ Whether I like training, coaching and daily management or not.

Management is the most important job in the dealership, because like the foreman on a construction site, management decides who gets the job and what they're expected to do. If you think about it, you make those decisions based on how you *feel* about everything.

Your attitude controls your *actions* – your actions control your *success*. Take demos for example; if *you feel* it's your responsibility to manage salespeople to ensure 75% demos, it will happen and you'll sell more. If you feel "they know what they're supposed to do", we all know they won't.

Choice of Customers (Lead Generation / Lead Management)

What does 'choice of customers' mean? Does that mean salespeople get to pre-qualify everybody on the lot and decide who they give presentations to? No, not at all.

Once there's a prospect in front of us, even if it's the worst looking, least likely person on the planet to buy – as a salesperson, we're committed. Our job is to follow those Basics, step-by-step and do our absolute best to turn this opportunity into a delivery.

You and the salespeople do get a choice though, on the *type of traffic* you focus on *generating*. It's the *type* of prospects dealers, managers and salespeople focus on that will ultimately determine your success.

Do you focus on the worst prospects?

As dealers, if your focus is advertising and tent sales, by default, you're focused on generating your worst source of business; expensive, price shopping strangers – walk-in traffic. That group is the toughest to close, lowest gross, lowest CSI, most expensive – and least likely to become a Service customer, or turn into future business.

Do you focus on the best prospects?

On the other hand, if you have solid prospecting, follow up and customer retention *processes and tools* in place, if your managers and salespeople are properly trained in those areas, and if you insist your managers focus on those activities every day – you'll generate more of your best types of prospects; repeat customers, referrals from all sources and more outside and inside prospects.

The *best groups* include; repeat customers, referrals, be-backs, outside prospects and Service customers. These prospects cost almost nothing to acquire, are generally not price-shopping pros, they close 5 times easier, pay you 40% more in gross profits, give you great CSI and are your best sources for loyal, future business.

Is it more trouble to build your business? No – in the long run, it's actually much easier and faster than focusing on walk-in traffic.

A 5-minute phone prospecting or follow up call takes a salesperson the same amount of time as getting a cup of coffee or calling their buddies around town to justify why they aren't selling more units.

Your decisions <u>today</u> as a dealer about your customer focus will affect your sales and your net profit for the rest of your life.

12

Are you willing to change, so you can improve and grow?

Before we worry about the challenges you face or before we get into the potential you have, I'll remind you of the first question I asked...

How would you like to sell more units, have more fun and make more money?

We all know we're *supposed to want to* sell more units, increase the gross, build our business, improve CSI, and retain more customers.

The problem is, while the answer is always, "Sure, we want to sell more," most people aren't willing to make changes in their skills or habits and they aren't willing to go to the trouble it takes to change.

So *seriously* – are you ready to make some changes so you can start selling more units, having more fun and making more money?

'Insanity' ... is doing the same thing over and over again, expecting a different result each time.

That means to grow – you have to change. But it isn't as tough as it sounds, and I'll walk you through it, step-by-step.

If you're a salesperson...

If you're a salesperson reading this, what if you really could figure out how to quickly move from selling just 10 units per month to delivering 15 consistently from now on? What if you really could raise your gross profit and commission by 40% on every deal overnight, just by learning how to work more effectively with customers in today's market and by changing your work habits?

With the extra bonuses and spiffs you'll pick up on those extra sales, those improvements mean *you'll more than triple your income.*

If you're a dealer or manager...

If you're a dealer or manager with 10 salespeople – take that last paragraph and multiply those results by 10 (or by how many salespeople you have). How would you like to move from delivering just 100 units per month at $2,500 per unit ($250,000 in gross) to delivering 150 units per month at $3,500 per unit ($525,000)?

Those improvements mean you'll more than triple your net profit.

Does That Seem Like A Highball?

If those results seem too high, and if you can't possibly see how you can increase sales 50% or how you could possibly improve gross 40% in a troubled market, just cut it in half.

Instead of a 50% increase in your unit sales and 40% in your gross, would you be OK with a 25% increase in sales (25 more units) and a 20% increase in gross ($500)?

Still too high? How about a 10% increase in both? Even at that, as a dealership you're still talking about moving from 100 units to 110 and $2,500 in gross to $2,750 – and that still adds up to $52,500 more per month in gross profit and $630,000 per year.

There Are Two Ways To Grow

If you think about it, there are only two ways to sell more:

1) You either buy more advertising to *try* to put more people on the lot (which isn't working very well in today's market) – or –

2) You improve the skills of your salespeople, so they can sell more of the prospects you already have on your lot and on the phone.

Recovery and Growth

Advertising is just a one-shot deal...

Even when more advertising generates more sales, it's a one-time deal. When you stop spending the extra money, you stop getting the extra sales. When you train and improve your people though, *the improvements continue after the expense of training is long gone.*

When you teach a 10 unit salesperson how to consistently deliver 15 units every month by developing their skills and improving their work habits, those improvements last. That means you keep getting the extra sales and gross, month after month.

It isn't a secret that advertising only generates about $1.^{50} for every $1 spent, while training generates $30+ for every single dollar you invest. There are dealerships and dealer groups who train regularly with us who earn *hundreds of dollars in return for every dollar invested.* When you train, you reach a new level in sales. When you keep training, you continue to improve to the next level and the next.

You should certainly advertise. But too many dealerships become *advertising dependent.* If they don't develop their selling skills, they can't reduce their advertising budget. Worse, most don't accurately track well enough to know which ads really work and which ads don't, so most of their ad budget is wasted.

What's that old saying...

> *"We know only half of our advertising works,*
> *we're just not sure which half."*

Even though most people hear it repeated again and again, we're so conditioned to advertise, we advertise even when we know it won't work. Example: I was in the sales office waiting to talk to the GM about training while he and his sales manager were trying to figure out how to sell more for the weekend.

GM: Run an ad in that paper this weekend.

Manager: But that paper doesn't ever work for us.

GM: I know, but we have to do something.

Did he train with us? No. He said sales were off and they couldn't afford it. Like most dealers, they just keep spending money that doesn't work, which in their minds justifies why they can't afford training, which is the only thing that does improve sales.

Let's Take A Look At 'Bad Gross' And 'Good Gross'

I'm always surprised at how few managers understand the connection between the *money they spend* to generate sales and the *type of return* they get. Like any investment, there are good returns and bad returns when you generate sales. Logically, if you can spend *zero in extra money to deliver 10 extra units,* you'll have more gross profit with lower costs per sale, which means more bottom line profit.

If you spend a 'ton' on an event to generate more sales, you have to subtract a 'ton' before anything can hit the bottom line. But too many dealers use bad math to justify big ad spending.

Example: A dealership that normally delivers 15 units on a weekend, has an event that generates 10 extra units. Management believes they had a 25 unit weekend from their event. They didn't; they had a 15 unit normal weekend and a 10 unit event. Worse; they take the cost of the event and divide it by all 25 units to help justify their overall expense.

That's just like a used car manager who protects their favorite ad source by counting every vehicle they sold over the weekend that was in *that* paper, as though it was sold because it was in their ad.

The Goal: Learn where and how to generate more low cost sales to lower your overall cost per sale, and increase your net profits.

That's what we're going to cover, because the best part of *training your way to higher sales* by improving your skills to improve your production, is that you don't add any new expenses to your bottom line. The floor traffic is already bought and paid for and you've already paid to make the phone ring.

When you sell more units to traffic you already have on the lot or more units to those prospects you already have on the phone now, or if you just raise the gross, there are no new expenses for the extra sales, only the normal sales and management compensation.

With training, you generate *good gross.* Why? Because you sell more to the prospects you already have now. By not adding more expense, you've lowered your overall cost per sale (which more than pays for all of the training you need). The same thought is true with gross profit. When you raise the gross by teaching salespeople to do a better job of building value, handling price, and a better job of negotiation, you're only out the extra commission.

Recovery and Growth

Good Gross = 60% To Net

We call this 'Good Gross' because when you improve sales without increasing expenses, 60% of the extra gross heads straight to Net.

After your initial investment in training, the only expense for the *continued extra sales and gross* is your sales and management compensation. The best part; your initial and ongoing training don't need to be an extra expense. Most of our dealers just pay for our classes and our online training from their ad budgets that aren't working that well anyway.

Improve Sales – Lower Costs Per Sale

In the end, you'll actually end up reducing your advertising and other hard costs of marketing. Why? Because you'll sell more units to the prospects you already have on the lot, on the phone, on your web site and to your own customers in Service and your database.

Assume $30,000 is your ad budget to deliver 100 units at $2,500 in gross per unit ($250,000 total). That means your overall cost per sold unit is $300. Your ad cost per $1 of gross you generate is 12¢.

Increase your sales to 120 units, though, and your cost per sold unit drops to $250. Then add the increase in gross of $500 per unit (120 units x $3,000 per unit = $360,000) and that drops your cost to generate every $1 of gross to just 8¢ (that's a good thing).

Isn't it great? When you learn how to sell more,
you actually pay less per sale, and earn more on every dollar.

But it costs to train! That's true, but with ads you pay for each extra sale. With training, other than a low monthly fee for JVTN®, you pay just one time to learn how to make extra sales from now on.

So where does our average dealer find the money for initial training in our classes and for our online virtual training? From advertising, of course. They use the money that wasn't working anyway to generate a much greater return. Most even end up cutting their ad budgets even more. Why? Because they realize their lack of sales wasn't from a lack of traffic, but from a lack of management and selling skills.

We'll get into the stats about today's market and your potential in later chapters, but the real facts in a 100 unit dealership are...

The dealership delivers 100 units and misses 200+ sales per month.
(Now that's some serious opportunity for YOU!)

RECAP OF THIS SECTION

Get <u>all</u> of your managers together for a meeting at least twice a week so you can work on recovery and growth as a team.

1. We do want to sell more units. ❏ **True** ❏ **False**

2. It is tougher to do business as usual. ❏ **True** ❏ **False**

   a. Make a list of all of the reasons you feel that it's tougher to do business in this market than in the past.

   b. Write out a common sense solution that doesn't include more price advertising to overcome the problem. Example...

   Problem: The gross is down.

   Solution: Build more value.

   Don't worry if you immediately assume, "Our customers won't pay more." ... We have solutions in this book. For now, just write out how you can counter-attack each problem in today's market.

3. We have less floor traffic now. ❏ **True** ❏ **False**

   List as many ways as you can think of to counter this problem:

   • Prospecting by phone. • Prospecting in Service.

   • Managers call everyone within 2 hours who didn't buy.

   • Be creative. We'll have solutions throughout the book.

4. Today's buyer is more cautious and more focused on *value* than they have been in years. ❏ **True** ❏ **False**

   Make a list of every example where you, your managers and your salespeople are dropping the ball on building value.

   Example: Every vehicle is marked down (this says none are worth MSRP). Hold the price on some, and explain the value to your prospect on why they should pay more for these vehicles.

5. We know our market better than anyone. Almost everybody has a vehicle and will buy more, and even if business is down 30%, that means 70% are still buying. ❏ **True** ❏ **False**

   I know a lot of you just said, *"Yeah, things on the list are true, but..."* Go back through this list and everywhere you catch yourself saying, "Yes, but...," force yourself to write out at least two common sense solutions to your own objection.

6. We agree that *with changes* in how we manage and in how our salespeople sell, we could sell more. ❏ **True** ❏ **False**

Same homework as #5. Again, don't worry if you don't *think* you can pull it off, we'll cover enough of the 'how to' in here, and you should attend our dealer / manager leadership course right away.

7. If our managers and salespeople have started cheap-selling our product in hopes that low pricing will get more people to buy, they're building even less value than ever. ❏ **True** ❏ **False**

Same homework as #4. Make a list, and write solutions.

8. My managers, my salespeople and I have developed too many bad habits in the last few great years. ❏ **True** ❏ **False**

Follow the directions at the end of Chapter 8, and write out a common sense solution to each bad habit you checked.

9. Discipline is a 'must' for recovery and growth. ❏ **True** ❏ **False**

If you aren't disciplined, this will be a tough assignment (as will be all of these assignments). Make a list of every area you personally bail on before the job is finished. Then do the same for all managers and salespeople. Identify your weaknesses, then fix them.

10. Being a Market Driven dealership in today's economy will either guarantee *slow* recovery or *no recovery* unless, and / or until the market changes and comes back around. ❏ **True** ❏ **False**

Check the boxes that apply (on page 28) and write your solutions.

11. All of the skills, work habits, attitudes and the types of customers that my managers, our salespeople and I focus on will determine our success today, and down the road. ❏ **True** ❏ **False**

No need for homework yet ... just know the answer is 'true'.

12. I am ready to make the personal changes, and the changes in how our managers manage and how our salespeople sell, so that we can recover and grow. ❏ **True** ❏ **False**

Note: Just mentally answering questions and checking these boxes won't change your habits. We learn from *hearing, seeing* and *doing.*

If you've ever seen or heard me speak, you can *hear* me as you *read* these words, so we have that covered. Now I just need you to *do* the things in here I ask – so I can help you develop new habits and reinforce the critical changes you need to make for recovery and growth.

SECTION 2

Key Responsibilities
Dealers – Managers – Salespeople

"You can't build a strong corporation
with a lot of committees. You have to be able
to make decisions on your own." – Rupert Murdoch

13

Dealer – CEO – GM
Vision – Planning – Action

Whether we're talking about a recovery plan to save a struggling dealership or just talking about how to grow year after year, there are three levels of "Core Responsibilities" in any organization.

In the military, business or even on a construction project you have three levels of people; the planners, the workers and the workers' supervisors. Every level has a completely different set of responsibilities and *success depends on everyone on the team doing their job.*

In dealership sales, these 3 levels of responsibility are...

- Dealer / CEO / GM
- Managers (All Categories)
- Salespeople

We'll start first with the Big Picture of each position's responsibilities and then expand on each position, throughout the book.

Logically this next statement should go without saying, but I'll say it anyway, just in case.

For a dealership to survive in this market,
and become successful or grow in any market...

Everybody has to do their job!

Core Responsibilities

To survive, recover or grow in sales in any market, every person at every level in the sales department has very specific responsibilities. We'll spend the rest of the book covering these responsibilities and the realistic potential you have in your dealership when everyone on your team does their job. First, here's *a condensed version...*

Dealer / CEO / GM

Vision – Planning – Action

The Dealer or upper management, has to have a clear vision of where the dealership is headed, create the specific goals and plans for everyone to follow – then hold every manager and their team in the dealership accountable to do their jobs, with no exceptions.

GSM / Sales Managers / Supervisors

<u>Training</u> Salespeople – <u>Coaching</u> Salespeople – <u>Managing</u> Activities

Management is responsible to take the dealer's goals and execute the plans given to them by upper management. They are responsible to hire, train, monitor and motivate the sales force – and they're directly responsible for managing every salesperson's activities, every day, to reach the goals they've been given.

'Sales Management' includes all managers in 'Sales'; GSM, desk, new and used car, ASM, team leaders, Finance, BDC, internet managers. (And anybody else in management I don't have on this list.)

Salespeople / Managers

Getting – Selling – Keeping

Salespeople *and their managers* have three key responsibilities in sales; get prospects *on* the lot, *sell* them the product and services you offer, and then *retain* them as customers forever.

Three Levels – Each With Three Key Responsibilities.
You will fail to reach your goals in direct proportion to the failure of any person, at any level, to fulfill these key responsibilities.

Dealer / CEO / GM

Vision – Planning – Action (Execution)

Dealers: What's your vision 1, 3 and 5 years down the road? What have you learned these last few years? What mistakes have you made that you don't want to make again? What do you want to see happen in your dealership in the future? Do you want to become the low price leader, focus on big events and marketing? Do you want to take the other route, stop advertising and build your business from within?

There aren't any right or wrong answers to those questions, and the only answers that matter are yours. You're the one who hocked your house and has all of your assets tied up in your dealership. Sure you should be open to management's input, but in the end, you need to decide on the direction you take. Therein lies the first catch: If you don't take the time to decide, you default to being market driven, nothing changes and the merry-go-round just keeps on spinning.

Once you decide on your direction, you have to lay out a step-by-step plan that will take you there. Planning for growth isn't much different than planning a trip across the country. If you're in California, you can't just head east, you need to decide on a final destination.

Once you know where you're headed, your plans start to look like a road map. You're in Los Angeles and you want to get to Baltimore. To the best of my knowledge, there isn't just one highway you can jump on, set your cruise control, and arrive 40 hours later. That means you'll have to do some careful planning before you get started.

If you envision your dealership going from delivering 100 units per month now, to delivering 172 in 3 years, the easy math says you have to improve 24 units per year, or 2 units per month.

That's just the math, though. Now you'll need to pull your team together, evaluate their current skills and activities, determine the realistic goals for each manager and salesperson, and create a step-by-step plan for each person to reach your goals.

Here's the second catch for dealers: It's great that you have vision, have set your goals, and created your plans – but if you don't personally step up and hold everyone accountable, you'll want to pick a comfortable seat on that merry-go-round, because you'll be there awhile.

As the dealer, this is your party – so make sure you plan it carefully.

Dealerships: Top – Bottom – Average

Before we go over the skills we need to turn on sales, let's take a quick look at the 3 levels of dealerships in today's market.

The top dealerships...

There are some super successful dealers in our business who do everything by the book. They aren't all super-sized or in the top 100, but whether they sell 500 or 10,000 per year, they have surrounded themselves with the best and the brightest. They run a tight ship, understand what it takes to grow and they have the money, the strength, the skills and the determination to pull it off.

Some of them have built tremendous organizations and are so successful they have teams of people at this point, who can take a *good idea* from a management meeting on selling more units or improving the gross profit, and turn it into a new process overnight.

They make up 5-10% of the dealerships.

The bottom dealerships...

You also have 5-10% of dealerships at the other end. Some shouldn't own a used tricycle shop, much less a car dealership. They're clueless about business, about selling or managing, and they attract some of the worst retreads in town. Somehow they stay in business, cost their dealership and their employees a ton, and make all dealers look bad.

Thank goodness, they make up just 5-10% of the dealerships.

Average dealerships...

Average is often described as the *bottom of the top* group, and the *top of the bottom* group. Average is where 80% of all people and all companies spend their lifetimes. Almost everybody I've met in this group works hard, has good intentions, wants to be successful, and wants to take care of their customers and their employees. They just lack leadership, training and a clear direction to follow.

If this is you, you're sitting on a gold mine!

Recovery and Growth

What I've learned about most dealers today...

I've been a business owner almost all of my life, including being a dealer. After meeting thousands of dealers in our 30+ years at the Joe Verde Group, here are some things I've learned about *most* dealers today...

- I know you most likely started on the line, worked 14/7 most days, did good in sales, got promoted, then got in on a buy-in or hocked your life to get your dealership.

- I know how hard you've had to work to get your business up and running initially and I know how much gut-wrenching personal effort you're putting into it in today's tougher market.

- I know how much personal time you've taken away from your family and friends, and how many of your kid's soccer games and birthday parties you've missed.

- I know how much money you've invested and how much more there is at stake, especially today.

- I know that even though you have some great employees, and that you feel responsible for their well being – we both know that even with great employees, nobody cares quite as much about your business, or stands to lose as much, as you do.

- I know you go home some nights so frustrated, that you wonder why you ever went into business in the first place.

- I know that ache you feel inside when you know what your company could do if everyone would just pull together, and I know how you feel when they don't.

- I know that nothing has come easy, and those 'lucky breaks' you really needed didn't come through for you most of the time.

- I know how much real effort you put out every single day you open the doors to provide employment for your people, and a great service to your customers.

- And I know that being in business is the most enjoyable, most exciting and most fulfilling thing you do, and I know that being a business owner is the only job either of us would ever consider.

I really do understand how you feel, I know the sacrifices you've made and what you go through daily, trying to run your business.

But there are a few things I can't understand, especially today.

- I can't understand why you'd put everything into your dealership, and not take charge when your leadership is needed more than ever.
- I can't understand why you'd sit still and let the market decide your fate when there is so much real opportunity and such a clear path to more success, especially today when so many have given up.
- I can't understand why you'd keep negative employees or those who can't sell or manage, or those who refuse to or can't do their job, when I know you're able to spot the difference between a valuable employee and an anchor that holds you back.
- I can't understand why you call an employee *loyal* for being with you for years, especially in sales or management, if they're negative and refuse to do their job.
- I can't understand why you'd strip a good manager of their authority by protecting a *loyal underachiever*, especially when everybody in your dealership knows they're hurting your company.
- I can't understand why you'd send a salesperson or manager to class, see their success and then just sit back and allow your most negative salespeople and managers to beat them back down.
- I can't understand why you would fire a porter for not doing their job, but justify keeping a salesperson or manager who can put you out of business by refusing to do some or most of their job.
- With so much invested, I don't understand why you'd just keep repeating, "I became successful on my own and they need to do the same thing," as your reason to justify not training your salespeople and managers, while you watch your dealership slowly fail.
- When a salesperson really improves their sales, I can't understand why you'd resent paying them the extra money and why you don't treat them better, so you can attract even more high achievers, instead of surrounding yourself with low achievers.
- I can't understand why you take every good salesperson off the line and promote them, and then give them no training.
- And I can't understand why you cling to old habits when you know they'll break you if you don't change, improve and grow.

None of this makes sense, because if the dealership doesn't make it, you're the only one who goes broke – everybody else just gets another job.

14

Basic Survival
And Growth Strategies

So what should dealers be doing
right now to recover or grow in today's market?

Survival – Recovery – Growth

We'll assume you're either one of the dealerships in serious trouble right now, or that from what you've read so far, you know you can grow and improve, and that's your goal.

That means these urgent decisions you have to make today about..

- Your Leadership
- Your Resources
- Your Strategy
- Your Direction
- Your Team

...are not that much different than the basic survival strategy and basic survival steps you'd need to take in any other emergency.

The Basic Steps To
Survival, Recovery and Growth

We'll spend the rest of this book covering survival,
recovery and growth ... but for now – just think 'survival skills'.

What would you do if you were the pilot on a 20 seater plane and
crashed in some remote mountain range? You hit your head, then
woke up and realized you were lost somewhere on top of a mountain
and in trouble. What would you need to do to survive?

1)   **Assess your situation.**

- **Are you hurt?** If you are, determine exactly where you're hurt
  or injured and where you aren't. Example: Your arm may be
  broken, but if your legs aren't, that's good luck in this case.

- **Are you rational or hysterical?** Are you able to control your
  stress so you can think clearly? If not, take a few deep breaths
  and calm yourself so you can think straight, you have a long
  trek ahead of you.

- **Is everyone else all right?** There were 20 people on the plane
  and we'll assume everyone is pretty beat up, but basically OK.

- **Take stock of everything you have.** Make a list of everything
  you have right now that you can use to help you survive.

- **Get your bearings.** Maybe you're not a wilderness survival
  expert, but you do know the sun comes up in the east and sets
  in the west. Go to your highest point and survey your options.

2)   **Be the leader.**

- **Take charge.** Even though some folks are pretty beat up, they
  are all OK, but they really need you to be the leader *right now*.

- **Who is on your side?** If you're lost in the mountains, you won't
  leave anybody behind, even if they're worthless (like you'll need
  to do in business). Just make sure you do a reality check and
  know who you can count on 100% – and who you can't.

- **Assemble your team.** 20 people is not a team. They're just 20 people, all with different ideas and agendas. They can't become a team without clear goals, a clear plan and a leader to keep them on track and headed together in the same direction.

- **Assign specific responsibilities.** Everybody doesn't need to watch one person try to start a fire. Determine exactly what needs to be done and assign every person a specific duty, and then make sure every person does the job they are assigned.

3) **Plan and prepare.**

- **Find your direction.** You can see a stream, you know streams run downhill, you know that's where the roads are, and if you know you need to head west – watch the sun go down, find a landmark downhill in that direction, and get a good bead on it.

- **Make a plan.** There is no trail, you'll have to make your own. Be careful trying to take shortcuts, there's always a catch.

4) **Always keep moving forward.**

- **Maintain morale and determination.** You'll all be fine, as long as *you* can maintain the *belief* in your ability to survive, as long as everyone does their *job* and as long as you *all charge hard every minute and make reaching your goal the priority.*

- **Check your bearings regularly.** It's easy to sit on the mountain and see that landmark. It's much tougher to maintain your direction once you're down in the woods, especially when it gets dark. Keep verifying that you're on the right track.

- **Avoid fatigue / stay fit for survival.** Survival takes its toll on everyone, both mentally and physically. While it seems like you should keep charging forward all through the night instead of stopping for rest and some food, it will more likely set you back than get you there faster.

- **Don't quit!** You're their leader, you have clear goals and you're determined to succeed. Hang in there, you'll be fine.

OK, we're not lost in the woods, so what does all that mean?

Well, whether you're talking about survival when times are tough, or about growth year after year, until you're actually 'out of the woods' in your dealership, the basic planning is the same.

Being in survival mode forces us to take a harder look at everything we're doing and not doing. We can make a few mistakes in good times, but if you're barely hanging on, there isn't much room for error. Let's focus on survival and recovery and if you're doing pretty well now, just adapt and adjust these points to grow even more.

What Is The Situation In Your Dealership?

• *How bad is it?* How much longer can you hang on at the rate you're going now? Set goals and deadlines, and stick to them.

• *How's your attitude?* Have you given up hope and are you just waiting for the ship to sink, or do you still believe that *if* you can pull your team together, get them all on a good plan and get them to perform their jobs, that you can still make something happen?

• *Your managers.* How many managers do you have that you can count on 100% to follow your directions? This is BIG.

Managers are your key employees and they will either make you or break you. Dealerships don't go broke because they lack good salespeople or other employees. Dealerships go broke because they lack good managers who can hire, train, coach, manage and develop good salespeople, and who will follow their leader's direction.

• *Leadership.* There's nothing more important than all of your upper-level managers and your mid-level managers becoming leaders, so you can reach your goals.

I have no statistics on this, but you and I have been doing this long enough to know *most* of your management staff is not able to pull this off by themselves, because they either aren't all leaders, haven't had enough education, because they're not all on board 100%, or because you won't give them the authority they need to do the job.

A catch: All dealers aren't necessarily great leaders. If you aren't, that's OK as long as you have a strong GM or GSM who *can and will* do exactly what *you* want done. Even if you're all great leaders, let's get you and your top managers to the leadership class *to quickly get everybody on the exact same page, with the same goals.*

Leadership requires making tough choices.

As the leader, you're always going to have to make tough business decisions. Decisions regarding employees are even tougher. You've made mistakes in hiring and then in keeping some of them – now most are like family. The problem is you have people in your dealership who shouldn't even be there. Some of them you hired out of necessity (or so it seemed at the time), and some were just plain bad decisions.

Whether your goal is survival or growth, you have to determine which employees you can count on to really step up to pull this off. *Those are the only people you can keep,* because if you hang onto anyone who isn't on board with you 100%, you risk total failure.

Time in service or being related *does not trump ability* when you're trying to survive. But before you fire anyone, try to fix them first by having that heart-to-heart you've been putting off and by getting them properly trained. Just know that if you decide to keep negative employees, or if you keep anyone who can't or won't do their job, you can't possibly develop teamwork. That flaw may be fatal and will likely cause total failure in your goal to recover or grow.

Management teamwork is absolutely critical, and the train is leaving the station today – so you guys have to all get onboard *now*. If you have a manager who isn't onboard 100%, it's because he or she has a different set of beliefs on how the car business works and on how it should work at your dealership. You have to fix them or leave them.

Coming to our Dealer / Manager Team Leadership Workshop with your managers is kind of like going to couple's counseling. In class, you have a third party to keep the discussion on track, point out potential and options you hadn't thought about, and help you and your staff discover the solutions to your problems *as a team.*

In 20 plus years of training dealers, their GMs and managers, we've found that at the beginning of our leadership workshop, *hardly any dealer and their entire management team is on the same page.*

Why isn't everyone on the same page? All the reasons we've talked about; poor initial training, bad habits, non-existent procedures and poor communication on goals, planning and proper execution.

In most dealerships, with a dealer and 5 managers, you have 6 different goals and agendas – and that won't work. So get to class fast.

In class, we spend two days *in a very structured environment* bringing your management team together. It starts with *common sense questions* about the potential and the problems in your dealership.

Even hard core, 30-year managers who've done everything differently, don't argue about anything we cover – they can't, because it's all common sense. We go through the most logical solutions to manage a sales force to improve sales, and we ask everyone about what would help them the most. When they answer, it becomes *their* decision on what would work for them. Because it's their idea, they take ownership of that task, goal, process or change.

We can help you pull your team together because we're able to hit on all the points in two days, in the right order, to generate the best answers, to get everyone pointed in the same direction with you.

By the end of class, everyone is almost on the same page. At that point, if the leader (the dealer or GM) takes charge, gets his or her team together after class and lays out clear goals, plans and requirements, turning on your management team is a done deal, 90% of the time.

At the end of class though, if any manager or salesperson *does not* agree with the direction *you* decide to take, if you don't eliminate them fast, they'll destroy any chance you have of reaching your goal.

> *This is your dealership, and running it cannot be a democracy. You should ask everyone for input, but once the discussions end, you're the only one who gets to vote on what to do next.*

If you're struggling now, these are critical decisions. If you don't get your management team onboard with a single goal, trained on exactly how to make and then execute the plans it takes to reach your goal – it can't happen, and you won't survive (or grow).

On the flip side, if you get everyone onboard, get them properly trained with a single goal and determination, you can turn your store around so fast, you'll be shocked you hadn't done it before.

• *About the rest of your employees, including relatives and friends...*

One year in my presentation at NADA, I was focusing on teamwork and was talking about how so many dealers have accumulated so many non-team, *negative* players over the years. In that class, I said, "If you feel *that* loyal to employees who *you know* are hurting your dealership, fire them and just keep sending them a paycheck every month, but get them out of your dealership so you can grow."

Recovery and Growth

How one dealer solved that problem...

One dealer came up to me at the end of the meeting and said...

"Last year, I did exactly what you just talked about. I started on the line with this guy and we became great friends. I got promoted to management, he stayed in sales, then I bought the store and that was always a sore spot with him.

"He was my best friend and our kids grew up together. But over time, he became the most negative employee we had, and everyone knew he was costing us sales. So I finally called him into my office and told him I just couldn't do it anymore. I told him he was fired but that I'd keep paying him for 6 months (because I felt so guilty)."

Then he said, "And it wasn't an hour after he left that several other employees came in to thank me for finally getting rid of him. When he left, the attitudes in my dealership changed completely, and we started selling more and making more than we ever had in the past. And at that point, everyone knew that if I was willing to fire my best friend, if they didn't perform, their jobs were on the line, too."

Tip: Give each of your negative employees the benefit of the doubt and train them first. If we can help you save them, their experience is invaluable. You have to be in class with them though, and by the end of class, they'll know exactly what you expect, and you will definitely know from their attitude whether they should be allowed to come to work tomorrow in *your* dealership.

• The rest of this book will be on the different areas of the Skills, Habits, Attitudes, the types of Customers you need to focus on in today's new market, and your incredible potential if you will.

STOP HERE! Whether you're a dealer, manager or a salesperson, read this section again. *It was either for you or about you.* Highlight every point that strikes a nerve and start writing out your plan to make those changes so you can improve, survive and grow year after year.

And whether you're the positive or negative person we're talking about, I'd really recommend you get to class on your own if your dealer won't send you. The car business offers so much potential, and most of us have been so under-trained, that once you learn the *core skills* of your job, success is simply a step-by-step process.

RECAP OF THIS SECTION

Get <u>all</u> of your managers together for a meeting at least twice a week so you can work on recovery and growth as a team.

Core Responsibilities...

1. It is logical for the dealer (the owner of the business) to decide where the dealership is headed, to develop the long and short range plans and to hold everyone accountable to do their job. ❏ **True** ❏ **False**

2. It is logical for managers to be responsible to implement the plans and activities required to reach the goals of their dealer, by training the salespeople, coaching them daily and by managing their daily activities to ensure results. ❏ **True** ❏ **False**

3. It is logical for the salespeople to be responsible for bringing prospects onto the lot through prospecting and follow up, to sell the prospect once they're there by following the Basics, Closing, Overcoming their Objections and Negotiating effectively, and then to retain (keep) each customer for life. ❏ **True** ❏ **False**

Survival and Growth Strategies...

1. We need to effectively assess our situation so we know exactly what direction to head and action to take. ❏ **True** ❏ **False**

2. Survival and growth require Leadership. ❏ **True** ❏ **False**

3. It is critical for the Leader to bring all employees together as one team, focused on reaching our goals. ❏ **True** ❏ **False**

4. Just working at our dealership or being in management is not an indicator of whether someone is *on* our team. ❏ **True** ❏ **False**

5. One key to survival and growth is to continually move forward in everything we do. ❏ **True** ❏ **False**

Tip: If management hasn't been involved as a group up to this point, it's a serious mistake and you should correct it right away.

To recover or grow, you need total buy-in to your goals and total teamwork in every department, especially from your management staff. If every manager is on the same page, you can pull this off. If every manager *isn't* on the same page, you risk total failure.

SECTION 3

YOUR SALESPEOPLE

Are your salespeople ready to help you recover and grow?

If you're ready to grow, we'll need to take a real life look at what your salespeople are doing now and at the changes you'll all have to make to grow.

15

A dozen things your salespeople may be good at, that will <u>not</u> guarantee your recovery or growth.

Most salespeople are very good at many things and have some or even all of the qualities of a great salesperson.

I'll cover a dozen things in this chapter that are extremely important if a salesperson wants to succeed in sales. These skills and traits describe them, their attitude and their goals in general.

However, these are only *the first dozen things* they have to be able to do well. These traits *do not guarantee* your recovery and growth – even though they're so important.

The Problem: Too many salespeople rely *solely* on these first dozen areas to make them successful. They never work on developing the *other technical selling skills* we'll cover in later chapters they must have to grow and succeed, especially in today's challenging market.

Recovery and Growth

First, grab that pen and paper...

If you're serious about growing in sales, as you read through these next few chapters, slow down, spend some extra time on each point, think about your team and make notes about each topic.

I'm betting just about everything on this first list fits most of the salespeople you have. How do I know? *Because I've met about half a million salespeople and managers personally,* since I started training. There are, of course, exceptions to the rule, but just about everybody I've met got into this business with good intentions and really does care about their customers.

At a quick glance, a lot of salespeople seem to be doing everything right to sell more cars. They're happy, they love their job, they love their dealership, they love their customers and they may even put in double shifts every day, just waiting to help someone. The problem is, they still end up with just average or below average sales for the month.

Here is our first list of 12 things your salespeople need to be good at to sell cars. Use that notebook or create a spreadsheet. List each salesperson and manager and rate each one, from 1-10 in each area.

Key Areas In Sales...	Rating
1. Loves cars and the business	(__)
2. Has tons of product knowledge	(__)
3. Has a great attitude	(__)
4. Has a professional appearance	(__)
5. Is outgoing, personable and friendly	(__)
6. Loves talking to people	(__)
7. Knows our inventory	(__)
8. Is a goal setter	(__)
9. Is extremely organized	(__)
10. Comes to work to work	(__)
11. Cares about our customers	(__)
12. Is a team player	(__)

So the question is...

> *If your ratings are high in each area on the
> list for just about every one of your salespeople,
> why aren't they selling more vehicles each month?*

That's an easy answer – it's because nothing on this list has anything to do with their actual *selling skills*.

All the attributes and abilities listed here are certainly important and everything on this list is critical to anyone who wants to become a high achiever in sales. But without the *dozens of other technical selling skills* they need that will turn a friendly relationship with a prospect into a delivery, they'll miss almost every sale your dealership could be making.

> *Stop again!*
>
> *Seriously, get out your notebook or spreadsheet,
> put each salesperson and manager's name on a row
> or column, and go back through this list and rate
> each person from (1-10) in each area.*
>
> *Then start helping them to improve in each area.*

16

SALESPEOPLE

Exactly what is their job, and how well are they really doing?

As managers, we've never actually been taught how to turn non-salespeople into the sales professionals you desperately need today. Plus in these last few great years – training and managing salespeople just hasn't been a top priority in most dealerships.

It's a fact, sales is one of the toughest professions to manage. There are so many different skills and work habits to train and manage, that for most dealers and managers, it always seemed easier to replace someone, rather than go to the effort to train and manage them.

There is so much to learn and so much to remember in sales, that even your most motivated salesperson really isn't any different than a $10 Million Dollar ball player. Now you'd certainly think that any ball player who makes ten million would be self-motivated and willing to practice on their own. They are motivated – *and* they're also continually trained, coached and managed every day of their career.

Most of your salespeople have potential, but until management steps up and treats their management position as seriously as a coach who wants to win the Super Bowl – you'll just keep missing easy sales every day and never even end up with a field goal in today's market.

Let's do a quick review of your salespeople's key job responsibilities and look even harder *at how they're doing their job* – especially in today's tougher market with today's more demanding buyers.

Why Were Salespeople Hired?

When we ask this question in our Dealer / Manager Leadership workshop, the answer: *'to sell'* is always the logical response, from everyone in class.

But while 'a sale' is what every manager hopes for and expects, that actually isn't correct. And understanding this *critical* key point is one of management's biggest problems; they're expecting, and usually simply hoping their salespeople will 'go sell something'.

Of course, there's no doubt about it, making a sale is the end result every manager wants. That's why managers yell, "Get out of here and go sell something," only to be disappointed later.

The short-list of a salesperson's critical job responsibilities:

- Follow the Basics: Give *every prospect* on the lot a great presentation and demonstration of the product

- Handle price and build value

- Close the sale and overcome objections

- Set up the negotiation properly

- Follow your negotiation process (if you have one)

- Complete the paperwork properly

- Deliver the vehicle properly

- Follow up after the sale

- Follow up if they didn't make the sale

- Prospect for new business

If you really do want more sales,
learn to better manage these sales activities.

Why? Because if you take a closer look at what a salesperson is supposed to do, making a sale is just the <u>end result</u> of everything on the list. These areas are critical *sales activities*. If they don't do the activities that create a sale, you won't deliver many units.

Recovery and Growth

Are your salespeople doing the job you hired them to do?

First, let's take a quick look at the critical job responsibilities they have and the 'short' answer on each area, then we'll go deeper...

- **Basic Steps Of The Sale**

  No ... Only 40% of your prospects get a demonstration.

- **Staying Off Price On The Lot**

  Most salespeople do the opposite and focus on price – not value.

- **Closing The Sale**

  80% of all sales are made after the 5th closing attempt, but 75% of your salespeople only know one closing question and 75% of the time, they only try to close one time.

- **Handling Objections**

  Salespeople only have one method to handle almost every objection they get; drop the price – and they use that same method, even when it isn't a price related objection.

- **Setting Up the Negotiation Properly**

  Just the opposite, they begin their negotiation on the lot with $844 as the *average* first discount they offer a prospect.

  By the time they write up the prospect, they've already given away $2,062 of your gross profit.

  They've already discussed trade value, what they owe, how much down they have and the payment they're looking for.

  (This is why you don't see as many write ups as you should, and why prospects go sideways when you hit 'em at sticker plus on your first pencil with nothing for their trade.)

- **Following the Negotiation Process**

  Two problems:

  1) Management has no process, or it's extremely loose.

  2) They work the 'desk' harder than they work the customer.

- **Delivering the Vehicle Properly**

  Only if you count this example as a good delivery, "Here are the keys, I put my card in the console, call if you have any questions and please give me a '10' on the survey."

- **Following Up After the Sale**

  A CSI contact for a 'Perfect 10' isn't Follow Up.

  An effective Follow Up process is *ongoing* for 'Retention'.

- **Following Up Unsold Prospects**

  Can't – didn't get their number over 70% of the time.

  Of the numbers they do get, 48% only call one time.

  If they do get a number, it's usually the home number. Then they call the home number one time in the middle of the day when people are at work and then tell you, "No one answered."

- **Prospecting for New Business**

  You do have a sense of humor on this; you're such a kidder.

In real life, the porter probably has a clearer job description than your salespeople, and the porter is held accountable to do his job.

Once hired:

- Salespeople get almost no *initial* training
- They get almost no *daily* ongoing training
- They get almost no daily 'sales *activity* management'
- They have no *requirements* to do anything on this list
- They have no *clear goals* for the day, week, month or year
- They have no *minimum* unit or gross requirements

Let's try to be realistic.
Without proper training to develop the skills they need,
and without the tools they need to do their job,
exactly what do you expect in production from your salespeople?

17

13 Critical Skills Salespeople
Need To Grow In This Market

In the last chapter, I didn't say that salespeople aren't putting in a lot of hours, and I didn't suggest they aren't trying as hard as they can with what skills they do have. What we *have* discovered on the last two pages is that for all the hours your salespeople work and their great intentions, in real life they're doing a poor job overall of handling the responsibilities on the critical list in sales.

Those were basic descriptions, so now let's go deeper and take a look at 13 critical skill sets that everyone in sales; dealers, managers and salespeople need to improve so they can sell more cars in today's changing market.

Note: Read through some of this section as if you were a salesperson.

Since dealers, managers and salespeople all 'sell', I'll go over the 13 skill sets your salespeople need to develop that you should be training on and managing daily.

As a dealer or manager, did you know that the more selling skills *you personally develop*, the more selling skills your salespeople will want to develop, too? You didn't 'get out of sales' as a manager or dealer, you're now *in charge of sales* and you have to know more about 'how to sell' than the salespeople you manage.

You're the leader – so always set the best example.
Always be first in class, first to ask questions, first to practice!

We'll assume *you see the potential* to sell more and we'll assume that *management is totally committed* to recovering quickly and growing. So let's look at some of the skills your salespeople need to improve to sell more units to today's buyer and maximize your gross.

Read and Rate: Let's use this section in two ways...

- First, read each description all the way through. Focus on the skill, the explanation and the tips on how to improve within each skill.

- Then after you've read and understand the skill and why it's important, go back and rate yourself, each manager and each salesperson from 1 – 10 on each skill set listed.

Don't bother rating yourself or anyone a '10' in sales.

Why? Because a '10' would be perfect and none of us are, so save yourself the trouble. Make 9 your maximum, or better yet, get really serious and realize that even if a salesperson is good, they're probably only closing 30% of the people they talk to.

In an accurate rating, selling 30% means they're missing 70%, and that doesn't sound like an 8 or 9, it sounds more like a 3.

Check your ego and rate yourself and your staff honestly.

Overrating their selling skills is one of the biggest reasons most salespeople stop growing. Some salespeople think they're so much better than their production proves, and some just can't admit they aren't perfect. Most salespeople and managers don't or won't open their eyes and their minds to see how much they could improve their sales and their incomes by developing better selling skills and making a few changes in their work habits.

Whether they honestly can't see how they could improve, or whether they just don't want to bother – they start making lists about why 'not selling more' isn't their fault. Big problem: No matter what job you have, once you head down the "no fault" road, you give up just about all of your future potential. Why? Because when you continually explain to everyone why you can't grow, it becomes a fact, at least in your mind. Once you've convinced yourself, it's downhill from there.

Managers also overrate and make excuses for their salespeople. Why? Because if salespeople can't sell, what does that say about management?

The Make It Or Break It Sales 'Skill Sets'

Common Question: What do we mean by *skill sets?*

A *single* skill is important to selling. Being able to combine single skills into a *set* of skills though, makes or breaks almost every sale.

A <u>skill set</u> is made up of multiple individual skills.

Example: A feature, advantage, benefit presentation.

A salesperson can't pull off a *great presentation* that builds value and helps close the sale unless they:

1) have the *product knowledge* to cover the *specific* features, advantages and benefits discovered in their *investigation of the prospect's wants, needs and hot buttons and,*

2) unless they can *bypass price, color and equipment objections* to stay focused on generating excitement,

3) and if they can't use 'yes' questions, they can't *confirm the benefits* of the features important to the prospect,

4) and they'll do all of this in their *walk-around (which is another whole skill set.)*

Plus they have to know how to ask a lot of different questions to do everything I just listed.

Most salespeople have some, but not all of the above skills. While they may give a walk-around, it's their lack of these *other* skills that keeps their *average* presentation from being a *great* presentation that helps them *close* more sales and deliver more units.

That's why as we go through these 13 *skill sets* they need with today's customer, remember there are also *dozens* of individual skills they'll need to master, too, so your dealership can deliver more units.

A Presentation is the BIG picture task, but success is in the details. It's these individual skills that determine how the picture comes out!

13 Critical Skill Sets For Salespeople

1. Control The Sales Process   Rating (_____)

Today's customer is more cautious than ever. They're there to buy, but if you aren't up to the task, you'll lose the sale. Plus, the more qualified they are to buy, the more likely they are to walk away from a bad presentation, arrogance, ambivalence or ignorance.

Buyers in today's market are way more concerned about value than price, and if you think cheap selling your product means more deliveries, you're wrong – 'cheap' will cost you sales. Your best bet to sell more units is to build more value than any other salesperson will. To do that, you have to learn how to control the sale.

Controlling the selling process means asking questions instead of just answering them. It means keeping the sale on track and continually moving the sale forward instead of losing it. Control means leading the customer through the Basic steps of selling and through the 4 steps buyers have to go through to purchase, *by asking questions*.

To control the sales process, you'll need to develop each of these skill sets on how to...

- Bypass price on the lot to focus on value.

- Use 'open end' questions to build rapport.

- Use 'either / or' questions to investigate, keep the conversation on track and close the sale.

- Use 'yes' questions to confirm the benefits of the features, advantages and benefits they said were important to them.

- Rephrase price when you close.

- Refocus price in the negotiation.

- Clarify, rephrase, isolate and close on every objection you get when you're in the final stages of the sale.

Everybody is a buyer, but very few will buy on their own without help from a professional salesperson.

Rate yourself (and your team) on your ability to control the selling process the way you've heard me describe it in my books, newsletters, in our classes and on JVTN®.

2. Follow The Basics With Every Prospect   Rating (____)

We cover the steps of the Basics again and again in my newsletters, books, classes and on JVTN® because more sales are made or lost because of the Basics than everything else put together.

About 90 pages in my sales book are on explaining the 3 Phases of the Basics. 75% of our new workshop, "How To Sell A Car And Close The Sale Today" is on how to follow the Basics and close the sale effectively to double and triple your sales. By now, you should understand what each step is and why it's important.

The 3 Phases: How We Teach The Basics

- **Warm Them Up**

  Great first impression

  Greet them properly

  Build rapport to find the common ground

  Investigate to find their buying wants and needs (not price)

- **Build Value**

  Present the features, advantages and benefits they care about

  Demonstrate the vehicle and those features

  Sell your service department and the people in it

  Prove what you've been saying with your evidence manual

- **Close The Sale**

  Start with your Summary Closing Sequence at the Landmark

  Use the Assumptive Sold Line Close at 100 yards

  Follow with 12 action closes for TMO (Total Mental Ownership)

  Ask your final 'either / or' closing question on refreshment, registration or accessories, not on price or terms

  Nothing will make you more sales or cost you more sales, than how effectively your salespeople follow the Basics.

Just showing a vehicle isn't the same as presenting it *effectively*. A ride around the block isn't an *effective* demonstration. Dropping price doesn't increase value. And you can't *effectively* follow the Basics if you don't know how to use the questions we teach.

A Super Skill Set: The Basics is an example of a super skill set that requires *dozens* of skills to turn *just following the Basics* into *following the Basics effectively*. It's that last word 'effectively' that makes or breaks the sale, every time you talk to a prospect.

To follow the Basics *effectively*, you have to know how to...

- Look, act and sound like a professional, so that when you first approach your prospects, you make a positive first impression.
- Greet the prospect *promptly* and *properly* ... with a smile and an open end question to get their name every time, immediately followed by an either / or question to move the sale forward.
- Ask open end questions to build rapport.
- Ask either / or questions to investigate to find their specific hot buttons that you'll focus on in your presentation later.
- Combine building rapport and investigating to put them at ease and learn more about what to cover in your presentation.
- Acknowledge a price question – bridge to another topic – ask an either / or question to pull the conversation back on track.
- Acknowledge – Bridge – Ask an either / or question to respond to any color, equipment or option objection or question that you aren't ready to discuss yet (sell the car, then worry about color).
- Control the 'wander-around' to get all of the information you'll need on your demonstration and walk-around later.
- Sell your Service department and introduce your prospects to several dealership employees, because the more people they like, the more likely they are to buy.
- Determine when it's time for a demo (after you've found hot buttons), and how to set up an effective demonstration.
- Use your product knowledge to cover the *specific* FABs each prospect is interested in, *as you trade drivers each time.*
- Demonstrate the FABs of each system *each* prospect is interested in (navigation / entertainment / adaptive cruise / etc.)

- Give a feature, advantage and benefit walk-around presentation to the *secondary driver,* that covers the specific features the secondary driver is most interested in.

- Give a feature, advantage and benefit walk-around presentation to the *primary driver* next, that covers the specific features the primary driver is most interested in.

- Use the Landmark Summary Close to start your closing sequence.

- Use 'yes' questions to get a minimum of 6 positive responses in the last 2 minutes of the demonstration.

- Use the Assumptive Sold Line Close when you're about 100 yards from the dealership.

- Use a combination of several Action Closes and either / or closes on registration, refreshment or accessories to get another dozen or more commitments to own.

- Use tone, inflection and body language and a Silent Walk-Around to help your prospect *devalue* their own trade to bring it to a more realistic figure before you go inside.

- Complete all of your paperwork properly.

- Rephrase any price objection to budget when you're closing.

- Clarify, rephrase and isolate on any objection you get to set yourself up for another close.

- Know how to close on "I'll think it over" with the 4-Step, 2-Step, 1-Step or 0-Step method.

- Use tone, inflection and body language to control the process as you ask your final closing question on the way to your desk.

You're correct. There's more to *investigating, presenting* and *closing* than, "What do you want to spend?", "Did you want to drive it?" and "Do y'all want to go inside and see what we can do on this one?"

Using this list, go through and rate yourself and each of your salespeople on how effectively and how often each person follows the Basics, with every prospect.

To learn more about Selling & Closing...
• 12 Specific Courses On JVTN® ... Just On Selling & Closing
• 2 Sales Workshops ... How To Sell A Car & How To Close The Sale

3. Ask The Right Questions   Rating (____)

From the last page, you can see that learning to ask questions is your key to success in sales. If you haven't read my sales book, been to class and aren't practicing on our Virtual Customers on JVTN® instead of on your expensive, real life prospects, understand this...

You don't tell your way to a sale,
you ask your way to the sale.

Almost every step of the selling process requires that you ask *the right questions, at the right time.* From your greeting to your delivery, it's a constant question and answer process.

Taking incoming sales calls requires that you get the information fast, control the conversation and end with an appointment that shows. That means you have to know how to ask questions on the phone, too.

It's the same with closing, handling objections, bypassing price, follow up, prospecting and getting more internet leads on the lot. Everything you do in sales revolves around questions.

There isn't enough space in this section or even in this book to go through all of the types of questions you need to ask, or the dozens of variations of those questions and specific closes.

We spend 30+ pages in my sales book and several hours in our sales class going over how to *ask the right type of question, at the right time* in the Basics, so you can continually move the sale forward a step at a time. Then in class we role play (practice) using these questions, closes, and objection handling methods for 5-6 hours over 2 days. When you leave, you can definitely use questions effectively.

You need good questioning skills, because without them, you can't stay off price, you can't build rapport, and you can't investigate to find each person's wants, needs and hot buttons. Without effective questioning skills you can't present effectively, close the sale, handle objections, get referrals or even schedule appointments that show.

How would you rate yourself on the questioning skills you have now?
What do you need to learn more about to improve your sales?

4. Close The Sale For Total Mental Ownership   Rating (____)

I hope I'm making selling, closing and negotiation sound easy, because it sure can be if you just develop the right skills, and then slow down and do all of this correctly.

People tell you "No" a lot when you're closing. They're nervous about spending 20 or 30 grand, and they didn't know you, like you or trust you an hour ago. So saying "Yes" in just an hour means really going out on a limb for most people. That's why you have to make it as easy as possible for them to agree to purchase.

If you close correctly, you'll never ask the dreaded, "Will you buy it today," question. Not only that, your negotiation will be about *helping them* fit this new vehicle they love into their *budget,* instead of whether you can "make them a deal today".

Oops! Salespeople have several problems with closing:

1) Most have only been taught the least effective closing questions that almost guarantee a "No" or "I'll think it over" every time.

   SP: Are you ready to buy it if we can work it out?

   Bob: No, we should probably think it over.

   SP: Are you sure we can't talk you into it today?

   Bob: No, we need some time.

   SP: OK, here's my card and make sure you see me before you buy anywhere else – we'll beat any deal in town.

2) They phrase it differently, but most only know one bad closing question, and they stop closing after just one *poor* attempt.

   • 75% of salespeople only know one close.

   • 75% of salespeople only try to close one time.

   • 80% of all sales are closed after the 5th attempt.

3) When they do ask their (bad) closing questions, they ask those bad questions at the wrong time. To sell a lot of cars, there is a specific time to start closing, and a step-by-step sequence to follow.

4) When they get an objection, most salespeople start dropping price, (even when the customer's objection has nothing to do with price).

What's the best closing question?

The most common question we get about closing is, "What's the best closing question to use?" While there are certainly *good* closing questions you'll ask, closing is a process, not a single question.

Closing isn't a question – the entire 'Basic Steps of Selling' is just one continuous closing process, from the curb to Finance.

Go back and read the steps of the Basics once more.

Doesn't doing a great job on each of those steps *close the sale,* a step at a time? Isn't each of those steps made up of dozens of individual skills, that once you master, literally close the sale for you so well that by the time you get to the *closing sequence*, it's more of a wrap up than a specific question you ask?

At the beginning of our 'How To Sell A Car And Close The Sale Today' Workshop, most salespeople and managers really can't see how they could *close 50% more of their prospects,* especially today.

By the end of class it's, "Holy smokes, this is easy!"

Think about closing the sale as a process, like building a house or anything else. Our process starts with a great first impression, a warm and friendly greeting, building rapport and investigating to find their buying motives. If we do those steps well, we move into an effective value building stage with our presentation and demonstration, which leads straight into a *Closing Sequence* at the end of the demonstration.

The closing sequence itself is a very simple 4-step process and it takes 10 - 15 minutes from the time you start your closing sequence until you're in your office starting the paperwork. In that short time, you'll get close to 20 *commitments to purchase,* all without ever talking price or even asking them to *buy.*

Quick Question: When you write somebody up, do you want a prospect in your office who is sitting there thinking...

❑ I might consider buying this – or –

❑ I'm ready to buy now – let's take care of the paperwork.

You definitely need a committed buyer before you negotiate. Otherwise, you'll just end up holding a price dropping contest.

Recovery and Growth

Closing means getting 'Total Mental Ownership'

People don't take delivery of a product until they make a mental commitment to purchase. When you ask these closing questions...

"Will you buy it if things work out?" or

"Do y'all wanna go inside and see what we can do?"

... you don't end up with a total mental ownership commitment. Both of those questions only ask them to *consider* purchasing, and both force the final decision to be based on the price.

Weak closes even cost you sales with people who are ready to say 'yes'. That's one reason you hear a lot of, "We'll think it over and get back to you later," when you're sure you were on the right car.

With Total Mental Ownership, you have properly closed the sale and you have a buyer sitting in your office for just one reason; they are ready to take care of the paperwork, so they can take their new vehicle home right now, today. Think back to your easiest sales; weren't they 'mental owners' before you started the paperwork? You just have to learn how to get everyone to become a mental owner.

Best of all, when you close with our process, their commitment to own is not contingent on price, trade, down, discount or payments!

Here are a couple of other quick facts on why it's so easy to increase sales when you follow our process and learn how to close properly...

- 78% of the people you talk to on the lot will buy (8 out of 10).
- 82% specifically came to your dealership to buy.
- 90% will buy within a week.
- 20% is the average closing ratio. (We sell 2 and miss 6 of 8 buyers.)
- 71% who didn't buy, said you had a vehicle in stock they would have purchased. (Wow – that's a real bummer.)

Why didn't the 71% buy?

Their answers are a combination of everything we've talked about. They didn't really like working with the salesperson, didn't feel the salesperson was very interested in *them*, didn't cover enough about the features that were most important to *them* and didn't get a very good demo, if they got one at all. Now toss in a bad closing question or two after all that and you're done.

5. Handle All Of Their Objections   Rating (____)

Handling objections is directly hooked to closing the sale. If 80% of all sales are made after the 5th attempt at closing, that means we have to close, get an objection, handle it, and close again, 5 times.

We were all taught the worst ways to sell, close and to handle our prospect's objections to buying. If you think salespeople have a hard time closing – *overcoming objections* is way out of their league. A price close, followed by a drop in price to overcome an objection will get you nowhere with most people, except into a hum-haw over price.

I was taught to do exactly that. My first five years in sales, every close I knew was a price close, and to overcome any objection, I was taught to keep offering a lower price.

Me: Whaddaya think – if we can make it work, will you buy it?

Bob: No, it's a lot of money.

Me: How about if I saved you $500?

Bob: Well, we really wanted blue instead of green.

Me: What if we dropped the price another $500?

Bob: We kinda wanted the automatic, too.

Me: What if we threw in a CD player – can we do it then?

Bob: I don't know ....

Me: What if we gave you $500 more on your trade, cut the price a grand, threw in the CD, got you in with nothing down and kept your payments under $300, would you buy it now?

What a way to lose a sale, or all of the gross profit in 5 quick questions. Worse, when salespeople close this way, describe the negotiation process once you're inside. Isn't it...

Grind – Grind – Grind – Lost Sales – Low Gross – Low CSI

After I really learned to 'sell', when I started selling cars again...

I sold more units and made more money my first 7 months back in the business, than I sold and earned my first 5 years combined.

Do you remember how much fun it really is to sell a car to someone who likes you, who is so excited about getting their new car, they can hardly wait to take delivery? Doesn't that seem like a much better set up for a negotiation than focusing on price?

Before we move away from selling and closing, I want to remind you about how important your timing is in making more sales ...

Speed Kills Selling

Slow Kills Negotiations

Speed Kills Selling. When you're in the Warm Up and Value Building stages, all the way up to that first closing sequence at the end of your demonstration when you're just a couple of minutes from the dealership; it's a fact that *going fast will lower your chances of making the sale.*

Time Spent on the Lot	Avg. Closing Ratio
60 minutes or less	6%
At 72 minutes	31%
At 100 minutes +	57%

Slow Kills Negotiations. Once you start closing, though, just the opposite is true. Going slow will cost you the sale and will cost you gross and good CSI scores, even if you make the sale.

From that Landmark Closing Sequence until they're headed for Finance to finish up the paperwork, you need a smooth, deliberate, fast and effective process. (And then you need a fast, efficient process in Finance, too.) *Closing and negotiation...*

- Summary Close / Sold Line Close / Dozen Action Closes
- Silent Walk-Around of their Trade
- Final Closing Question
- Start the Paperwork / Get the Trade Appraised
- First Pass in the Negotiation (Pull their highest budget figures)
- Second Pass (Go for the gross)
- Wrap it Up (Last bump close) and Head to Finance

Total Time: 30–40 Minutes Max (75% of the time)

For more info on the sales process, the basics, bypassing price, closing & handling objections, jump on JVTN® our online training network, or get to our two sales workshops, How To Sell A Car and How To Close The Sale.

6. Handling Price   Rating (____)

Salespeople: There are three things you have to learn to do with price...

Bypass – Rephrase – Refocus

You have to learn how to *bypass* and move away from price on the lot. You have to learn how to change the objection (rephrase) when you're closing. You have to learn how to *refocus* the Negotiation back to budget and away from price, trade, discounts or rates.

Why is that important? Because...

*Selling is Emotional
Negotiation is Logical*

On the lot...

Haven't you heard you're supposed to be enthusiastic when you're selling? Haven't you also heard you're supposed to get your prospects excited about owning the vehicle you're showing them? Haven't we all heard we should "sell the sizzle, not the steak"?

Enthusiasm, excitement, sizzle – don't those describe emotions?

To sell the sizzle and build the excitement, you *enthusiastically* use those questions we've been talking about.

- Won't this be fun with the top down on those warm summer evenings up in the mountains?

- With that new cruise control and that adjustable seat, you can sit back, relax and enjoy those long drives, and won't that be a lot better than those uncomfortable seats you said you have now?

- Don't you guys just love that stereo system, plus with the hook up for your iPod, you can listen to all of your favorites?

- Having this camper gives you the freedom to roam, and sure beats the high cost of staying in hotels every night, doesn't it?

On a demo you also get to use the prospect's five senses to help you get them even more excited: *see, feel, hear, touch and smell.* Isn't a demonstration the most emotional step in the selling process? Wouldn't that be the reason we select the vehicle we plan to send them home in, demonstrate that vehicle, and close the sale at the end of that demonstration? *This is easy – plan your sale so it's easier to close.*

Your goal in the first 90% of the selling process is to build so much excitement in owning your product, they can't wait to take it home.

That means on the lot and during your presentation and your demonstration, you have to learn how to bypass price so you don't get bogged down in a *logical* discussion about pricing, trade values, rebates and all the other money conversations.

When you're closing, you 'rephrase' price...

Again in closing, you're using the emotions you've built along with the value you've created to get your commitments to own the product. When price comes up as an objection during *closing,* your goal is to change price to an objection that's easier to close. The objection you want to hear is *budget,* and changing price to budget is one of the easiest things to do.

You: (1) (At the end of your demo) It sounds like we've found the perfect car, go ahead and park in the Sold Line and I'll pull the keys so nobody else can drive your new car.

Bob: We like it, but it's a lot of money – what can you do for us on the price?

You: (2) Bob, it sounds like you guys are like me and everybody else, it sounds like you're on a *budget,* am I right?

Bob: Yeah, who isn't these days and we can't afford to spend any more than we have to – what will payments run?

You: (3) Beats me, but I'll get some information real quick and we'll go over all of your payment options.

Bob: That's fine, but if they're too high we're not getting it.

You: (4) I completely understand – I know you both really like the car and I know it has everything you said was important, so *other than* making sure this fits your *budget,* is there any other reason we couldn't wrap this up right now and get you guys out of here so you can start enjoying your new car?

Bob: No, if we can make it fit our budget, we're ready, but we're using our trade as a down payment, what do you think they'll give us for it?

You: (5) We'll have my manager take a look at it right away, I just
need to get some information real quick – Betty, do me a
favor and grab your insurance card and registration on your
trade from your glove box and we'll get started.

Betty: Sure, but can we get in with nothing down?

You: (6) Let's go see. Oh Bob, can you read me the exact mileage
on the new car real quick, I need it for registration.

What were the numbers 1 to 6 for?

Those are situations where average salespeople would have switched
to price to try to get a commitment. That means they would have
started their negotiation before they had a commitment to purchase
and they would have started generating objections immediately.

Here are some of the most common responses average salespeople
would have used at each point to cost themselves sales...

(1)   First, they would have used a bad close: *Well, what do you
think, do you want to go inside and see what we can do? (or)
What do you think, are you ready to take 'er home today?*

(2)   "What can you do for us on price?" ... *How low do we have to go
(or) what do we have to do ... to earn your business today?*

(3)   "What will payments run on this?" ... *Probably around $500,
depending on how much you put down – what were you thinking?*

(4)   "If they're too high, we're not getting it." ... *Bob, we never
miss a sale because of price, we're real flexible and we'll beat
any deal in town, plus we have real good rates and a $2,500
rebate, plus $500 cash as a customer loyalty bonus because
you're trading in one of our products.*

(5)   "What do you think they'll give us for our car?" ... *Probably
somewhere between 10 to 11 thousand, what do you owe on it?*

(6)   "Can we get in with nothing down?" ... *I don't see how,
you're upside down about $2,000. I know you don't want to,
but can you come up with $4,000 or $5,000 down payment?*

In the 'right way' example, we *rephrased* price to budget, *bypassed*
their other pricing questions and continued closing. The 'wrong
way' responses above would have turned a serious buyer who saw
the value, into a dissatisfied price shopper in 2 minutes or less.

In the Negotiation...

You bypassed price on the lot, built *value* in owning the product and got them excited enough to want it <u>now</u>. You started closing the sale, got a price question / objection and you rephrased it to *budget* and got back on track closing.

After doing such a great job building value and excitement and bypassing price, and then rephrasing their price question or objection to budget – why would you flip everything back around to *price* in your negotiation, make it tougher to close and cost yourself gross?

I'm trying to squeeze enough in here on selling and closing from our 2-Day "How To Sell And Close" class to make sense, but there's no way I can squeeze enough information from our "How To Close & Negotiate" class in here to cover negotiating.

Let's leave it with this general thought...

If you've done a great job on value and budget in the Negotiation, just continue to keep *refocusing* every objection they bring up on trade or pricing or terms, back to down and payments.

Bob: The price is too high!

You: So you're OK with $6,000 down and the $586 per month?

Bob: No way – I don't have $6,000, but the price is too high.

You: We can try to work on that a little, but how close to the $6,000 can you come, can you put down $5,700 or $5,800?

Just keep bringing price and trade objections back to the down and the payment. If you will, you'll end up selling more cars, having more fun, making more money, and keeping your customers a lot happier. Side Benefit: High Gross = High CSI.

Within 30 to 60 Days, You Can Easily Learn To
Deliver 20 to 30% More Units – With 30% to 40% More Gross.

Dealers and Managers: If you want to increase your units and gross quickly, just get your entire team through our complete series of classes and get on JVTN®. We'll teach you how to sell more units, with higher gross profits and we'll put the fun back into selling cars!

7. Follow Up With Unsold Prospects   Rating (____)

First the facts…

   a. 78% of the people who walk on your lot are going to buy

   b. 90% of them will make their purchase within a week

   c. With a 20% closing ratio, that means 80% leave without buying

   d. 33% will come back in with good follow up

   e. 67% of them will purchase on their 2nd visit

If the prospect just left without buying, how much time has your salesperson already spent trying to make this sale? If they did a decent job, we're talking about an hour or so, give or take.

Urgent Reminder: 78% will still be buying a vehicle whether your salesperson contacts them again or not.

If they come back in to your dealership, your closing ratio jumps from the 10%-20% *chance* you had with them the first time, to a real 67% *probability* this time.

How long does that 3 to 5 minute follow up call take? Exactly, only about 3 to 5 minutes. How long does it take to address an envelope, put in a preprinted thank you note (below), or to send an email that says the same thing? (Tip: Use a template.)

"Thanks for giving me a chance to show you our products.

*I know getting a vehicle is an important decision and
I know that people make decisions on who to purchase from,
as well as what to purchase, and I hope you'll give me another
chance to earn your business when you're ready.*

Call me if you have any questions. Have a great day – Joe

p.s. – Hope your kids won the ball game!"

How long does it take management to make sure this happens? Less time than it takes to complain about salespeople not doing their follow up. The question isn't will they buy. We know 78% *will* buy, either from you or your competitor. The question is this: Since you've already paid to buy the prospect, since your salesperson has already invested an hour, *are you willing to make them follow up* so you can have a 67% chance of making this sale to pick up an extra $2,500 in gross profit – or not?

Please Note:

> *If your salespeople follow up with every unsold prospect,*
> *you will almost totally eliminate your competition.*

Why would that eliminate the competition? For a few reasons...

The first five years I sold cars I really thought I, personally and *we,* as a dealership were competing with the dealership down the street. I assumed because they'd be talking price, we would have to have the best prices in town to have any chance at making the sale.

After I learned how to actually *sell* (instead of just hoping people would *buy*), I also realized that I was not competing with the dealership down the street, and your salespeople aren't, either.

You may not have thought about it this way, but people don't talk to *dealerships*, they talk to salespeople. Most prospects will never even talk to a manager at that dealership down the street. That means your salespeople are only competing with the other *salesperson* your prospect will talk to at that dealership across town.

As a reminder – here's what will happen to the prospects over there...

• They'll talk to a 6-car guy, not a pro (the pro is busy with a referral)

• 72% won't be greeted properly or have a positive 1st impression

• 85% of the time, the salesperson won't build rapport or investigate

• 88% won't get what they feel is a good presentation or demo

• 75% will only be asked to buy once, and it will be based on price

• 70% won't be asked for their contact information

• 90% will never be contacted again by that salesperson

Let's be serious here, the 6-car guy down the street isn't even in the running as a competitor for a salesperson willing to do a great job of the Basics, control the process, avoid price so they build value, close the sale and handle the objections. Even if your salesperson doesn't sell it the first time, you have a tremendous advantage. Today's buyer wants to talk to a trained professional in sales, not some amateur who just keeps repeating, "Do you have any questions?" and offers cheap prices.

Ask us about our follow up and prospecting training on JVTN®
or get to our Internet & Phone Business Development Workshop.

8. Follow Up Previous Customers   Rating (_____)

How do you spell Gold Mine?

R – E – T – E – N – T – I – O – N

All of the highest achievers I know in sales (30-40-50 units per month) do almost all of their business with repeat customers and referrals. There's just no way to snag enough floor traffic to consistently earn a six-figure income.

If you'll learn how to, and then focus on building a solid customer base, the sky is literally the limit on your earnings. Right now, if you're struggling, your dealership database is your least expensive, most productive list of buyers you can hope for. They already like you or your dealership, and are very open to buying their next vehicle from you, and you have FREE access to the list – today.

It's too easy in tough times to lose sight of the real potential you have in sales, in every community.

1) Your Existing Customer Base: Even when times are tough, try to remember that somebody in your customer base...

   • Wrecked their vehicle yesterday.

   • Is paying too much on repairs and needs to trade.

   • Needs a vehicle for a new driver in the family.

   • Is helping their son or daughter get a new / used vehicle.

   • Has a lease expiring soon.

   • Just wants a new vehicle, and can afford to buy it.

2) Your Market:

   • If new vehicle sales are off 30%, then 70% are still buying.

   • If unemployment reaches 10%, then 90% are still working.

   • If 30% are concerned about losing their job, 70% aren't.

   • And anytime you really think "nobody is buying", for a rude awakening, order the free R.L. Polk & Co. Market Report we provide for our customers at www.JoeVerde.com/Polk

Key Facts About Retention

The Good News...

- 95% of the people you've sold to in the past are going to buy again, either from you and your dealership, or from your competition. Either way, they'll be buying again.

- 50% *plus* are product loyal, and my bet is that it would be closer to 90% with effective follow up.

- Average families will purchase a total of 36 vehicles. This is a 20-year old fact that is probably higher now.

The math...

Families have about 3 vehicles and *were* trading about every 4 years, but let's assume it's every 6 years right now. That means each family is still buying a vehicle every 2 years.

Not including sales to walk-ins, if you want to deliver 1,000 *extra* vehicles per year just to repeat customers, you need 2,000 families who are 100% loyal to your dealership who buy a vehicle every 2 years. Or you need 4,000 families who are 50% loyal, or 8,000 families who are 25% loyal, buying from you.

Your walk-in business will be consistent with market trends. If you've been selling 1,000 units per year for 10 years, that's 10,000 people in your customer base. Even after the duplicates, you already have 6,000 or 7,000 families you could be selling to on top of your walk-in sales, and these extra sales cost nothing.

You could have practically stopped advertising years ago.

- 70% is the closing ratio on repeat customers with 'active follow up'. Why is it so high, and why *active* follow up?

It's so high because people like *familiarity* and dealing with people they know and trust. If you don't follow up, *a few* still come back and buy. If you do follow up though, three to four times as many come back in to buy, and that extra oomph with follow up also raises your closing ratio from 40-50% to 70%+.

- Gross is 40% higher on repeat customers than on walk-ins.

- They're cheap! 20 years ago, manufacturers discovered it was 5 times cheaper to *keep* a customer than to get a new one. In today's market, I'm betting that's closer to 10 times.

The Bad News...

- 90% of your sold customers are never personally contacted again by the salesperson about *buying another vehicle from you.*

  (Sorry – your bulk mailers and bulk emails offering cheap prices don't count as follow up or a personal offer to do business. That's just an ad and they know it.)

- 80% of sold customers never become service customers. This is a biggee, because it takes more than sales follow up for total retention of your customers.

  Note: A *continuing, satisfying business relationship* along with great, consistent follow up is the key to retention.

  Wow – as a potential repeat customer with a 70% closing ratio, with service only 100 steps from the showroom, you'd think scheduling their first service appointment would be a part of the sales process.

- 78% of your service customers *would* consider buying where they have their vehicle serviced (a gold mine).

- 80% of service customers never make it back to 'sales'. It takes a continuing relationship <u>and</u> effective follow up.

- CSI is a score on the sale, not on your customer loyalty. You can score 100% on CSI – and still only have 30% retention.

- CLI is your Customer Loyalty Index. This is your % of sales to repeat and dealership customers. (Your most important number.)

- 70% of the average dealership's monthly sales are made to the most expensive, most informed, lowest gross, price shopping prospects on the planet: Walk-In Prospects.

- If you'll work hard to flip the numbers to 70% repeat and dealership customers and 30% to walk-ins, you'll lower expenses, increase your net 4 to 5 times and selling will be fun again.

How do you build your customer base?

  1) Make a commitment and develop a retention process

  2) Learn how to effectively follow up and prospect

  3) Manage your salespeople's daily activities

*We have a 2-day class and 4 complete training courses on JVTN®
on this topic. Call today and we'll have you online training tomorrow.*

9. Prospecting By Phone Or In Person — Rating (____)

*30% of 'all' people have a family member
who will be trading vehicles within the next 90 days.*

Dealers: Read that again and again, to see the potential impact
this single fact can have on your sales volume and income.

*For one thing, it means you're missing more buyers who are on your
service drive every month than you even deliver in sales right now.*

It also means if your salespeople knew how to prospect, and if your
managers knew how to coach them and manage their in-person and
phone prospecting activities each day, you could cut your advertising
bill 50-75% and your gross would go up 40% or more per unit.

Let's do the math at *your* dealership...

• Your Service Drive (enter total # of customers per month)

     _____   # customers on the drive per month

  x   30%   have a family member trading in 90 days

  = _____   potential sales you *could* make in the next 90 days

• Your Database of Customers (enter total units & years in business)

     _____   units (# you sell per year)

  x_____   years you've been in business

  = _____   people in your database

  x   30%   have a family member trading in 90 days

  = _____   potential sales you could make in the next 90 days

Now we're using *your* numbers. That makes it easier and more fun
to start seeing where you really can start improving, doesn't it?

*On every example I cover in here, grab your notebook
and take some time to meet with your managers. Go over the
statistics in each example and how it affects sales in your dealership.*

10. The Telephone   Rating (____)

How do you spell 'key' to the gold mine?

T – E – L – E – P – H – O – N – E

The telephone is the single most important selling tool you have in sales, yet it's the sales tool most salespeople dislike most. Why is it so important? Because 90% of your total selling opportunities require the use of the telephone.

- Today, 90% of your Unsold Prospects are never contacted again. To follow up Unsold Prospects quickly and effectively, you need phone *selling* skills.

- Today, 90% of your Sold Customers are never contacted again about buying another vehicle. To build Customer Retention, you need phone *selling* skills.

- Today, each of your salespeople *could be making* 5 outgoing prospecting calls each day to bring in more traffic. To Prospect by phone, you need phone *selling* skills.

- Today, a 100 unit dealership gets about 150 incoming sales calls, of which 135 are buyers, and 121 of them will buy within a week. Average sales per month to those 135 buyers: 6. To turn Incoming Sales Calls into appointments, you need phone *selling* skills.

  Important: Based on the average salesperson's and sales manager's phone *selling* skills on incoming sales calls (setting appointments that show): to see more prospects on the lot, *statistically* you're much better off letting the phone ring than answering it.

- Today, 75% of internet leads include phone numbers, but 75% of salespeople send only <u>one</u> email. You need phone *selling* skills to turn 50% of these leads into appointments that show.

One of the most important points to make about working the phone more effectively on incoming sales calls and outgoing follow up and prospecting calls – is to remember that phone skills are just *selling* skills that you use on the phone.

Your 20 or 30 car guy doesn't have any problem with controlling the call, getting the information he or she needs, or scheduling a firm appointment. Why? Because they can sell.

11. Negotiate Successfully   Rating (____)

Buying is <u>Emotional</u> ... Negotiating is <u>Logical</u>.

The 'nots' first...

- You can *not* negotiate if you don't have a commitment to own.
  All you can do without a commitment is to continually drop
  the price, *hoping* you can get a commitment at some lower price.

- Negotiation is *not* running back and forth from the 'desk' to the
  customer dropping price. That's called "running back and forth
  from the desk to the customer dropping price."

- While *price is generally the objection* most salespeople and even
  customers focus on, *price is not the deciding factor.* Price should
  not be the focus in effective negotiations, especially if you
  want to sell more units, and maximize your gross profit on the
  vehicles you do sell.

- Negotiation is *not 'working the desk'*, harder than the salesperson
  works the customer.

So what is a negotiation?

- Ben Franklin said it has to be a win-win for everyone.

- Ben Franklin also said the negotiation starts as soon as the
  first person throws out a figure. He also said the first person to
  throw out a figure has the advantage in the negotiation.

  By that, he meant if you ask a customer on the lot, "What kind
  of payments are you looking for?" the negotiation just started.
  More importantly, you just handed the advantage to your
  prospect when they said $375. Then as a typical salesperson's
  response goes, it continues downhill from there with...

  ... $375 is kinda low – how much down do you have? ($500)

  ... That's not much, hopefully you have some equity in your
  trade, what do you want for it? (Way more than it's worth.)

  ... It doesn't sound like you're close on a $25,000 car. (Oh, we
  saw an ad and only want to pay $19,500 for it.)

In that example, you have given up the advantage in all four areas of the negotiation; price, trade, down and payment – and now your presentation isn't on value, it's on price.

As soon as the *money talk* starts, you also move from the *emotional* stage of generating *interest and desire* in owning the product, to the *logical* stage of the *financial decisions* that have to be made to purchase the product.

At this point in a typical salesperson's presentation, you have no relationship, no idea *why* they want it, no *value* has been created, no *ownership commitments* have been made, and you're on the lot trying to negotiate a (logical) car deal.

After they've already opened the negotiation on the lot and handed prospects the advantage, then the average salesperson uses the *worst 'close'* of all when *no value* has been established, "If we could do that, are you ready to buy it now?"

Then you write it up and they commit to $500 down, $375 a month, wanting $15,000 for their trade (worth maybe $9,000) and only wanting to pay $19,500 for a $25,000 vehicle.

When you bring back your first pencil from the desk at sticker price plus fees ($27,954), $5,000 down, $7,500 for their trade and $784 a month ... they go ballistic.

You need to learn to sell – this stuff is costing you sales every day!

- People, especially walk-ins who've done their homework online and in the paper, sit down at the kitchen table and figure out what they *think* they can spend on a car. They start low on payments (like at $375), then keep adding their higher *'if we had to'* numbers. They do this for down, payment, trade and price.

When a salesperson talks price on the lot, they hear the lowest *hope to* figures from their prospect's Kitchen Table Budget; not their range from low to high, just their lowest numbers.

They don't say, "We want to pay $375, and if we had to, we'd go to $400-$425 but we know that's not very realistic either. So if it really got down to it, we'd go up to $450-$475 and if we get really, really excited, we'd go to $500, but that's it."

- Once you have a proper commitment with TMO (Total Mental Ownership), the Negotiation Process is a simple 3 step process.

1) 1st Pass ... Should always start at *sticker price* with the correct *large* down, the correct *large* payment for a *short term* loan, with a close low *guesstimate* on their trade. (If it's an ad car, make sure they know the 'should be' price, with the same down and terms.)

The Goal in this 1st Pass: Pull the *highest* figures from their Kitchen Table Budget that they figured they could afford.

2) 2nd Pass ... If you do a good job in #1, you're profitable, or very close to it. So the goal in the 2nd Pass is to bring in the gross. This is where you'll spend the majority of your time in the negotiation. You'll close, handle objections, present and defend your numbers, keep the negotiation off of price and on down and payments (budget), focus on the difference and reduce the difference to the ridiculous, and close and overcome objections.

3) 3rd Pass ... This is the Wrap It Up stage of the negotiation, and time for your Final Bump.

Once they're inside, this entire 3 Pass Process shouldn't take more than 20-30 minutes, including appraisals, etc. (75% of the time).

Please remember...

- Speed Kills Selling and Value. Trying to go fast in the Basics will cost you sales almost every time. It doesn't matter if it takes four hours, do your job, build value and start closing properly.

- Slow Kills Closing and Negotiating. Once the Closing Sequence starts, now it's time to work a very deliberate and very efficient and effective process. You sold on value (emotion) and once the numbers start flying, you start to lose that emotional glue that's holding this deal and your gross together.

  URGENT NOTE: To get your salespeople and managers on the same page in how you Negotiate; dealers, managers and salespeople attend our "How To Close & Negotiate" workshop *together*. Dealers and managers also need to attend our workshop for managers, "How To Negotiate & Desk Deals For Maximum Gross".

Remember how great it is when you work a deal that's set up perfectly? It's easy, it's fun, it's profitable, and customers love you afterwards.

12. Track Everything You Do   Rating (____)

You can't grow, if you don't know!

In all sports, the coach tracks and knows every statistic on each player and so do the players. They know how far they hit the ball, how many yards they run on each play, how high they can jump, how fast they can run, how many putts per round.

The coaches and players realize they need this information to know *exactly* what to work on, so they can improve everything they do.

13. Set Clear Goals   Rating (____)

We all know you can get lucky now and then and you'll make some sales without any of these skills we've covered. The problem I've found with relying on luck though, is that *luck is never around when you really need it the most!* You need clear goals, a specific plan and you need to take action – every day – especially in this market.

- Do you set monthly, quarterly and yearly goals?
- Do you have a written plan to achieve each of your goals?
- Do you have a daily plan of action and do you review your goals daily to make sure you stay on track to hit each goal?

Rate yourself carefully using these three questions as your guide, because goal setting controls your success in sales.

There will be more information on
Tracking and Goal Setting in later chapters.

• *Tools to help you and your salespeople Track & Set Clear Goals:*

JVTN® and our Weekly & Monthly Planners track everything we've covered to help you train, forecast, set and reach your goals.

• *For more information on Tracking, Forecasting & Setting Goals:*

Call us and we'll show you and your sales team the easiest way to track your activities and results to increase sales right away.

Go to JoeVerde.com/Calculators to set your goals.

RECAP OF THIS SECTION

You may need a bigger notebook from here on out and longer management meetings to discuss your problems and create your plans.

"A Dozen Things Salespeople Can Be Good At"

These are *core* traits and basic habits and attitudes everyone in sales *must have to succeed*. That means salespeople who score low on this list are less likely to make it in sales.   ❑ **True**   ❑ **False**

"13 Critical Skills Salespeople Need Today"

Now the work and the fun really starts. Get ready to make some serious improvements in your team's ability to recover and grow.

➤ On the left side of a blank page, or in an Excel® spreadsheet, list your salespeople, then your managers.

At the top of the page or in the spreadsheet, recreate the list of 13 skills to rate your salespeople and managers. (Refer to pages 68 through 92.) Using a 1–100 rating per skill (1 low – 100 perfect), rate each person in each area. Because this is so important, be *brutally honest*. The goal isn't to fire anybody, it's to improve them.

➤ The total possible score in 13 areas would be 1,300. A typical 8 to 10 unit per month salesperson (or manager) will score in the 300 – 400 range. Because their scores are so low, that means you can *easily improve* everyone *some*. And *some,* means more units and more gross profit for your dealership.

➤ Now create a training plan to improve every person. If you haven't been tracking everything by salesperson, for the fastest increase in sales right away, just start with: Basics – Closing – Negotiation.

Tip: Keep this original list and update their ratings every 90 days and you'll be amazed at the improvement every salesperson and manager will make with continuous training, coaching and daily support and management of their selling activities.

➤ Note: *Rate you and your managers*, too. Why? Because you and the managers are in charge of the salespeople and if you only score 350, how are you going to help them get to 500?

"I went from averaging 14 to 22 units"

"I have sold cars for 6 years now and was averaging 14 units a month. My dealership got JVTN® and Joe's Book 'How to Sell a Car Today'. For one month I trained, practiced, and applied what I learned out on the lot daily and had one of my best months ever selling 22.

I have had other sales training and I must say, nothing comes close to the Joe Verde way!" Keith Tiedtke, Salesperson, Hyundai

"From 2 cars out to 12!"

"I attended Joe's Closing and Negotiation Workshop on 3/9/2009. Before the class I had 2 cars sold. After I came back I started closing on the appointment to get customers in and then doing a focused presentation/ demonstration and finished the month with 12 units sold. Everyone should attend Joe's Workshop; it makes you realize that even in tough times, getting back to the Basics can really turn things around!" John Marsh, Salesperson, Mercedes–Benz

"I sold 8 cars last week and made $6,000"

"Since I have been training daily on JVTN®, I've learned how to build value and stay off price. In one week I sold 8 cars and took home $6,000! I could have never grossed that much without JVTN®, so Thank You, Joe!" Mike Hansel, Salesperson, Ford

"I sold 6 units my first week after class"

"After attending Joe's 2-Day Sales Workshop and training with JVTN®, I learned to ask my way to the sale and I sold 6 units my first week after class! I just started asking the 'right' questions, both on the lot and at my desk. I never knew selling could be this easy. Thanks, Joe." Nathan Kowalski, Salesperson, Honda

"I tripled my sales"

"When I started selling cars I was the youngest salesperson there and only averaging 3 units a month. Then I started training weekly on JVTN® and I learned that selling is a process, not a game of luck.

I started following the steps to the sale and now 2 months later I tripled my sales and sold 9! I could not have done it without the training! Thanks, Joe." Greg Hart, Salesperson, BMW

SECTION 4

YOUR MANAGERS

*How prepared are they
to manage your dealership
to recovery and growth?*

*If you're ready to grow, we'll need to take a real life
look at what your managers are doing now and at the
changes you'll all have to make so that you can grow.*

18

MANAGERS

Here Are A Dozen Great Skills That Won't Help

(Unless You Also Train, Coach And Manage Your Salespeople)

Even though we didn't get any training as managers, most managers are very good at a lot of things they have to accomplish, and most have some or even all of the qualities of a great manager.

The Problem:
Most managers lack the technical skills that separate a <u>potentially</u> great manager from a manager who <u>accomplishes</u> great things.

I don't believe there are people who work longer, harder or who have better intentions than managers in the car business.

You're in charge of millions of dollars in inventory, and in charge of generating millions of dollars in revenue each year. To top it off, you were given these responsibilities, and then probably given less training than the poorly trained salespeople who work for you.

You wear a lot of hats, and you're willing to adapt and adjust what you're doing at any time to try to make a deal. You're able to do ten things at once; control the crowd at the desk on a busy day, and at the same time, grab a deal and head out to the showroom to close it yourself. Then late at night, you're very likely to be the one who washes that last vehicle of the day, so you can deliver it tonight.

Recovery and Growth

As with the 'Dozen Things Salespeople Can Be Good At', this first list is also about your attitude, your intentions and your willingness to step right up and do this job, day after day – most often with too little success on the board for so many hours worked.

I also know you see way more potential than you're getting right now from your salespeople. I know you think about that on your way home every night, and shake your head at the deals you could have made *"if the salespeople had only..."*

So I want you to do the same thing we asked in the salesperson section. Go through each area and rate yourself. If you know you need work in any area, go for it and start improving.

Next, we'll also go through the job description and responsibilities you weren't told about when you were promoted. Then we'll go over the skills you need, so you can improve production right away.

The skills below control your day.
The technical skills we weren't taught, control your future.

Key Areas In Sales Management...	Rating
1. I can appraise trades with the best of them	(___)
2. I can order cars or buy used cars that sell	(___)
3. I can write great ads	(___)
4. I can quickly settle down an upset customer	(___)
5. I can desk deals and hold a ton of gross	(___)
6. I do a great job of merchandising the lot	(___)
7. I know my inventory	(___)
8. I know what I want to accomplish	(___)
9. I can work multiple deals at the same time	(___)
10. I come to work to work	(___)
11. I care about our customers and salespeople	(___)
12. I am a team player	(___)

19

MANAGERS

Exactly what is their job?
How well are they really doing?

Why were managers hired?

Just like 'to sell' is the common answer for a salesperson's job, 'to manage' is the logical answer to this question, too.

So again, let's take a quick look at *what* every manager involved with any salesperson was actually hired to do.

Before we start, we need to clarify:
Who counts as a manager for this discussion?
'Managers' – includes all managers in charge of salespeople.

- Sales Department: GSM, Sales Managers, Assistant Sales Managers, New Car Managers, Used Car Managers, Desk Managers, F&I, GM and Dealer if they involve themselves with 'Sales'.

- Business Development: BDC Managers, Internet Managers.

- Service & Parts: Service Director, Service Managers, Parts Managers.

    Yes, Service Managers are Sales Managers, too. One reason service writers and parts people don't sell more is that most of them don't realize they're in sales. They don't have a GSM or Sales Manager to teach them how to sell more service or parts every day.

    They're really nice people and sure work hard. I bet they'd like it if you helped them sell more and make more *money*. JVTN® can help!

Basic Management Responsibilities

1. Establish the Processes and Procedures for everything that happens with salespeople, the sale and customer retention.

2. Properly Staff the Sales Department. This includes Recruiting, Interviewing, Hiring and Firing.

3. Train every newly hired salesperson initially. (Both Experienced and Inexperienced.)

4. Ongoing Daily Training and Daily 1-1 Coaching.

5. Track every Opportunity, every Sales Activity and every type of Result in sales every day.

6. Monitor and Manage each salesperson's sales activities throughout the day to keep them on track.

7. Keep salespeople Motivated and eliminate the demotivating factors in the dealership.

8. Set clear annual, quarterly, monthly and daily Goals for the department and each salesperson.

9. Lead the team to success, month after month.

10. Plus ... Then of course, comes the list of *other duties* every manager in sales is also responsible for.

    The other *stuff* managers are supposed to do each day ...

• Appraise Trades	• Order Vehicles
• Desk Deals	• Write Ads
• Handle Heat	• Do Dealer Trades
• Stock in Inventory	• Merchandise the Lot
• Wash Cars if Needed	• Everything Else

Of 1 – 9 above (managing), or of #10 (stuff), which is *most important* for the stability and growth of the sales department? ❑ 1–9 ❑ #10

Which do most managers in sales spend 99% of their days focused on and doing, 1-9 (managing) or #10 (stuff)? ❑ 1-9 ❑ #10

Are managers doing the job they were hired to do?

Like we did with your salespeople's job description, let's take a quick look at the short answer to each responsibility below, then we'll spend more time on most of these topics.

Basic Management Responsibilities

1. **Establish the Processes and Procedures** for everything that happens with salespeople, the sale and customer retention.

   Your 15-car guys are doing their thing, your 6-car guy skips steps, does no follow up and has lousy CSI, you have a couple of high and low achievers who are doing it sorta right, and the rest of the group is out there right now doing whatever they want.

   You need consistency to grow. Without clear guidelines in *writing* that they're *trained* on and that you *enforce*, salespeople (people in general) will always take the path of least resistance.

2. **Properly Staff the Sales Department.** This includes Recruiting, Interviewing, Hiring and Firing.

   Recruiting ... Running ads isn't recruiting, that's passive, not active. Recruiting means going out and finding people you'd like to hire. It's like Prospecting for new business – I guess that's why managers don't do it, most never liked Prospecting, either.

   Interviewing ... 20 minute interviews, bad questions and *telling candidates what you want them to tell you* before you ask the question, isn't interviewing. Key word: Properly.

   Hiring ... It's a process – not, "OK, when can you start?"

   Firing ... Do you have any salespeople on staff who aren't any good, never were any good, and should never have been hired in sales? Who hired them, and why are they still there?

3. **Train New Salespeople Initially.**

   Quick Question: How long should an effective 60-90 day initial training program for new hires last?

4. **Ongoing Training and Daily 1-1 Coaching.**

    Sales meetings aren't training meetings. Daily would mean *daily*, and it would mean daily for *each person*, even with shift changes, etc. Coaching doesn't mean yelling, that's just what they do on the field – they actually work with their team to get them good, and in their case, the yelling is actually support.

5. **Track every Opportunity, every Sales Activity and every Result in sales every day correctly.**

    Tracking is the single most important thing you aren't doing.

6. **Monitor and Manage each salesperson's sales activities throughout the day.**

    This is the daily coaching that keeps your salespeople focused and doing the activities you need them to do to sell more units.

7. **Keep salespeople Motivated and eliminate the demotivating factors in the dealership.**

    In the leadership class, dealers and managers discover that *demotivation* and other *stuff* that gets in the way of salespeople selling more, runs 5:1 over *motivation* in most dealerships.

8. **Set clear annual, quarterly, monthly and daily Goals for the department and each salesperson.**

    You track in #5 so you can set clear goals for improvement.

9. **Lead the team to success month after month.**

    Your salespeople can reach levels in units and gross profit you've never seen before, and they will when your managers become leaders instead of being 'desk managers' or the boss.

10. **Then in #10, comes that list of all the other duties (the stuff) every manager in sales is also responsible for.**

    Are we doing 'the stuff' well? ... "YES!"

    Managers do #10 the best and they work hard trying to make sales every single day. It's just those first nine that hold things up, so let's look closer at each of those skills in the next chapter.

20

MANAGERS

What other critical skills do your managers need to grow in this market?

As a manager – you literally determine the success or failure of your dealership. While mid-level management doesn't get much of the spotlight in any industry, it really is mid-level managers who do the grunt work that controls the success of an entire organization.

Easy Question: Can any salesperson improve by at least one unit and improve their gross by at least 10%?

Sure, and if one salesperson decides to improve and sell one more unit and raise their gross 10%, that's great, and overall that's a 1% improvement for a 100 unit dealership.

From experience, we know that *all* of the salespeople won't decide to improve on their own, though. ❑ **True** ❑ **False**

The Power of Management: When managers decide to improve all 10 salespeople by just one unit and 10% in gross, now you have a 10% improvement in sales and gross for the entire dealership.

In a 100 unit dealership with $2,500 gross per unit, that 10% improvement means the dealership goes from 100 units and $250,000 in gross to 110 units at $2,750 for $302,500 in total gross. That's a 21% improvement in gross with 60% of the extra $52,500 headed to 'net'. Go for a 20% improvement instead – and total gross goes up 44%.

Believe it, you really do control your success, and you're sitting on a gold mine. Now it's time to find out how to get the gold.

The 10 Technical Skills Every Manager Needs
(An evaluation of what's going on now)

1. **Establish the Processes and Procedures** for everything that happens with salespeople, the sale and customer retention.

    ☑ Check <u>two</u> boxes in each area below. First, are procedures *written* or just *implied?* Check one. Then check if *not enforced.*

    Ten common sense procedures everyone should have...

    *   Salespeople are *supposed* to come to work to work. Waiting around all day for an "Up" isn't working. Work is "doing something all day that has to do with selling a vehicle right now, or at some point in the future."
        ❑ Written Procedure ❑ Implied Procedure ❑ Not Enforced

    *   Salespeople are *supposed* to dress professionally. Recommended: a dark suit, white (or blue) shirt and tie. No cheap slacks, wrinkled shirt, stained tie, un-shined shoes. (Women: professional dress, also.)
        ❑ Written Procedure ❑ Implied Procedure ❑ Not Enforced

    *   Salespeople are *supposed* to follow the Basics. The average: 72% poor 1st impression and greeting, 85% no rapport or investigation, 88% poor presentation and demonstration, 90% no Service presentation and 90% no Evidence Manual to prove what they've been telling the prospect.
        ❑ Written Procedure ❑ Implied Procedure ❑ Not Enforced

    *   Salespeople are *supposed* to have a commitment before you work a deal. "Do you wanna go inside and see what we can do?" is not a commitment to buy the product, and working the desk harder than the customer isn't what we mean by working the deal.
        ❑ Written Procedure ❑ Implied Procedure ❑ Not Enforced

    *   Salespeople are *supposed* to follow the procedures to turn the customer to Finance if they sell it. Too often it's, "Hey Jim, are you ready for the Smiths?"
        ❑ Written Procedure ❑ Implied Procedure ❑ Not Enforced

- Salespeople are *supposed* to introduce every delivery to Service before they leave, so the dealership can retain the customer until their next purchase, but 80% of new vehicle sales never become service customers.

  ❏ Written Procedure ❏ Implied Procedure ❏ Not Enforced

- Salespeople are *supposed* to put every sold customer on a regular follow up program for long term customer retention. However 90% of buyers are never contacted again about purchasing another vehicle.

  ❏ Written Procedure ❏ Implied Procedure ❏ Not Enforced

- Salespeople are *supposed* to 'touch the desk' or turn every prospect before they leave without buying. Excuses, excuses, excuses = lost sales every day. Then again, management shouldn't be waiting until a deal is lost to get involved, why didn't they get involved sooner?

  ❏ Written Procedure ❏ Implied Procedure ❏ Not Enforced

- Salespeople are *supposed* to follow up every prospect they don't sell. The average: 90% of unsold prospects are never contacted again, even though 78% are buyers, 33% would come back with good follow up and 67% of those buy.

  ❏ Written Procedure ❏ Implied Procedure ❏ Not Enforced

- Salespeople are *supposed* to prospect for new business. Even though 30% of all people have a family member who will trade vehicles in the next 90 days, salespeople don't call or even walk the 100 paces to your own Service drive.

  ❏ Written Procedure ❏ Implied Procedure ❏ Not Enforced

So much opportunity.
So much money invested to get people there.
Too little control ever exercised over what happens!

2. **Properly Staffing the Sales Department. Staffing includes Recruiting, Interviewing, Hiring and Firing.**

   Please ✓ every box below that applies to your dealership...

   ❑ We *don't do* a good job of recruiting the best people in town when we hire. (Tip: Stop saying there aren't any good salespeople to hire – that's always untrue. Now, with higher unemployment, there are more *good people* everywhere.)

   ❑ Our interviews are *too short*. (Minimum should be 1 hour.)

   ❑ We don't have at least 2 managers in every interview.

   ❑ We *don't ask very effective questions*. They're more general like, "So why do you want to sell?" or "Why should we hire you?" instead of, "Describe a situation where..."

   ❑ We spend *more time selling the job* and us than we do having the candidate sell us on their qualifications and desire.

   ❑ We're so anxious to hire, we treat the interview like a *selection process*, rather than the *rejection process* a good interview is supposed to be.

   ❑ When we hire, we *don't* take the time to clearly explain our most important procedures (assuming we had some).

   ❑ We have a *very loose process* once we do hire someone. It's kind of like, "Jim, this is Bill, the new guy we just hired, show him around some and tell Ann to do his paperwork."

   ❑ After we do hire someone, we *do not* have a formal 60 to 90 day initial sales training process.

   ❑ We have a salesperson on our staff now who isn't any good, never was any good and will probably never be any good no matter what we do.

   Who recruited/interviewed/hired him or her? _____

   Based on the above, how <u>properly</u> is your sales department staffed today?
   (1 is real bad, 10 is perfect) 1 – 2 – 3 – 4 – 5 – 6 – 7 – 8 – 9 – 10

3. **Train New Salespeople Initially. (✓ each box you agree with.)**

   a. How many skills does a salesperson need to develop if you want them to produce an *above average* # of units?

      ❏ 10-15 major skill sets ... dozens of individual skills

   b. Check the definition of *initial training*...

      ❏ It's where you teach new salespeople everything you expect them to know *how to do* well in sales.

   c. Check which salespeople need *initial training*...

      ❏ All salespeople (new or experienced) need to be taught what we expect them to do in sales at our dealership.

   d. How long does it take to teach even a single skill or skill set like Building Rapport, Investigating, or Closing?

      ❏ A minimum of one week initially, with continued focus for several weeks to fully develop the skill.

   e. How long should a good 60 to 90 day initial training program last for new hires?

      ❏ Between 60 and 90 days.

   f. Check the 3 stages of skill development...

      1. ❏ Recognize. This is the, "Ah-ha, I get it – I see how that works and how it would benefit me."

      2. ❏ Duplicate. This is the practice and role-playing part of learning how to do what you just taught them.

      3. ❏ Master. This means they completely understand the information and have developed the skill well enough to use anytime, anywhere.

   g. Has every salesperson and manager in your dealership had a formal *initial training* course to teach them all of the core skills they need, especially in today's market? ❏ No

   h. Do you want your salespeople to improve? ❏ Yes

   Congratulations!
Yeah, I know it was a trick to get you to check each right answer.
But now you know why training salespeople *initially* is so important.

4. Ongoing Training And Daily 1-1 Coaching.

Train...

a. Check the best dictionary definition of the word *Train*, as it applies to managing your salespeople:
- ❑ A locomotive with railroad cars behind it.
- ❑ To teach someone the skills necessary to do a particular job, or to improve something, especially the mind.

b. How long does *ongoing* training last?
- ❑ 7 days.   ❑ Forever – that's why it's called *ongoing.*

c. How long should a 45 minute to 1 hour training class last?
- ❑ 45 minutes to 1 hour, except on the last day of the month, and then it's just a 5 minute stand up meeting.

Coach...

a. Check the best dictionary definition of the word *Coach* as it applies to managing salespeople:
- ❑ A railroad car or bus designed for long distance travel.
- ❑ To give someone private training in a particular subject.

b. How many people are involved in 1-1 coaching?
- ❑ 2 people.   ❑ 11, if you leave out the dash (-).

c. How often should you do *daily 1-1s* with each salesperson?
- ❑ Only on workdays, except for the last day of the month.

d. How long should a 20 minute 1-1 last?
- ❑ About 20 minutes.

e. Check all words and phrases that apply to *1-1 coaching...*

❑ Be Prepared	❑ Care What Happens
❑ Do Not Cancel	❑ Be Supportive
❑ Discipline	❑ Role-Play / Practice Skills
❑ Praise / Recognition	❑ Create 'Wins' In Practice
❑ Get Involved	❑ Control The Meeting
❑ Listen to Understand	❑ Be Motivational

5. Track Every Opportunity, Sales Activity And Every Result Daily.

Tracking is the *single most important task* that isn't being done in your dealership. You need to be tracking everything every salesperson does, every single day.

Why? Because tracking is the only process that tells you *exactly* what you need to do, or *where to focus* in your training, or what to cover in your 1-1s and goal setting *with every individual and for the dealership,* so you can continually improve and grow.

- In sports, they keep score: 100 to 94.
- We keep score, too: 100 units and $250,000 in gross profit.

The difference is that in sports, they have all the stats on *how* they got to 100. In dealerships, all we know is the final score.

We know next to nothing about the type of prospect we're selling to, we don't know where (ad sources) they came from, we have no idea how many are really getting a presentation or demonstration, we don't track write ups, we don't track the gross on deals by the manager who worked the deal, we don't track where our used cars came from (source) and the average we spend on 'get ready' by source and the average gross by source, we don't know how many times the phone rings, how many web leads we got, how many appointments were made, how many appointments showed on the lot, how many people showed up for the event last weekend, or even how many units each person sells on average.

In sports, they count everything that happens so they can grow. In sales management, we count almost nothing because we say, "It's too much trouble." We throw incredible amounts of money on the advertising wall or to a lead generation company to try to put more people on the lot, then we work people long and hard and hope something comes from the shotgun effect.

Instead of looking out and seeing salespeople that aren't very good; track what they do, turn them into a team, and coach them to the top.

There's more information on 'Tracking' in Section 7. And you'll find a FREE training segment on tracking and daily planning on JVTN® at JVTN.com/ManagersMPG. JVTN® and our planners also have tracking built into the system and the process.

6. <u>Train</u> And <u>Coach</u> People – <u>Manage</u> Their Activities.

This is BIG. Most of us, through experience, and a lack of training, were taught to do just the opposite of these three things.

My first five years as a salesperson, I was never taught anything about how to sell. And even though I had gotten early promotions in the Army because I attended one training school after another and kept learning more, I never associated *training and education* with something you do in automobile sales to improve.

When I did have a question on how to do something, if I asked my manager, I usually got, "Get out of my office and go sell something!" This conditioned me to believe managers don't train, and that I was supposed to figure things out on my own. (After I did learn how to sell, I realized my managers *didn't know the answers*, so they huffed and puffed and intimidated us, instead.)

Other than training on how to take a customer statement and write up a customer, I never remember a manager *coaching* me on any of the steps of selling or role-playing on anything we were supposed to know. For example; they said I should prospect, but they never picked up a phone once to show me *how to* prospect or follow up.

The only role-playing or training we did was to practice taking credit apps and doing write ups every day when we came on shift. One salesperson would be the customer, the other would be the salesperson and we even had a flip chart printed with our write ups and customer statements, so we could practice in front of the group.

I couldn't present, demonstrate, build value or close the sale, but I sure did learn how to control the negotiation stage of selling. We learned how to take a customer statement on every person we wrote up – period. We didn't have a choice. If we brought a deal to the desk without a complete credit app, a completed write up, keys, registration and money, they simply turned our deal to another salesperson and we got zip, nada, nothing.

I wish they had worked as hard to teach me everything about selling, closing, prospecting and follow up as they did on *working deals*, but I'm sure glad I learned how to control the negotiation step of the sale.

Working deals is almost a lost art in this business. If you aren't good at it, get to our new class and we'll show you how. This is something you do daily, and you make or lose sales based on your skills.

For five years, I learned nothing, received no coaching and nobody even considered managing any of my daily activities. Management's attitude about salespeople was, "They have to eat – don't worry, they'll figure out how to sell something."

Management's motivational tool seemed to be to get us all to take on as much debt as possible so we'd be driven to succeed. I guess that worked because at one point I had a demo, a motorcycle, a personal car and two boats. Those payments sure gave me the incentive to work 14/7 most weeks and I couldn't use my boats. It's a shame I wasn't trained, because I could have easily doubled my sales back then *for them* and still had time *for me* to go to the river.

So if that's what I got from the receiving end of management, is there any question on the type of manager I became? Do you think I did training? Do you think I was supportive? Do you think we did role-playing and practiced other skills?

You wouldn't think so, but after so much Leadership training in the Army, once I was promoted to Closer, we trained every day and we became the number one team in the store every month, and usually with nobody even close to catching us.

There is nothing that will make you more sales faster,
than educating your salespeople and managers.

• *Training* means educating your people when they're hired, to get them up to speed fast. *Continuing education* means you teach them something new, or retrain them on something every day they already know so you can help them improve even more.

• *Coaching* in sales means the same thing that it means in your favorite sport. Coaching means *working with* your salespeople to make them better. It's practice, drill and rehearse for our game in sales – so when a selling opportunity comes along on the phone, on the web lead, in service or on the lot – they're ready to win more often.

Too many people assume that once they're pretty good at selling, they don't need to learn anymore and don't need to practice. Oops, that one isn't working too well right now in this market, is it?

110

In sports or sales, there's a big difference
between being good and being prepared.

Most people who are already 'good', would never play in a local tennis tournament, or enter a semi-serious golf tournament or play and compete in a local baseball league without practicing before the game, so they'd have a chance at winning.

Our tournament in sales is on the lot, *every single day*. If we don't win out there each day, there's no paycheck for salespeople or managers, or for some of those other employees who have been laid off lately. With everything on the line every day in this market, why wouldn't we practice and make sure our salespeople are prepared for every opportunity they'll have to make a sale?

"Luck is what happens, when preparation meets opportunity."

– Elmer G. Letterman

Activity Management

After they're trained and ready to go, now we just need to help salespeople plan their day and *monitor their activities* to make sure they're doing the most productive thing possible.

How many times have you heard managers running stores with 6 and 7-unit averages say, "I'm a manager, not a baby-sitter," as they just shake their heads and watch salespeople do nothing all day?

By example, most of us were taught to believe it's the salespeople's responsibility to manage themselves and not ours. Wow, when you think of some of the dumb stuff we were taught or learned through experience, this one has to be right up there close to the top.

I was on a plane once, sitting next to a sales manager at a copier company. We talked about selling and you could just tell by the things he was saying *indirectly* that his salespeople weren't very good at selling their products. I asked some questions about his *daily management* activities and he blurted out...

"Oh, I don't get involved with the salespeople that much,
I prefer to be more of a hands off manager."

We were at 30,000 feet, so maybe he had too much air in his head.
To clear the air – sales management is a very 'hands on' job.

So what activities should you focus on each day? Focus on everything they should be doing – but for recovery, here are the top five activities.

A. **Unsold Follow Up Calls.** 90% are never contacted.
  - In a 100 unit dealership, 500 people come in, at 20% closing; 100 buy and 400 don't. Salespeople only get 30% of prospect's contact information. That's only 120 names and #s out of 400.
  - 48% of salespeople only make one call, then stop. That means only 60 of the 120, out of 400 will be contacted, even one time.
  - 25% make two calls and quit. We're down to 30 out of 120.
  - 12% make three calls and stop. Now we're down to 15 of 120.
  - 10% keep calling. Only about 12 of the 120 prospects you paid so much to get on your lot will be contacted more than 3 times.

  With training, requiring 75% names and numbers is very realistic and then 75% contacts is realistic. But if you don't train, coach and manage this activity every day, this is all you can expect.

  Unsold Follow Up is a Gold Mine!
  See Section Six for more on follow up.

B. **Presentations and Demonstrations.** 99% won't buy until, and unless, they've driven the vehicle.

  If you sell based on our selling process, the demonstration is where you make your formal presentations and where you start your Closing Sequence. ... Step 1 to improving: count demos *accurately.*

  If your average salespeople sell less than 15 units per month, please stop pretending you have a 75% demo ratio. If by chance they are doing 75% demos, and only selling 8 or 10 units each, they're either working their own deals on the lot, or can't close.

  In real life, just know that 75% is almost never correct. And if you don't believe me, no big deal – hire a spotter.

  Or just save your money. Salespeople freely admit they only give about 40% of the people a demonstration. That means they've guaranteed 6 out of every 10 prospects won't be buying a vehicle – they can't, because they didn't get to drive it.

We also know that overall, 50% of the people said they bought *on the spot* when they got a good presentation and demonstration of the product (this average includes walk-ins). 'Good' is a relative term that doesn't depend on product knowledge, but depends on if the salesperson investigating finds their *hot buttons* and then *pushes those buttons* in their product presentation.

Is the 50% statistic correct? Absolutely, the numbers prove it:

Closing Ratio		Demos / Closing Ratio	
Talk to 10		Talk to 10	
x 20%	Closing Ratio	Only 4	Demos
		x 50%	Close Ratio
= 2	Deliveries	= 2	Deliveries

Same 10 prospects, same 2 deliveries (who got a demo).

• Your demo activity goal: 75% good demonstrations.

Once you track accurately and know *your* numbers, selling more is just a math problem. If you deliver 100 now with 40% good demos, if you get to 60% demos, you deliver 150 units instead.

To improve your demonstrations, get on JVTN® and attend our How To Sell A Car And Close The Sale Today workshop.

C. Incoming Sales Calls.

Recap...

• A 100 unit store gets about 150 incoming sales calls per month.

• 90% of callers buy within a week. That's 135 of 150.

• 129 is the average number of missed sales per month.

We'll never sell them all, but only delivering 6 out of 135 buyers is worse than terrible. Why is this so bad? Because almost none of the salespeople have any kind of training on selling skills. So instead of setting appointments that show, they educate prospects on pricing, trade, down and payments – and cost you sales daily.

Your Incoming Sales Call Activity Management...

a. Track your incoming calls:

Don't argue – this is too easy. Have the receptionist keep a log or enter the information. She just needs to always be sure to ask the customer their name before she transfers the call and then she needs to enter their name and which salesperson took the call. That way you can follow up to make sure the salesperson set an appointment.

b. Incoming Call Goals (An average, OK job on calls):

150 = Total incoming sales calls
135 = 90% names and numbers
90 = 60% of appointments on all incoming calls
54 = 60% of appointments that show
27 = 50% of appointments that show, buy

c. Track Calls by Salesperson:

- Total calls
- Total appointments
- Total appointments who show
- Total who buy (and the gross)

d. Pull salespeople off the phones who aren't meeting your goals and put them through more training and coaching.

*Use JVTN® to certify each salesperson before
you let them take calls. Or get them to our 2-day
workshop on how to use the phone to build your floor traffic.*

D. Daily Prospecting.

How long does a 5-minute prospecting call take?

If each salesperson knew how to prospect, if you managed this activity and each salesperson contacted 5 people – with 10 salespeople, you would have 50 prospecting contacts per day, 250 per week and over 1,000 prospecting calls per month.

Since 30% of all the people have a family member who will be trading vehicles within the next 90 days (even in this market), that's 300 buyer opportunities they'd contact.

If 50% of those 300 were interested and salespeople scheduled an appointment, that's 150 appointments per month (5 per day).

If we use the same stats as on incoming sales calls and 60% show, that's 90 extra people you'll put on the lot each month.

If you close 50% of those, that's 45 extra units per month or about $100,000 in extra revenue. Too high? Cut it in half.

Don't argue, don't find excuses ... just train and manage these calls.

E. Touch the Desk.

I agree that every prospect on your lot these days should be talking to a manager before they leave. But in real life, that isn't even close to happening.

Maybe 1 out of 5 actually talk to a manager on a good day. Unfortunately, that's only after the salesperson has blown everything and completely lost any chance of making a sale.

This is a management responsibility and activity, not a salesperson activity. *This was explained to us incorrectly.* It isn't that salespeople should touch the desk before the sale is lost and the prospect blows out. It should be...

Managers touch every prospect
very early in the process!

Don't wait until it's too late...

Stop waiting for the salespeople to touch the desk when they're about to lose a sale.

Instead, management needs to get out from behind the desk so they can go *touch the prospect* early in the process. Meeting the prospects early on has a ton of benefits...

- By introducing yourself sooner than later in the process, you'll know the people, get a chance to build rapport and know what's going on, just in case you need to get involved later.

- You can get people to take demonstrations who didn't really plan to drive the vehicle.

- Meeting you gives the prospects *another person* for them to *like* at your dealership and that alone helps close more deals.

- Your *management title* helps reassure them, especially the more cautious prospects in today's market.

- If price comes up, your salesperson can hand it off to you on the spot and you can bypass it with, "Don't worry about the price, I'll take care of that later. You just find the perfect vehicle and we'll find a way to help you fit it in your *budget."*

- Now you've already changed the objection from *price to budget,* and they'll be happy knowing you're on their side.

- By knowing them, it's easy to step in and nudge the sale *back on track* if there's a problem at any stage of the process.

This is so much more effective than waiting until your 6-car guy has negotiated price on the lot, blown the deal, and tells you to hurry because his customer is 'walking'.

7. Keep Salespeople Motivated.

How would you rate the positive *motivation* in your dealership, would it be a 5 or 7 or even an 8 or 9? That's great, and means you probably work hard to keep your salespeople pumped.

When you come to class, and we spend an hour or so talking about motivation and *demotivation*, the ratings change fast. Ratings drop down to 2 and 3 overnight as dealers and managers go through a couple of homework sections with checklists on demotivating things they do in their dealerships. The two sections are:

- "Old School Thinking" ... things like...

    Keeping and rewarding those *loyal (negative) underachievers* who are protected by upper management. Keeping them and rewarding them really demotivates the rest of your salespeople, especially the good ones who work hard to improve.

    That bad schedule. That schedule you're most likely on now; the split shift, mornings and nights, with a long day or two in between, is really bad for growth. It's terrible for your high achievers, it helps your low achievers and kills your sales production. I started on that schedule in 1973. It was worthless then and it's worthless now.

Get to class and learn to write a work schedule *to increase sales* for your dealership, and provide effective coverage and you'll motivate people to sell more – and they will.

Protection on deals. Way too complicated to talk about here.

Rules. Making the 25-car guys conform to the 6-car guy rules, schedules and management in the dealership. This thought should be completely reversed and the 6-car guys should be required to conform to the 25-car guy rules.

And a dozen or so other 'old school' problems.

• 22 Quick & Easy Ways To Demotivate Salespeople, like...

  • Can't find a manager to work a deal, or managers who don't make working deals a priority, or aren't good at it.

  • *Demotivating* 'motivational' meetings.

  • Constant errors on paychecks.

  • *And 19 more easy ways to turn their heads and cost you sales.*

The goal in management is to develop high achievers, not keep low achievers happy. But by day two in class, most dealers and managers realize they've set up just about everything in their dealership: their processes and procedures, and how they pay, treat and schedule their salespeople – to attract and keep low achievers.

With all of the class discussion on this topic, most attendees add another dozen things to their *demotivation* list. Once the dust settles, the score in the average dealership is usually around ...

  • Motivation 1
  • Demotivation 5

Don't think that's true in your dealership? If you have no turnover to speak of and your average salesperson is delivering 15 to 20 units per month, you're right. If they're averaging under 10 or 12, you may be motivating people all right, just the wrong ones.

8. Setting Clear Goals.

I said earlier that, "Tracking is the most important thing you don't do in your dealership." Why is tracking so important?

It's simple, you can't set clear goals if you don't have all of the information you need.

Example: You sell 100 units now with $2,500 gross per unit.

Answer these questions: *Exactly* what can you do today to...

> A) Increase the gross $200 per unit
>
> B) Increase sales by 5 units

We were all taught so many ineffective things about how to run a business, it's amazing some of us are still at it. In my first dealership, annual goal setting was a ritual we did about the 15th of January after they got through backing deals into last year to pretend it was better.

We'd have an early morning management meeting with coffee and donuts and start planning our goals for the new year. We had no information, except that last year, we delivered 500 new units and 700 used and that the gross was $2,500.

So everybody would take their turn either being very negative, or highballing the rest of the group on what they thought we should be able to do. Soon though, the coffee got cold, the donuts ran out and somebody would bring in a write up, and that was that. Whatever the last highball was became the goal.

We had no plans, nobody was assigned any specific tasks to reach the goal, and nobody was held accountable – it was just, "OK, I'm gonna hold you guys to it, let's have a great year!"

Our annual goals were never discussed again until around September when somebody would notice how far behind we were. Then our meetings turned to "Blame Storming" sessions, because somebody obviously hadn't done their job.

Monthly goals were worse, and when everything trickled down to the salespeople – we're talking stupid stuff like 15 car goals for 5 car guys.

> *Goals control your future and it's time to learn to do it right.*
> *Get to our Dealer & Manager Team Leadership Workshop*
> *and go through our Goal Setting course on JVTN®.*

9. Lead The Team To Success Month After Month.

To clear up one critical point on Leadership, are Leaders...

A) Out front leading their team?

B) Out back, telling them what they should be doing?

We were definitely not taught to be Leaders, that's for sure. Most managers in the sales department (includes working Dealers, GMs, GSMs, Service Managers, Finance Managers, New and Used Car Managers and Desk Managers) sit behind their desks most of the day, waiting for something to happen, or they're busy doing 'stuff'.

Yes, they're busy, I didn't say they aren't. They're just not busy training, coaching, or managing their sales force ... they're busy doing "stuff" like they were taught to do. The only reason they aren't Leaders, is because they haven't been taught those skills yet.

You promoted a decent salesperson, but they didn't even have *all* the selling skills we've talked about in here, and then you put them in charge of the other salespeople who don't know much, either.

In the dealer class, we try to laugh at the dumb stuff we do and this is a biggee. We all agree that *salespeople are pretty poorly trained* overall, so here's the question...

Who has had even less training in your dealership than the poorly trained salespeople?

Exactly – the people who are in charge of the poorly trained salespeople are the only ones with less training on how to do their job. Everybody laughs in class, but this is so costly, it isn't funny.

If you're only going to train one person, make it a manager.

Why? Because if you only train one salesperson, you only affect one person's production. If you train a manager in charge of 10 salespeople, you affect the performance of all 10 salespeople.

You're going to have to actually apply the things we've been covering in this book if you want to grow. Everyone; dealers and all managers, will have to take a serious leadership role to pull off recovery or growth in today's market.

Don't worry, you can do it. I watch dealers and managers become leaders all the time as they walk out the door after class.

10. And ... Do All The "Other Stuff" Managers Have To Deal With.

The first time I got promoted to management, my training was about the same as when I got hired in sales ... zip. It was...

"Joe, you've done good in sales and we're promoting you. I want you to take charge and turn these guys around. Now get out there and make me proud ... and oh, by the way, don't forget to do all the other things expected in management...

- Appraise trades
- Order cars
- Desk deals
- Write ads
- Handle any 'heat'
- Do the dealer trades
- Stock in the inventory
- Merchandise the lot
- Wash cars if you have to
- Do whatever it takes to sell a unit

... and don't forget to manage the people."

Of a sales manager's responsibilities, which is most important? Is it managing the people or doing the other stuff (above)? Which is most important to selling more units?

> *Answer ... Managing the people and their activities.*

Of managing the people or doing the other stuff, which of these have sales managers had almost no training?

> *Answer ... Managing the people and their activities.*

Which activities do they focus on? Answer ... *The Stuff!*

> *This is bad. It's the perfect set up for disaster...*

Too many responsibilities, no training, no authority to counsel or fire bad employees, and no personal accountability to perform.

RECAP OF THIS SECTION

This homework is virtually identical to Section 3, except now we're focusing on management skills.

"A Dozen Great Skills That Won't Matter"

Even though this is the list of "stuff" managers have to do besides training, coaching and managing the salespeople's activities – their skill level in these areas is critical, too. ❑ **True** ❑ **False**

"Managers' 10 Critical Skills"

The 10 Factor: Here's where your skills and results are multiplied by 10. When a salesperson develops or improves a skill and grows, it affects just one person. When managers develop their management skills, it affects all 10 of the salespeople's production.

➔ On the left side of a blank page, or in an Excel® spreadsheet, list your managers.

At the top of the page or in the spreadsheet, recreate this list of skills to rate you and your managers. Using a 1 to 100 rating per skill (1 is low and 100 is perfect), rate each person in each area. Because this is important to your recovery and growth, *be brutally honest*. The goal isn't to fire anybody, it's to improve them.

➔ The total possible score in 10 areas would be 1,000. In a typical dealership with an 8 to 12 unit per month salesperson *average*, management will score in the 200 to 300 range. Why so low? Go back and *really* read the last 20 pages.

➔ Now create a training plan to improve every manager in every area. Save time: this *critical list* of responsibilities is exactly what we cover in our dealer / manager workshop, so get to class quick.

Tip: Keep this original list, keep rating everyone regularly and you'll be amazed at the improvement every manager has made and at the increase in your units and gross profit.

Remember 'The 10 Factor'.
Train management – improve all salespeople.

"Our Gross is up $800 per unit in just 45 days."

"We have only had JVTN® training for a month and a half and already see and feel a difference in our dealership. Our salespeople learned how to avoid price on the lot and our gross has gone up $800 per unit. With Joe Verde our future keeps looking brighter and brighter!" Chris Reade, UCM, Putnam Lexus

"I couldn't have done it without your training."

"Joe, I've been selling cars and managing dealerships the Joe Verde way since 2001. I have attended multiple workshops and have JVTN®. I take your training to heart, master it, believe it, lead and motivate others with it. As a result, 80% of the people I've trained using your information sell 18-25 units per month and average over $10k+ per month. I recently opened the doors to my now accomplished dream, Reyton Auto Sales, and I could not have done it without your training, staff, and support.

Thank You, Joe, for taking my career to a new level. I'll see you at the top!" Miguel Reyna, Reyton Auto, WA

"We are #1 in our region for new car sales!"

"We believe in Joe Verde Training 100%. All of our salespeople go to the sales workshop and all of the managers attend the managers <u>and</u> sales workshops. We train continuously; it's not an option. After attending the Train The Trainer Workshop, it put training into perspective and I have a game plan to succeed and I execute it as I have practiced. We are currently # 1 in our region for new car sales! Again while everyone is falling to the side we are not only surviving, we are growing! Thanks, Joe!" Rick Ramirez, GSM, Boggus Ford-L/M

"Sales are up 38% – gross is up 29%."

Our Mercedes-Benz and Cadillac stores in Easton are up 38% in sales and 29% in gross this year over last year in a supposed recession. The Joe Verde classes and JVTN®, along with our daily training and one-on-ones have been a large part of our success. We are pacing to be considerably more profitable this year (2009) than last year. Keep up the good work." Brian Kramer, General Manager, Germain Mercedes–Benz / Cadillac / Smart

SECTION 5

Pros Are 'Strategic'
Amateurs Are 'Hopeful'

*In this section, let's look at the statistics on today's buyers,
how we're doing in real life selling to these buyers, and find out
which group of buyers we should be focusing on the most
for a faster recovery and continued growth.*

How To <u>Lose</u> Consistently

*Amateur gamblers don't understand the odds of winning.
They have no plan and they pull the handle or play each hand based
on 'possibility', 'hope' and a 'hunch' – and they consistently lose.*

*Amateurs in sales and in management hope for a great day, a lot of
traffic, good credit, plenty of money down and a lot of equity in
every trade – and they're usually disappointed.*

How To <u>Win</u> Consistently

*Professional gamblers understand the odds of winning and have
a plan. They place their bets and they play their hands based on the
'probability' of winning – and they consistently win.*

*Pros in sales and in management hope for the best, too. To back up
their 'hope', they also set goals, create plans, train, and manage the
activities that will make it happen – and they consistently win.*

21

Learn The Stats

Then Just Play Your 'Best' Odds

A Quick Question

If you were going to gamble in Las Vegas and you saw two tables with the exact same game, but one only offered you a 10% chance of winning *a small amount with a higher minimum bet,* while the other table offered you a 50% or higher chance of winning with *a larger payback and lower minimum bet,* which table would you play?

Of course, any logical person would play the best odds with the lowest ante and higher payback – to do otherwise wouldn't make sense.

Because there are so many statistics that can point you toward that "winning table" in sales, you can take the guesswork out of what you need to do to sell more units, have more fun, make more money and control your success, *especially in this tougher market.*

You're trying to *win* the sale and beat your competition and it took me years in sales to finally understand this next point …

> *You aren't competing with the dealership down the street or with their pricing. You're only competing with the salesperson your prospect will talk to at the dealership down the street.*

That untrained, poorly managed salesperson down the street with a stinky little attitude, will pre-qualify their prospects before they give them a presentation, focus everything they say and do on price, and even if they think they have a 'live one', they'll still take every shortcut they think they can get away with and they won't follow up.

The 6-car guy down the street is no competition for a pro in sales!

Think Of These Facts As Your 'Odds Of Winning'

(Learn how to play the best odds and you'll deliver more units.)

First we'll look at the statistics that reflect your prospects today.

We'll break these facts into different categories so we can look at snapshots of each area that will determine whether you make a sale or miss the sale, and lose the gross that goes along with it.

Your Prospects

As we said earlier, prospects in today's market are more cautious than ever about making a major purchase, especially a purchase the size of a new or used vehicle. *Cash outlay* is very important to people these days, and everyone is more careful than ever because they're *watching their budget.* When you dig deeper though, when they buy, what you discover is they're really more concerned about *the value they get in return,* and *who* they buy expensive products from now.

Even in good times, *price questions* and *price objections* were almost always the things prospects brought up first. Sure, they cared about price then, and even more so now. But in real life, most wouldn't buy a cheap vehicle they didn't like, and most wouldn't buy a product with a terrible reputation, then – *or now* – just because it's cheap.

In fact, if everything was about *price*, then the average consumer would only buy your *cheapest* vehicle – but they aren't. Most of us could do fine with the least expensive, most economical vehicle, but we *choose* larger vehicles with other features and equipment.

In the 35 years I've been in the car business, I have *never* had a single prospect walk in and say, "I have \$____, I'll take whatever you can sell me at that price." Buying is always about *wants* and *needs* (value) and then about *price.* The order is never reversed. Even when they say, "I want to know your best price," just remember the first part of the conversation with them. It went something like this...

"I want something that seats 6, I need room in the back for the soccer gear, we want it in blue, with 22" wheels, a navigation system, the rear entertainment system, and *I want to know your best price.*"

Price is always last – not first. Even then it really isn't about price. Whether they buy or not will depend on this vehicle fitting their budget. Stop talking about price – sell the car – and close on budget.

Recovery and Growth

I'll tell you up front, these statistics aren't pretty. They paint a very dismal picture of the actual skills we've developed in sales, and they clearly point to a ton of bad habits and below average performance.

Poor skills and bad habits just mean lost sales. One indisputable fact is that when you develop more skills, and do a better job with each prospect, in the end you'll sell more units and make more money.

Habits and attitudes are hard to break, though, and skills take time to develop. When I started selling cars again after being the 8-car guy for 5 years, I knew I had my work cut out for me. I started selling again *with new skills*, but I still had 5 years of habits and attitudes to overcome. My first 5 years I saw 4 groups of people who walked on the lot; *lookers, shoppers, bad credit* and only a very few *buyers.* My habits were pre-qualifying, focusing on price and not giving a great presentation or demonstration unless I thought I had a 'live one'.

> *Before I could change my results in sales, first I had to change my mind and stop pre-qualifying, and I knew I had to change my habits and start giving everyone a chance to buy.*

Here's what I did...

(Get some 3 x 5 cards.) I wrote out the statistics we'll be covering (and about 50 more we cover in our classes) on 3 x 5 cards, and carried them around in my pocket for a couple of months and read them a dozen times each day, *until I believed them completely.*

Why? Because repetition is how we learn!

After reading these facts and statistics day after day, I really started to see buyers everywhere instead of those lookers, shoppers and people with bad credit. If you want to grow and improve, that's your first step, too. Just start seeing buyers, and only buyers when someone is on the lot.

The easiest way to double your sales overnight is for your salespeople to stop trying to *"guess who the buyers are"* and just start giving *everyone* their most enthusiastic and their very best value building presentation and demonstration of your product.

> *If they will – you'll definitely sell more cars, have more fun and make more money!*

22

What are the real facts about today's buyers that we can use to help us improve our skills, so we can quickly recover and grow?

Today's buyer is just like you and me when we buy something expensive. They want to make sure the product is right for them.

They've done some research, they've analyzed their Kitchen Table Budget to figure out how much they think they can spend, and it's a fact, when they walk on the lot in today's market, you have a serious prospect ready to buy now.

Instead of *trying to sell to them,* if you'll teach your salespeople how to *work with them* to find the perfect vehicle *first*, get them really excited about how much they'll enjoy that perfect vehicle and then just help them find a way to fit that perfect vehicle *into their budget (down, payment and terms, not 'price')*, you'll deliver more units, at higher gross profits. It's just a combination of common sense and effective selling skills.

Play the best odds and you'll consistently win.

Recovery and Growth

1. *99% of the people want to drive the vehicle before they buy it.*

    Surely they must be kidding on this one. Why would anybody need to see how a $30,000 product works before they make a commitment and agree to buy it?

    Just like you looking at that new sofa, big screen TV or cell phone, people want to see how things work before they buy.

    Buying is *emotional*, especially when you're buying a car, and the demonstration is the *highest emotional point in the selling process*. That's why you demo the vehicle you plan to send them home in. That's also why the Closing Sequence logically starts at the end of the demonstration and continues straight into the office to do the paperwork.

    The Basics are a series of continuous steps that lead straight to a delivery and the demonstration is one of the most critical steps. I can't imagine why any salesperson would skip the step that raises the prospect's emotions higher than any other.

    I got an email yesterday from a manager who had just used JVTN® in his meeting on closing. He said a salesperson took a customer and to *prove it wouldn't work*, he avoided price and started closing like we had just covered online. He said, "Park in the sold-line," and they did. He said, "Grab me the registration on your car," and they did.

    He got in a few more of the *action closes* we cover, asked his final closing questions, went inside, presented the first set of numbers and they said, "OK, let's do it." His manager said the salesperson was *blown away* by how easy it was to close the sale at MSRP.

    I'll show you some quick math on the importance of demos here in just a few pages. But the quickest and easiest way to increase your unit sales, is to increase your demo ratio.

2. *90% (give or take) do some type of research on the internet before they start looking at vehicles on the lot.*

    We are continually bombarded with this stat and it implies everyone is online diligently comparing prices all over town. From that assumption, we logically figure we better have the cheapest prices in town, so that's what most dealerships focus on.

Prospects go online to get information about buying cars, no question about it. Is price on their list? Of course.

They'll check features, equipment, color, options, etc., etc. on a BMW compared to a Mercedes or a Ford to a Toyota. They'll find their local dealers, click 'map it' and yes, some of them will send an email, "Do you have this vehicle and how much is it?"

The problem with their online adventure is the average person knows as much about cars as you and I do about computers.

To understand what they go through; go online and start with a simple Google search on 'computers' and you'll get 381,000,000 hits. Then narrow your search to just 'Apple Computers' and you'll only get 26,200,000.

Live in Boise? Narrow your search to 'Apple Computers in Boise' and you get 40,100 hits. Soon you just give up, go to your local computer store and say, "I want to look at an Apple computer."

I know, that's computers and you sell Toyotas. So do the same search: Toyota, 169,000,000 ... narrow it to Boise ... 420,000. Click on Local Toyota Dealers ... (3) ... Click on 'New Car Quote' on the first dealership (Peterson) ... you end up with 46 units listed in their inventory (today), and you'll get a banner ad from Hometown Toyota that keeps distracting you.

About now Bob says, "I can't figure it out, let's just go look at cars."

Keep it simple. When you get a lead, focus on the appointment, not the price. When they get there, or when any prospect on the lot says, "I was online, etc.", just say, "That's great," and follow the Basics.

3.   ***78% of the people who actually take the time to go out and look at a new or used vehicle, end up buying one (soon).***

Seems logical – why would people go to all the trouble in #2 and then just kick tires – especially in today's market?

Actually, we have less traffic now than ever, and because of that, this percentage makes even more sense. People are not spending their evenings or weekends *just looking* at expensive products they can't afford to buy.

If they're on the lot, they came to buy.

4. *71% of the people bought because they liked, trusted and respected the salesperson they dealt with.*

This goes back to that "fearful and cautious" attitude our buyers have today. Read my sales book, or get to class and learn to use this stat to help you sell, because it will *make or break* your sale.

71% bought from a salesperson they liked, and exactly the same number walked, because they didn't. 71% found a vehicle, but didn't buy, because they <u>didn't like</u> or feel comfortable with the salesperson, manager or the process.

If your prospects like your salesperson, your chances of making the sale are much higher. That's why the first four steps of the Basics – your "Warm Up" steps are critical:

Good 1st Impression – Positive Greeting – Build Rapport – Investigate

5. *58% of the people buy the same product they looked at first.*

Wow – another burst of logic! Does this mean if a prospect goes to a Toyota or Ford or Mercedes dealership first when they go out looking for a vehicle – that they may actually be most interested in a Toyota, Ford or Mercedes?

I think common sense says this fact means that if someone is on your lot, you don't have to worry about why they're there or if they're interested in buying a car, or interested in buying your product or whether they're interested in buying from your dealership. They're on your lot because they have a serious interest in buying your product, from you, today.

Assume everyone will buy if you do your job correctly; stay off price, get them excited, follow the Basics and learn how to close based on value. Then set up the negotiation as a win-win, based on fitting this in their budget, not on how cheap you can sell it.

No Pre-Qualifying Required!
The prospects who walk on your lot today are buyers,
and they're looking for a professional in sales.

Snapshot of Today's Buyers

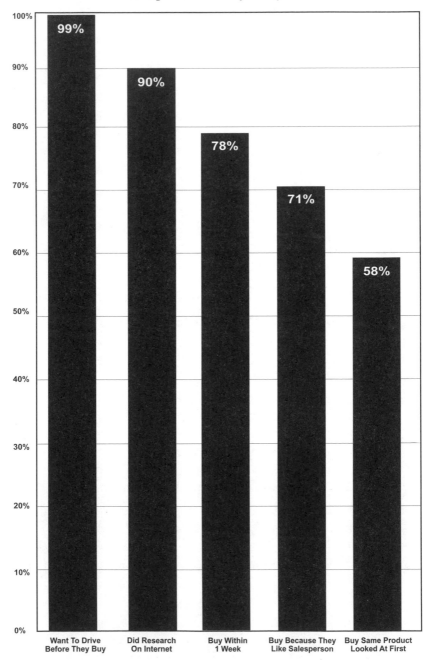

Wow - today's buyers sure seem serious!

23

Key Statistics
On How We Rate With
Today's New Buyers

We know who our buyers are and what they want.
Now let's look at the facts on how we're doing.

Key Stats On How We "Sell"

1. *28% of the time, salespeople make a good first impression and greet prospects promptly and properly.* (*The flip side: 72% of the time they don't greet them properly or make a good 1ˢᵗ impression.*)

    A good first impression and an effective greeting go hand in hand in making that positive first impression that determines if they feel comfortable working with your salesperson. The *"like"* is what your customers have said is so important.

    72% of the time they don't feel that your salespeople greet them promptly (within 2 minutes) or properly (approach, attitude, smile, etc). To make matters worse, 72% of the time salespeople also use some form of, "How can I help you?" as their greeting.

    Why is that a problem? Because, "Can I help you?" solicits your first buying objection and 90% of the time their response will be some version of, "We're just looking." Even though 'just looking' is simply a reflex response to 'can I help you?', salespeople have started down the wrong road and have created their first objection within 10 seconds of meeting a new prospect.

    What should we do instead?

    First, they have to look, act and approach the prospect like a professional in sales to make a good first impression.

    Their greeting is also meant to start the warm-up process. In their greeting, the idea is to get everyone's name and move the sale forward – not stop it dead in its tracks.

    They need to use this greeting with every new prospect...

    • *Welcome to ___ Motors, I'm ____ and you're ... ?*

    They'll get their name 90% of the time instead of hearing *'we're just looking'*. Then move the sale forward with...

    • *You sure picked a great day for looking at cars, nice out, isn't it?*

    They'll get a positive response in return, which sets them up for another question to keep the sale moving forward...

    • *So Betty, who's the lucky one this time, will this be for you or Bob?*

    Now just keep things moving right along with more questions to build rapport and to find their wants and needs (next stat).

2.   *15% of the time, prospects said the salesperson built rapport and investigated to find their personal wants and needs. (The flip side: 85% of the time we didn't build rapport or find out what was important to them on their new vehicle.)*

Building rapport (finding the common ground) establishes the *like, trust* and *respect* that 71% said was critical to buying.

But ... just *liking* a salesperson doesn't guarantee a sale – it just opens the door so they have the opportunity to make a sale.

If they don't like the salesperson – the door to the sale is closed.

Too many people in sales confuse being likeable and having a lot of product knowledge with success in sales. Investigating to find out *exactly* what is important to each prospect and *why* it's important is just as critical, because 80% of the buying and selling will take place in their presentation.

Being likeable and having a ton of product knowledge is great, but 80% of the buying and selling is based on just 20% of the features on your vehicles that are important to your prospects. *Prospects don't care about everything your salespeople know.*

Sales psychologists clearly explain why *'walking, talking, smiling, product knowledge experts'* don't sell many cars:

- Every time they talk about something that is *important to your prospect* (a feature, advantage and benefit that's on their Top 20% list), they move a step closer to the sale.
- Every time they talk about something that *is not important to your prospect,* they move a step farther away from the sale.

3.   *40% of the people get a demonstration of the product.*

(If 99% want to drive it before they buy it and if salespeople only give 40% a demo, they've guaranteed 60% of the people you put on the lot will not buy, even if they like your salesperson and even if you have the vehicle they want.)

Salespeople in every class and in our surveys, freely admit that if you count everyone they talk to, *at best* they only give 40% of your prospects a demonstration. We're not talking about a good or bad one ... just whether they do a demonstration at all.

Like we talked about before, the demonstration is the single most important step in the selling process. Even if they like your salesperson, even if you have the vehicle in stock they want to buy, even if the price is the lowest on the planet – 99% said they won't buy until, and unless, you let them drive it.

If your salespeople were going to skip all of the steps to the sale except one, the demonstration is the step you'd want them to take every time they could, with every prospect.

Keep this simple: No Demo = No Sale!

4. **12% of the people felt they got a _good_ presentation and a _good_ demonstration of the product (that was specific to them).**

(Here we are again – 88% of the time, prospects do not feel that salespeople are giving them what they want.)

If you take #3 into consideration, "Salespeople only give 40% a demonstration," this stat shouldn't come as a surprise.

Of the four out of ten we let drive a vehicle, this stat says only one of those four gets that bang up, quality presentation the prospect is looking for so they can make their final decision.

When we cover potential, I'll show you why this fact is accurate.

5. **10% are introduced to Service as part of their presentation.**

The more people they meet and like, the higher your closing ratio. Cheat; introduce them to everyone in the dealership.

6. **Note: 90% of Walk-In prospects don't buy on their first visit.**
(After what we've seen in the first 4 stats – why would they?)

I know some of your reports say your closing ratio is closer to 20% or maybe even 30%, not just 10%. But oops, there's a fatal flaw in the process. Salespeople are only logging half, at best, of the opportunities they have to do business.

So unless they count every breathing person they talk to in person each day who even mumbles the word *car,* your numbers aren't correct. If you want to find out how good (or bad) you're really doing – use our Planners or JVTN® and track everything you do.

Track accurately and you'll sell more units!

How Does The Average Salesperson Rate Selling To Today's Buyers?

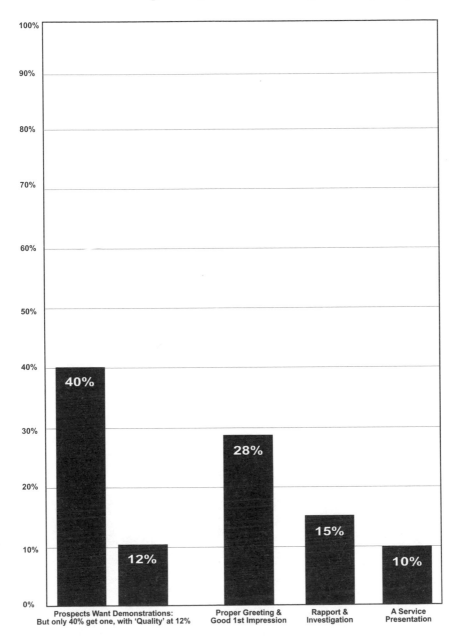

If you were the prospect, would you buy from this average salesperson?

24

Closing Ratios Of The
Five Different Types Of Buyers
In Today's Market

We don't have just one type of buyer.
We have five different groups of people who buy
from us. One group is tough to work with,
and the other four are easier.

The best part – you get to pick which groups
your dealership focuses on in sales.

Closing Ratios By Type Of Buyer

The average closing ratio across the board is 20%.

That's the combined average of all types of prospects.

20% is not the average for any specific group.

1. *Walk Ins ... 10% is the average closing ratio for walk-in customers.*
   (That means we are not closing 90% of walk-in traffic.)

Can you improve your closing ratios and sell more to walk-ins? Absolutely! *Results* in sales are relative to the quantity and quality of sales *activities*. To improve the percentage of people who buy, just improve the *activities* that affect your salespeople's closing ratios.

Go back to the last chapter and focus on improving the quantity and quality of the percentages in each of those areas for each salesperson, and those improvements will logically improve your sales and gross.

Note: 50% of *all* of the people buy on the spot when they get a good presentation and good demonstration – even walk-ins.

But ... salespeople can't give a good presentation or demonstration *if they didn't complete the first four steps of the Basics effectively* (Great 1st Impression / Greet / Rapport / Investigate). They have to get to know each prospect and what they want and why they want it, so they know what to focus on in their presentation, demo and closing.

This is what confuses and frustrates your warm and friendly product knowledge experts who don't sell many units. They just can't figure out why they aren't selling more; they know their product inside out, they tell everybody everything there is to know about their product, plus they love people and the car business.

Product knowledge is absolutely critical, and salespeople need a lot more of it than most of them have right now. But prospects don't care about everything your salesperson knows – they only care about the things most important to them. That's why you investigate.

Remember: 80% of the selling is done in the presentation steps, on just 20% of the features on your product. Think *targeted* presentations.

To sell more – they just need to ask more questions in the Warm Up to find their Hot Buttons, before they start presenting and demonstrating.

2. *50% is the average closing ratio for phone and internet prospects <u>that you get on the lot</u>.* Read that again – your closing ratio <u>is not</u> 50% on the phone, you close 5 out of 10 that show up 'on the lot'.

One of the biggest mistakes salespeople make on incoming and outgoing sales calls and internet leads, is they forget that their goal is to set *a firm appointment* that shows up on the lot.

The goal <u>is not</u> to educate the prospect on the phone...

Salespeople certainly need to be positive, answer general questions and they need to get the prospect excited about coming in to look at the vehicle. But if they don't get the prospect on the lot, they won't sell them anything, no matter how nice and helpful they are.

> *You have one goal on the phone or with a web lead,*
> *set an appointment that will show up on the lot.*

The steps to set up an appointment that shows...

• Warm and friendly greeting
• Congratulate them and get control with questions
• Get their number then name
• Confirm that you have the vehicle (or can get it)
• Get the appointment with 'Either / Or' questions
• Firm it up on the quarter hour, "Can we make that 5:15?"
• Anchor the appointment and repeat the time 4 to 5 times
• Confirm every appointment you *think* you have

Note: The shorter the call, the more likely you are to see most (75%) of them on the lot.

On Internet Leads ... Most include a phone number, so send a quick email, "With a customer – I'll call you soon." Then call them in 5 minutes and stick with the plan above.

Big Misunderstanding!

Most people think *phone skills* are a unique set of skills. Phone skills are just *selling skills* that you use when you have a phone in your hand. You control the conversation, build some light rapport, bypass price, and *close* on a firm appointment. You use the same type of questions to control the conversation, build rapport, bypass price and close the sale on the lot. That's why you have to learn to sell.

*3.   60% is the average closing ratio for referrals, or through
      prospecting in person or on the phone.*

(Why are closing ratios getting higher as we go?)

Selling expensive products is almost always a *relationship based*
process and once you *communicate* with someone in person,
by phone or through the mail or email, *you start to develop a
relationship*. Once that happens, the *'like'* part of the buying
process carries you through to higher closing ratios.

Think about the walk-in closing ratio at 10% versus the phone
or internet prospect at 50%. By the time they show up on the lot,
salespeople have already been through some of the Warm Up Phase
with them on the phone or online. They talked awhile or went back and
forth in a few emails and now the prospect feels more comfortable.

That means if everybody just called in first and your salespeople
had those 3 minutes of conversation before your prospects walked
on the lot, your closing ratio would go from 10% to 50%.

Remember: 71% buy because they like their salesperson.

Here are the two most important statistics everyone forgets:

*30% of all the people have a __family member__ who'll trade vehicles
within the next 90 days, and 62% know __someone__ who'll trade.*

The car business didn't die – it slowed down, but almost all of your
market is still intact. If business is off 30%, 70% of the people are
still out buying, and all you have to do is find them.

Sure, the 30% are out of the market at least for awhile – but even
they'll be back before long. Most dealers, managers and salespeople
who are down in the dumps about today's market, have forgotten
about all the other people in their database and community who *are*
still buying today. If you think about it...

- Somebody's lease is expiring right now
- Somebody just wrecked their car and needs a replacement
- Somebody has to buy one of their kids a car today
- Somebody spends too much on repairs and will buy today
- And some people will buy because they can and want one

Salespeople always ask ... "Where do you find these prospects?"

That's the benefit of selling cars – just open your eyes. Everybody has a vehicle now, and they'll be getting another one when they're done with this one. Plus, everybody they know also has a vehicle and will eventually trade it in, too.

Referrals at 60% Closing Ratio

Referrals aren't usually price shoppers like walk-in prospects. Even if they are, salespeople have the edge when they're referred to them. The person who referred them also transferred the salesperson's credibility, which means they've already started to establish the *relationship* with that referral, before they even meet them.

How do you get referrals and where do you find them?

You have a computer full of customers and prospects. Now salespeople just need to make a list of everyone else they know or deal with at the grocery store, gas station, laundry, etc. Remember – 30% have a family member who'll be buying in 90 days, and 62% know someone who will.

How long does a 3 to 5 minute prospecting call take? How many of those calls could a salesperson make when they aren't with a prospect?

Service Customers at 60% Closing Ratio

Do this: Count the steps from your showroom floor to your service drive. That's how far you are from a gold mine of opportunity. Why? Because 8 out of 10 customers out there would *strongly* consider buying at your dealership (but don't). They're comfortable in the dealership and just need a salesperson to get involved.

Unfortunately, 80% of sales never make it to service and more than 80% of service customers never make it back to the sales department.

Since average families buy 36 vehicles in their lifetime, why would you spend so much more money on advertising than on training your managers and salespeople? If they were trained and focused on selling within your customer base, they could just walk the 100 paces to your service drive or pick up a phone and flood your floor with great traffic.

Dealers spend a ton of money to attract the most expensive, price focused, lowest closing ratio prospect (walk-ins), instead of developing a retention process, teaching everyone to follow it and then holding everyone accountable to bring service customers back to sales.

The service department is one of your best sources for business. They're convenient, you don't have to spend any extra money on advertising to get them in, and best of all, when you do prospect in service and bring a customer up front, they haven't done any shopping to compare products, and aren't price focused. They're easier to close and your gross profit skyrockets.

We have sales training modules on JVTN® for Sales, Service and Finance and all three focus on building a loyal customer for the future. Use JVTN® to teach Sales, Finance and Service a consistent process that will ensure customer retention. Retention in dealerships should be a continuous process.

Sell → *Service* → *Sell* → *Service* → *Sell* → *Etc.*

Orphan Owners at 60% Closing Ratio

90% of the sold customers are never contacted again about buying. Those 'Perfect 10' calls to get better CSI scores don't count. If the real question was, "Did anybody from the dealership ever personally contact you again about purchasing another vehicle?" The answer is, "No," 90% of the time.

Since 95% of your previous customers, Service customers and orphan owners will buy more vehicles, why aren't dealers prospecting in their customer base for cheaper, easier, high gross deals instead of spending a ton on advertising to buy expensive, tough, low gross deals?

Important Note: When you say 'orphan customers', most dealers and managers only think about customers whose salesperson isn't there any more. Whether salespeople left or still work there, if the customer isn't being contacted regularly, they've been abandoned.

Big Problem: Dealers and managers protect salespeople who don't follow up. When that previous customer comes in, doesn't ask for their last salesperson (who doesn't follow up), and Johnny, the new kid sells them the car, he's called into the office and told, "That's Bob's customer, he sold them their last car, and he gets half a deal."

Wow – talk about 'two birds with one stone'. You can turn a new guy's head for doing his job right, and at the same time reward a salesperson for doing their job *wrong* (no follow up). This isn't even a *mixed signal*; you just said, "Even though you refuse to do your job, we'll protect you and you'll be rewarded whether you follow up or not."

Friends / Acquaintances / People you deal with every day at 60%+

Salespeople: Don't you hate it when you find out that a friend, a neighbor, the kid at the pizza place, the couple at church, or the counter person at your dry cleaners tells you about the new car they just got – that you didn't sell them?

It's always the sad face and, "How come you didn't see me first?" which is followed by, "I forgot (or didn't know) you sold cars."

There's gold in your service drive, customer base and with all of the people you deal with outside the dealership.

But like the big Gold Rush in California back in the 1800s, not everybody grabbed a shovel and headed west. Back then, just like with most dealers, managers and salespeople now, most of the people just said ...

> "That's too much trouble."
> "I'm too busy."
> "I don't have time."

Just like dealers, managers and salespeople today, they had a ton of excuses to justify *not going for the gold.*

In fact, one of the prospectors who did head west and struck it rich sent his friend a telegram that read...

"There's gold everywhere, buy a pick and shovel and get here quick."

His friend replied...

"Can't afford to, picks and shovels are too expensive these days!"

Dealers: You don't have to just *hope* you get lucky in today's market. The gold is in your customer base every day and you can start cashing in, anytime you want.

Make retention your focus and everyone's requirement.

Then you just need to train and manage everyone on the process you want them to follow from the curb with a new prospect, to your service drive after delivery, and back to sales when it's time.

Really learning how to build your own business to work with friendly people turns a hard job into a very enjoyable, high paying profession.

4. *67% is the average closing ratio for unsold prospects (be-backs) you bring back into the dealership through follow up.*

(Closing the sale with 'be-backs' is 6.7 times easier than closing the sale the first time they were on the lot. Such a deal!)

YOUR HOTTEST PROSPECT! You talk about wanting a hot prospect – the people you didn't sell a vehicle to today are the hottest prospects you have in your system. There is a...

- 78% probability they're a buyer
- 38% chance they'll buy within the next 4 hours
- 57% chance they'll buy within 3 days
- 90% chance they'll be burning gas within a week in their new (or used) vehicle – hopefully from you.
- 33% chance they'll come back to see you with good follow up
- 67% chance they'll buy on the spot on that second visit

Other than a repeat customer you bring back in, no other group is this easy to close. Not only that, both the dealership and the salesperson have already done 95% of the work to sell this prospect.

You've already paid to get them on the lot the first time, so there's no extra expense to get them back in. The salesperson has already spent 1 to 2 hours with them, and when they come back in, it's usually a very fast process. *Who could ask for anything more?*

I forgot, how long does that 5-minute follow up call take?

About 5 minutes. And remember, the goal is always to get the appointment. Salespeople aren't calling to educate them on pricing or product, the only goal is to *set an appointment that shows.*

The worst follow up call you can make is ...

"Bob, this is Joe down at the dealership – have you guys given any more thought to getting a car?"

Stop using that type of question unless you don't mind hearing, "We decided to hold off a while," to which most salespeople respond with, "Well, make sure you see me when you're ready – we'll beat any deal in town." (Get a grip and learn to sell!)

> *With our scripts in the system and our training on JVTN®*
> *you'll be able to continually improve sales.*

5. *70% is the average closing ratio for a previous customer you bring back into the dealership through follow up.*

We work with half of the top 500 dealers in the US, half the top internet dealers and 3,500 of the other most motivated dealers of every size. And they all have one thing in common; they focus on building their organizations from within.

The highest achievers I know in sales also focus on their repeat and referral business. None of the 30, 40 and 50-car a month salespeople I know make the majority of their sales from walk-in traffic.

In fact, it would be virtually impossible for a salesperson who only closes 10% of the prospects they talk to on the lot – to sustain a 40 unit average with just floor traffic. They'd need 400 people on the lot every month to deliver those 40 units. Even if they got much better and closed 30% of all the people they talk to, for them to deliver 40 units, they'd still have to talk to 133 people on the lot each month.

High achievers also spend less time in the dealership. Not only do the highest achievers sell a ton of units and make the most money, most of them spend less time in the dealership than average and even above average salespeople who depend on floor traffic. They come to work, say "Hi" to old friends all day and deliver vehicles.

Added benefit: The gross profit on repeat and referrals is 40% higher.

Salespeople: If you're closing 20% of your prospects; to sell 15 units to walk-ins, you'll need to talk to 75 people on the lot, mostly price shopping strangers. If you average $400 per sale in commission and bonuses, that's $6,000+ per month which is a great income, no question.

But what if you did all your business with repeat customers? With a 70% closing ratio, to sell 15, you'd only need to put 22 people on the lot each month, and you'd make 40% more – $8,400 total.

Friendly people – almost no grind – and you'd earn over $100,000 per year ... just from following a daily process that includes those 5-minute phone calls to keep 'em coming in to see you.

You're going to go to work tomorrow, either way. From these stats, though, it sure looks like everyone has a choice about how easy or how tough it's going to be, and how much or how little money they make.

Recovery and Growth

Closing Ratio – % of Sales by Group – Cost by Group

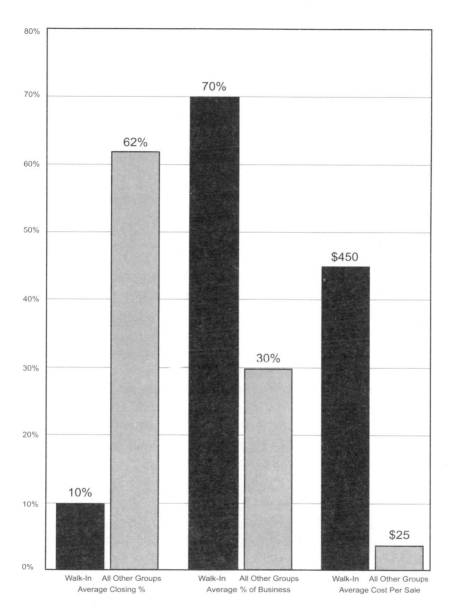

Flip these stats around and you'll get (really) rich.

*This is backwards. Dealers spend 95% of their time and money
on the least productive, but most expensive prospects – and practically
ignore the least expensive and most productive prospects. Go figure!*

RECAP OF THIS SECTION

This section was about logic. Understand who your prospects are, sell to their wants and needs, and focus on your best prospects.

1. Amateurs lack skills and hope they sell. Professionals have skills and play the best odds of making a sale. ❑ **True** ❑ **False**

2. We've gotten away from playing our best odds and have instead spent too much time and money on 'hope'. ❑ **True** ❑ **False**

3. If I really look at the 'buyer stats' and the chart, most of our customers want and expect the same things we all do when we're buying an expensive product. ❑ **True** ❑ **False**

4. When I buy expensive things, 99% of the time, I want to *test drive* the new product (DMS, TV, CRM, Car Wash, JVTN®) before I make my purchase, just like our prospects do. ❑ **True** ❑ **False**

5. It's pretty logical to assume most people are serious when they walk on the lot these days, and it's logical to assume if we don't do a good job, they won't buy from us. ❑ **True** ❑ **False**

6. If our salespeople aren't taught how to do a good job 'in sales', then try as they might, a previous plumber, porter, waiter or waitress, or my nephew turned salesperson, won't have the skills they need to do a professional job in sales. ❑ **True** ❑ **False**

7. If our management staff doesn't learn how to train our salespeople, coach them to develop their skills and manage their sales activities daily, we'll lose sales we can't afford to be losing in today's market. ❑ **True** ❑ **False**

8. When we look at the closing ratios by group, and then at the breakdown of our % of business by group and cost, we've sure been taught (through experience) to focus our time, money and efforts on the least productive customers. ❑ **True** ❑ **False**

9. If we take the prospect's buying logic into consideration, train and require our salespeople to sell professionally, we can increase sales in today's market. ❑ **True** ❑ **False**

10. If we just keep doing what we're doing in how we sell to today's buyer, we'll just keep getting what we're getting now, or less.
❑ **True** ❑ **False**

SECTION 6

Your Five Quickest Ways To Recover & Grow

Your Greatest Potential Actually Lies
In The Areas That Are Easiest To Improve!

Recovery and Growth

Yes – We Have Less Floor Traffic

Everyone agrees there are fewer people on the lot right now and having said that, there's still a ton of potential to increase sales and gross, anytime you get serious.

When you look at the buying and selling statistics we talk about in our classes, the only thing that's really changed about buying vehicles is that there are fewer people on the lot buying, these days.

Since there are fewer prospects in the market today, once you have a prospect on the lot, the facts on how *serious* they are, and how *soon* they'll buy, and *what they want* from us, and *how we sell* the product, are more important than ever.

In this section, I'll go through the profit potential that you and your salespeople have in 5 strategic areas...

1. Selling to the prospects you already have on the lot now

2. Turning your unsold prospects into be-backs

3. Turning your incoming sales calls into deliveries

4. Prospecting for referrals with the easier groups

5. Improving your gross per unit – across the board

Our Sample Dealership

For all of our examples, I'll use a typical 100 unit dealership, that has 10 salespeople, closes 20% of their traffic, and has an average gross of $2,500 per unit, including Finance.

We'll look at each of these 5 profit centers two ways...

- Your Current Lost Sales and Gross Profit

- Your Realistic Potential Improvement in Sales and Gross

*Grab a pen and paper, and do the math on your dealership
as we go through these five areas to focus on for growth.
You can also go to JoeVerde.com/Calculators*

25

Profit Center #1

Sell More Of The Prospects

You Already Have On The Lot

We'll look at your...

- Current Lost Sales and Gross Profit
- Realistic Potential Improvement in Sales and Gross

Our Sample Dealership

For all of our examples, I'll use a typical 100 unit dealership, that has 10 salespeople, closes 20% of their traffic, and has an average gross of $2,500 per unit, including Finance.

Lost Sales On The Lot Today

We aren't missing sales from lack of opportunity.
We're missing sales from lack of training, lack of coaching,
and lack of managing the selling activities that will generate sales.

The Facts

Here's the math on what we know in a 100 unit dealership...

500	people were on the lot
x 20%	bought
100	deliveries per month

Which means...

500	people were on the lot
− 100	bought
400	people didn't buy

Which means...

400	people didn't buy
x 78%	are buyers (90% buy within a week)
312	additional sales were missed
x 71%	found the vehicle they would have bought
221	lost sales on vehicles that were *in stock*

Which means...

221	sales missed for sure, each month
x $2,500	average gross per unit
$552,500	**lost gross profit each month from lost sales**
x 12	months
$6,630,000	**lost gross profit each year from lost sales**

Dealers and managers complain about training being expensive!
Lost sales (on the lot) are 2 times higher than deliveries in most dealerships.
Losing $6,630,000 is the budget for <u>not training</u> managers and salespeople.

Realistic Potential Improvement
For Sales And Gross Profit On The Lot

Two Easy Ways To Increase Sales
To Your Current Floor Traffic

1. Do A Better Job With The Basics – Increase Your Closing %

One of the easiest ways to increase sales is to simply do a better job 'within' the Basics. The math below <u>does not</u> include giving more demos, it just reflects doing a better job overall of selling, building value and closing with the customers you're already making presentations and demonstrations to now.

Assume a 20% closing ratio, a salesperson who delivers 10 units per month, and talks to 50 prospects per month.

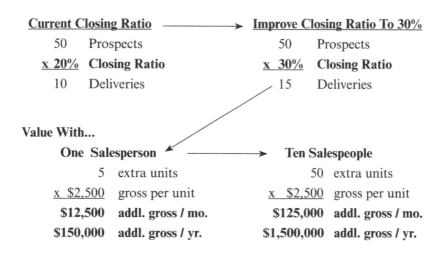

Current Closing Ratio			Improve Closing Ratio To 30%	
50	Prospects		50	Prospects
x 20%	Closing Ratio		x 30%	Closing Ratio
10	Deliveries		15	Deliveries

Value With...

One Salesperson		Ten Salespeople	
5	extra units	50	extra units
x $2,500	gross per unit	x $2,500	gross per unit
$12,500	addl. gross / mo.	$125,000	addl. gross / mo.
$150,000	addl. gross / yr.	$1,500,000	addl. gross / yr.

Wow – a 50% improvement by closing just 10% more.

*Just train on the first impression, greeting, rapport,
investigating, presenting, demonstrating ... and close more sales.*

2. Just Increase The <u>Number</u> Of Demonstrations

Everybody wants a shortcut to selling more units. If that's you, here's the easiest shortcut around.

Logically, you'll sell even more if you do a better job, but you can *increase sales overnight* if you increase your current demo ratio by 50%. And please save the, "We're doing 75% demos right now," story because if you hire a spotter, 90% of you will find your salespeople are only logging half of their prospects.

Why will you increase sales?
Because 50% buy on the spot with a good demonstration.

Again, assume a 20% closing ratio, and a salesperson who delivers 10 units per month by talking to 50 prospects per month.

Improving Sales
By Improving The Number Of Demonstrations

<u>Sales By Demo Ratio</u>		⟶	<u>Improve Demo Ratio To 60%</u>	
50	Prospects		50	Prospects
x 40%	**Demos**		x 60%	**Demos**
20	Demos		30	Demos
x 50%	Buy with good Demo		x 50%	Buy with good Demo
10	Deliveries		15	Deliveries

Value With...

One Salesperson			**Ten Salespeople**	
5	more units		50	more units
x $2,500	gross per unit		x $2,500	gross per unit
$12,500	**addl. gross / mo.**		**$125,000**	**addl. gross / mo.**
$150,000	**addl. gross / yr.**		**$1,500,000**	**addl. gross / yr.**

Holy Smokes – another great return on investment.
Double down on demos – double up on sales!

The Realistic Potential In A 100 Unit Dealership
By Improving The Basics And Closing Ratio

1. Improving Closing Ratios From 20% to 30%

Realistic Annual Potential

$1,500,000

----

2. Improving Demo Ratios From 40% to 60%

Realistic Annual Potential

$1,500,000

----

*Wow! Train your salespeople to give a few more demonstrations, teach them
how to close properly and pick up an extra $3,000,000 this year!*

= $3,000,000

Total Realistic Potential

So far, your Total Realistic Potential from...

1. Demos and Closing (Above)................... $3,000,000

$3,000,000 Per Year

26

Profit Center #2

Unsold Prospects

"Your Hottest Prospects"

We'll look at your...

- Current Lost Sales and Gross Profit
- Realistic Potential Improvement in Sales and Gross

Our Sample Dealership

For all of our examples, I'll use a typical 100 unit dealership, that has 10 salespeople, closes 20% of their traffic, and has an average gross of $2,500 per unit, including Finance.

Sales Potential With Unsold Lot Prospects

We aren't missing sales from lack of opportunity, we're missing sales from lack of training, coaching, and activity management.

The Facts

Assume a dealership sells 100 units per month, has an overall closing ratio of 20%, with $2,500 gross profit front and back.

Here's the math on what you could be doing in that 100 unit dealership...

500	people came on the lot in one month
x 20%	people bought
100	deliveries per month

Which means...

400	people didn't buy, but assume we got...
x 75%	names and numbers with good skills
300	who didn't buy – but we got their info

Which means...

300	didn't buy – and we got their info
x 33%	who come back with good follow up
100	come back in (be-backs)

Which means...

100	come back in (be-backs)
x 67%	who buy on their second visit
67	sales with unsold follow up
x $2,500	average gross per unit
$167,500	**additional gross profit each month**
x 12	months
$2,010,000	**additional gross profit each year**

Wow - Talk about easy sales you could be making.
Dealerships or salespeople can increase sales 67% today, with just
2 good phone calls and one thank you note to everyone who doesn't buy.

The Realistic Potential In A 100 Unit Dealership
With Unsold Lot Prospects

Because most dealerships kinda, sorta try to follow up Unsold Prospects, to be realistic, just cut the statistical potential in half...

Statistical Annual Potential

~~$2,010,000~~

We'll assume you do some follow up now, so cut it in half.

Realistic Annual Potential

$1,005,000

Total Realistic Potential

This brings your Total Realistic Potential from...

1. Demos and Closing $3,000,000

2. Unsold Follow Up $1,005,000

$4,005,000 Per Year

27

Profit Center #3

Incoming Sales Calls

Turn More Calls Into Deliveries

We'll look at your...

- Current Lost Sales and Gross Profit
- Realistic Potential Improvement in Sales and Gross

Our Sample Dealership

For all of our examples, I'll use a typical 100 unit dealership, that has 10 salespeople, closes 20% of their traffic, and has an average gross of $2,500 per unit, including Finance.

Lost Sales And Gross From Incoming Sales Calls

We aren't missing sales from lack of opportunity, we're missing sales from lack of training, coaching, and activity management.

The Facts

Dealerships don't track incoming sales calls, appointments they set and appointments that show. If you do track *accurately*, use your numbers. If not, figure (deliveries x 1.5) to get a close guesstimate of the number of incoming sales calls you get each month.

Here's the math on what we know in that 100 unit dealership...

100	deliveries per month
x 1.5	number of incoming calls per month
150	incoming sales calls
x 90%	will buy within a week
135	buyers call in each month

Which means...

135	buyers call in each month
– 6	sales on average from incoming sales calls
129	lost sales from incoming sales calls

Which means...

129	lost sales from poor selling / phone skills
x $2,500	average gross per unit
$322,500	**lost gross monthly from poor phone skills**
x 12	months
$3,870,000	**lost gross each year from poor phone skills**

Talk about easy sales you could be making...
Dealerships or salespeople, can increase their sales easily just by learning what to say on this 1 to 2 minute incoming sales call.

The Realistic Potential In A 100 Unit Dealership
From Incoming Sales Calls

You'll never hit *perfect* on incoming calls, so let's use
just *an average return* with training on sales to incoming calls.

Statistical Annual Potential

$3,870,000

Cut it – Cut it – Cut it!

Realistic Annual Potential

From just 30 additional units per month at $2,500 each.

$900,000

Total Realistic Potential

This brings your Total Realistic Potential from...

1. Demos and Closing $3,000,000

2. Unsold Follow Up $1,005,000

3. Incoming Sales Calls.............................. $ 900,000

$4,905,000 Per Year

28

Profit Center #4

Get More Referrals

Through Daily Prospecting

We'll look at your...

- Realistic Potential Improvement in Sales and Gross

Our Sample Dealership

For all of our examples, I'll use a typical 100 unit dealership, that has 10 salespeople, closes 20% of their traffic, and has an average gross of $2,500 per unit, including Finance.

Prospecting Opportunities Each Month
The Facts

30% of all the people have a family member who will be buying or trading vehicles within the next 90 days. 62% of the people know someone who will be buying or trading within 90 days.

Here's what you could be doing in that 100 unit dealership...

1. Prospecting In Your Service Drive

250	contacts (10 SP at 1 each x 25 days)
x 30%	family member trading in 90 days
75	Hot Prospects in Service

2. Prospecting In Your Existing Sold Customers Database

2,500	contacts (10 SP at 10 calls each x 25 days
x 30%	family member trading in 90 days
750	Hot Prospects

3. Prospecting Calls by Salespeople to Friends / Unsold Prospects / Etc.

1,250	contacts (10 SP at 5 calls each x 25 days)
x 30%	family member trading in 90 days
375	Hot Prospects

Total Above : 1,200   Contacts With Hot Prospects Per Month

Using the statistical average, you'd get 60% appointments = 720.
Let's cut 720 in half, just to make sure we're totally realistic...

360	Schedule appointments (30% of 1,200)
216	60% show for their appointment
108	50% of those who show, buy (average)
x $2,500	average gross per unit
$270,000	**potential monthly from prospecting**
x 12	months
$3,240,000	**potential each year from prospecting**

Why worry about running more cheap price ads???
Just teach your salespeople to prospect by phone and in service.

**The Realistic Potential In A 100 Unit Dealership
From Prospecting In Those Three Areas**

You may not be able to make every call listed,
but you can certainly improve your unit sales today.

Statistical Annual Potential

$3,240,000

Realistic Annual Potential
(This was already low at only 30% appointments.)

What the heck – cut it in half, anyway.

$1,620,000

Total Realistic Potential

This brings your Total Realistic Potential from...

1. Demos and Closing $3,000,000

2. Unsold Follow Up $1,005,000

3. Incoming Sales Calls............................. $ 900,000

4. Prospecting (All three areas)................... $1,620,000

$6,525,000 Per Year

29

Profit Center #5

Raise The Gross

On Every Sale You Make

We'll look at your...

- Realistic Potential Improvement in Gross

Our Sample Dealership

For all of our examples, I'll use a typical 100 unit dealership, that has 10 salespeople, closes 20% of their traffic, and has an average gross of $2,500 per unit, including Finance.

Gross Profit Improvement Opportunities

The Facts

- Gross profit is 40% higher overall with Joe Verde Training.

- The average first discount *by a salesperson* is $844, and by the time salespeople have a commitment and are ready to work a deal, the average discount is $2,062.

- Gross is 40% higher on repeat and referrals than walk-ins.

Here's the math on two easy ways to raise the gross...

1) **Stop Talking Price.** Let us teach your salespeople how to avoid price, build value, close on value, turn price objections into budget objections, and refocus price back to down and payments in the negotiation, so you can raise the gross 40%:

100	units
x $2,500	average gross per unit
$250,000	total gross
x 40%	increase
$100,000	**additional gross per month**
$1,200,000	**additional gross per year**

2) **Build Your Repeat Business By 20 Units.** Even if you don't sell more units, you'll pick up $1,000 (40%) in extra gross profit for every repeat, referral, or service customer you develop and sell to.

   Example: (Read this slowly.) If you're selling 30 repeat, referral and / or service customers, and 70 walk-ins now – if you do follow up and increase repeats to 50 and walk-ins drop to 50, you still pick up...

20	additional rep/ref/serv. customers
x $1,000	in additional gross per unit
$20,000	**additional gross per month**
$240,000	**additional gross profit per year**

Additional Gross Profit potential is everywhere you look.

We lose gross by focusing on walk-in traffic, by salespeople selling price not value, and by closing on price and focusing the negotiation on price.

The Realistic Potential In A 100 Unit Dealership
From Raising Your Gross Profit In These Two Areas

Gross is one of the easiest things to improve,
and you can do it almost overnight.

Statistical Annual Potential

$1,440,000

Realistic Annual Potential

(This is realistic – this is what you should expect.)

$1,440,000

Total Realistic Potential

This brings your Total Realistic Potential from...

1. Demos and Closing .... $ 3,000,000

2. Unsold Follow Up .... $ 1,005,000

3. Incoming Sales Calls............................. $　900,000

4. Prospecting .... $ 1,620,000

5. Raise the Gross (Two ways) .... $ 1,440,000

$7,965,000 Per Year

I know it's a lot – so if you can't quite see...

$7,965,000

---

*If $7.9M is bigger than your imagination,
no big deal – just cut it in half.*

~~$7,965,000~~

$3,982,500

*Still too high at $4M, cut it again,
to just 25% of your real potential.*

~~$3,982,500~~

$1,991,250

Still too high at $2M – cut it to 12.5%.

~~$1,991,250~~

$995,625

*Still too high at $1M – cut it again to
only 6% of your real potential.*

~~$995,625~~

$497,813

*And in real life, you'll still probably
triple your net in that 100 unit dealership.*

---

*No matter how you cut it – you have potential.
Step one: Start believing you can improve in today's market.
You can – the key questions are "will you?" and "by how much?"*

RECAP OF THIS SECTION

Cut It – Cut It – Cut It
No matter how (far) we cut it, there are sales to be made
and more gross profit to be earned, right now – in today's market!

1. We do not sell all of our floor traffic and we can increase sales to people who are already on our lot now.   ❑ **True**   ❑ **False**
   I think we can increase by _____ units per month within 60 days
   We can do that by... (___Answer this in your notebook___)

2. We do not sell everyone on the first visit and we'll sell more if we get more unsold people back in for another chance. ❑ **True**   ❑ **False**
   I think we can increase by _____ units per month within 60 days
   We can do that by... (___Answer this in your notebook___)

3. We do not sell all of our incoming sales calls and we'll sell more if we get more of them on the lot.   ❑ **True**   ❑ **False**
   I think we can increase by _____ units per month within 60 days
   We can do that by... (___Answer this in your notebook___)

4. We do not prospect, or prospect well enough, and we will easily improve sales by prospecting more effectively. ❑ **True**   ❑ **False**
   I think we can increase by _____ units per month within 60 days
   We can do that by... (___Answer this in your notebook___)

5. *Gross is relative to value* so when we learn to build more value and sell the vehicle, not the price, gross will improve.   ❑ **True**   ❑ **False**
   I think we can increase by $_____ per unit within 60 days
   We can do that by... (___Answer this in your notebook___)

Tip: Use Your Ad Money To Cut Your Ad Expense By 75%

You aren't missing sales because you lack traffic – you're missing sales because your salespeople and managers lack skills. If you'll use 25% of your advertising money to teach them skills, your units will go up, your gross will improve, your expenses will drop and you'll eliminate the need to advertise for more hard to close walk-in traffic.

If your ad budget is $400,000 – use $100,000 over the next 12 months to train, and in about 90 days (based on your efforts) you will come close to eliminating your need to spend the other $300,000 on advertising.

"From 2.5 to 13.3 units per month…"

"Joe, I started my career in sales 5 months ago and was averaging 2.5 units. I started watching JVTN® and learned the basics, then I went to your 'How to Sell a Car Today Workshop', got really pumped and started implementing your processes.

With the skills I learned from JVTN® and the Workshop combined I'm now averaging 13.3 units!" Scott Hourie, Salesperson, Ford

"From 8 to 38.5!"

"When I first started selling cars my average was 8 per month. In the last two years I have attended two Joe Verde Workshops, I use his Monthly Planning Guides daily and his VSA® (software) to manage my customers. Now my 90 day average is 38.5!

I do well because I eat, live and breathe Joe Verde methods, training and processes. I am proof it works and I can honestly say I do not know where I would be without Joe!" Trent Bright, Salesperson, General Motors Products, Utah

"On track for 20 units…"

"Joe, I have been at the same dealership for 30 years and less than a month ago, I was averaging 14 cars a month, and then I attended your 2 Day Sales workshop.

Now instead of struggling all month to get to 14 units, I'm only half way through the month and I've already sold 10. From a man who has been in the business for 30 years I cannot thank you enough for opening my eyes and making it so easy!" Pat Fortin, Salesperson, Toyota, BC

"From 6 to 16 units."

"Joe, your workshop changed how I sell cars. Before your class, I was averaging 6 units per month and struggling to maintain that.

In your course I learned the importance of investigation and finding my customers' wants and needs. Now instead of just finding them a car, I help them to find their 'perfect' car and price isn't even an objection. I also started tracking, using your Monthly Planning Guides and setting monthly goals. I sold 16 units my first month back!" Paola Catalan, Salesperson, Ford, Kentucky

SECTION 7

Your Recovery

Step One

All of this potential may sound great, but as a dealer, there are a few more hard decisions you'll have to make before you can move your dealership from the "having potential" stage of recovery and growth, to the "we're making it happen now" stage.

If you're on the brink of failing, the steps to recovery are like sending out an elite strike force to save the world. To recover, you have to have a team you can count on that *can* and *will* do the job you need them to do *right now*. You're out of *tomorrows* and can't take any more chances, because a failure at this point may be irrecoverable for many dealers reading this.

One of the toughest tests for you will come up somewhere in these next two chapters, because we'll take a hard look at whether all of your employees are helping you recover and grow – or not.

If they're helping you, of course you want to keep them. If they're hurting you, they have to be willing to learn and change, or they have to go. If you falter here, you risk everyone's job in your dealership – including your own.

30

You Can't Keep People
Who Refuse To Do Their Job

*"The only thing wrong with common sense
is that it just isn't that common." – Zig Ziglar*

In good times, we all have the latitude to do some 'dumb stuff'. We can lose focus, make bad decisions and still sell cars in spite of our poor choices. In times like these, we lose those 'dumb stuff' options.

Our Training Support team is an integral part of our company. We know training is only step one, and that we have to support our training to get results for our dealers. So we created a stand-alone department with the sole function of supporting our JVTN® customers who will use over a million virtual training chapters online this year.

Our support staff will make dozens and dozens of calls to each dealership throughout the year to give managers tips from class, tips from other dealers and to keep managers and salespeople using the training system effectively, so they can continually improve.

I met with our Training Support team last Thursday to talk about how we can improve our support even more – especially now when dealers, managers and salespeople need all the help they can get. Because they talk to managers and salespeople in 200 to 300 dealerships *per day,* they have a real bead on what's going on in dealerships across the country. They hear just about everything that's happening in sales today in every market – whether it's good or bad.

*Two common problems
that could put you out of business.*

Here are the 2 biggest challenges our Support people are running
into that are costing your dealership a ton, and they're costing you
money every single month that you'll never see in your paycheck.

1. First Problem: Allowing salespeople to *refuse* to do their job!

Some dealers and managers tell us that as hard as they try, some of
their salespeople just won't do "it". So what is the "it" that they won't
do? *You name it – if it's important, some salespeople won't do it.* Go
ahead and ✓ the critical areas below that any of *your* salespeople aren't
doing, or aren't doing correctly and write their name(s) beside it...

❑ They won't give demonstrations to *everyone* so we can see more
write ups, and sell more units.

❑ They won't stop pre-qualifying and won't stop talking price, so
they can build value and hold more gross.

❑ They won't get solid commitments or write up people correctly.

❑ They won't follow up people they don't sell to get them back in.

❑ They won't prospect for new business to increase traffic and sales.

❑ They won't answer incoming calls correctly to set appointments.

❑ They won't do their paperwork correctly on every sale.

❑ They won't take their new customers to service before they leave.

❑ They won't follow up sold customers to build customer retention.

❑ They won't even come to work to work every day.

❑ They won't watch a 6 to 10 minute online training chapter.

The last one sounds so trivial, especially when you look at how many
chapters Travis Haldeman trains on monthly. Travis is a salesperson
from Pennsylvania on his second tour in Iraq, and he averages 75
chapters a month on JVTN® (from Iraq). While he's doing that, some
dealers and managers say they just *can't* get their salespeople to do
their training online, and admit they're losing sales because they won't.

At our company, we hire good people, we train them properly when
they first start and we train them daily. When we decide on a process,
everyone does it, because it's our process.

That's why one woman in our support department just laughed when a dealer told her he couldn't get some of his guys to use JVTN®. He couldn't believe she had just laughed and said, "Why are you laughing?" She said, "Because where I work, when my manager or Joe says to do something, we do it, or we can't work here."

This dealer got so angry at himself for not requiring his managers and salespeople to do what they were told, that he held a meeting right away. It was the 10th of the month and he told everyone they would either start training online with a minimum of 8 virtual training chapters per week, or they wouldn't qualify for spiffs or bonuses, and if they missed the goal twice, they'd be fired.

His market was way down for General Motors. He was selling around 120 units a month, but by the end of that month, they had a record month and delivered 217 units, all because somebody finally took charge of the sales department. We know that nothing positive changed in his market to increase sales, but something *new* did happen in his dealership. The dealer took charge of management, they took charge of the salespeople, and everyone had their best month ever.

With 24/7 password access for everyone on JVTN®, and with most chapters in the 8 to 10 minute range, it is very realistic to require salespeople *and* managers to complete 8 to10 training chapters per week. This is such a low minimum requirement it's silly. We're in a profession with pros earning $100,000+ and we have a bunch of 6-car guys and 6-car managers complaining because they have to spend eight minutes to learn more, so they can earn more money.

If managers have salespeople who refuse to do their job,
one of them needs to be replaced right away.

Still using JVTN® as an example ... what's the benefit to your dealership of having your salespeople practice on a Virtual Customer instead of one of your (expensive) live prospects out on the lot?

Exactly – it makes more sense to turn on an interactive video, take a quiz to make sure they 'got it', practice in a virtual role play session and then finish with a timed "Power Drill" than to practice on an expensive, tough to find prospect, and risk a $2,500 sale.

You'll either spend money to put prospects on the lot they can't close or on
training your salespeople to sell to today's prospects. If you're a 100 unit
dealership, JVTN® is less expensive than one lost sale every 3 months.

*Management is always the root problem when
employees refuse to do the job they were hired to do.*

If you're afraid of your sales force or intimidated by them (actually
a common problem), get over it. Or if you have the, "I'm a manager,
not a baby-sitter" attitude, stop complaining and do your job. Some
of you demanded the promotion and got it, or promised you'd do it
right if you got the job – now you have it, so step up.

If you're serious about becoming a more effective manager, call us
today at 1-888-835-5187 to sign up yourself and your managers for our
new 2-Day Team Leadership Workshop. This workshop specifically
focuses on how to *double your sales and triple your net profit*, by learning
to manage your salespeople's activities and by leading your management and sales team to recovery in the toughest market in decades.

*I know that 'doubling sales' sounds like a highball,
but that's only because you haven't been to our class yet.*

2. Second Problem: Allowing managers to refuse to do their job!

Oops! Same problem we have in sales. Some managers say, *"I'm not
doing some parts of my job, and you can't make me."*

It really shouldn't come as a surprise that we have managers who
refuse to do their jobs, too. After all, they were salespeople before
they were managers. In sales, they didn't do everything then either,
so why would you think that all of a sudden you'll have a follower
when you didn't have one before?

You could even have the same root problem with upper management. If
you're a dealer and don't have a clear vision of where your dealership
is headed and clear goals and plans to get you there, and if you don't
hold upper management responsible and accountable for reaching
your goals, all accountability below you just falls apart.

That's why when someone buys out a failing company, the first
person to go is the previous CEO. Why? Because if the company
is failing, it doesn't fail from the bottom up, it fails from the top
down. Getting rid of the real problem is the only solution.

Everyone needs to remember: You can't be a good leader of the
people who report to you, if you can't make yourself follow the
directions you're given from the person *you report to*.

Here are two solutions to both problems.

Plan A ... My 1st choice – Train Them.

Assume every manager and salesperson will come around with proper training. So make sure you, your managers and your salespeople attend our 2-Day Team Leadership and then Sales workshops (together).

We turn about 75% of your problem salespeople and managers around, and that's true even if they come to class *alone*. If your managers and salespeople *attend as a group*, we'll turn 99% of them around, and you can expect a minimum of a 20% improvement in units and 30-50% in gross profit *within 30 days*.

Plan B ... Dealers: This is never the first choice. But if you all came to class in Plan A, and someone still refuses – I'd go straight to Plan B.

If you've done Plan A, had everyone through training and you still have a manager who can't or won't fix themselves or the problem salespeople you have – I'd end it today.

Take the decision away from management and either fire the manager who won't solve the problem and / or fire the salesperson who is most resistant to doing their job. Do it today, so you can get back on track!

Important ... If you have more than one problem person, I'd fire the most protected salesperson or manager that nobody thinks you'd ever mess with and get rid of them first, to get everybody else's attention while you still have a chance to save your dealership.

Again, always start with Plan A first. Remember, we turn 75%-99% around and it's way cheaper to train them and save them, than to fire and replace. Besides, you have to train their replacement, anyway. If Plan A doesn't work, you don't have time to mess around, though. If they don't respond immediately, I'd go straight to Plan B.

It's time to recall every 'get out of jail free' card
you've handed out to salespeople and managers over the years.

Explain what you expect to everyone, then get them to class so they have the information they need to improve. If they refuse, it's time to put someone in the position (that you train) who will do the job.

If you're a struggling dealer and if you just cringed at
firing someone for not doing their job, try real hard to understand;
these people will break you, then shrug it off and just go find another job.

31

Three Types Of Employees
You Can't Afford In Today's Market

With luck, you only have one or two people who aren't doing what they're supposed to be doing – and with training, they'll come around and jump on board 100% to help you grow.

You also have to take another hard look at three types of employees most dealers and managers have always kind of accepted and tolerated in the car business. In good times, we even laugh at how worthless some salespeople really are, and how they just won't do their job. Most dealerships also have that salesperson or manager who purposely spins everybody else's head now and then.

In good times, we all overlook way too many things we should be correcting and improving. In today's market, if you're struggling and are serious about recovery or growth, you're going to have to take a hard look at every one of your employees, especially in sales and management, and deal with the areas listed below that will absolutely stop your recovery and growth dead in its tracks:

- *Incompetent Employees*

- *Employees Who Resist Change*

- *Destructive Employees*

#1 – Incompetent Employees...

Wow – now we're using words that have normally been off limits when we're talking about salespeople or managers. We know the 3-car guy can't sell, but declaring him or her 'incompetent' – whoa, this is a serious breach of protocol.

Sorry, but it's time to pull your head out of your heart. Incompetent employees will break you in today's tough market.

The dictionary defines 'competent' as, "Having the skills or ability to do something properly." Incompetence means just the opposite.

And yeah, it almost sounds mean or demeaning to even say, "You're incompetent". The dictionary doesn't say anything about being mean or hurtful, it just describes *incompetent* as, "Lacking the skills, qualities, or ability to do something *properly.*" It's not about the person. *Competence* just defines their ability, or inability to function *effectively* in the job.

Complacency is sorta the same problem – they *could* sell more or do more, they just don't care enough to bother. That means by being too complacent, *most salespeople become incompetent, by default.*

We may not use the word very often, but no dealership would ever keep a clearly incompetent receptionist, technician, DMV clerk or accountant. Incompetence would destroy the department or cause a ton of damage to the dealership.

To determine *competence*, if every job were rated on a scale of 1 to 10 and *10 was competent*, a dealer would never keep a tech who only scored a 6, or a receptionist who only scored a 4, and they'd be in big trouble if their bookkeeper was only a 5.

In the sales department though, (the department that will make or break a dealership today), nobody focuses much on competence. Plus most didn't realize we have a 'competence rating' to go by.

Logically, though, if the average salesperson delivers 10 units per month, and if there are salespeople regularly delivering 30 or 50, even in the market we're in today, obviously *average* production can't be called good – so at best, *9 or 10 would be called competent.*

Common sense says if they're producing higher than average sales, they are more competent. So lower than average logically equals less competence. If a salesperson sells 25 units per month, they're certainly more competent in sales than someone who only delivers 8 or 9.

So what *competency rating* would a salesperson get who only averages 7 units? What about a salesperson who sells 6 or 4 units per month?

Whether you look at the average salesperson's *technical skills* to do the job or their overall *performance,* it's clear that close to 75% are *less than competent.*

Apply that same thought to an entire sales team. To rate sales management's competency level, if the team averages 15 units per person, that would mean management is competent in its "skills and ability" to hire, train, coach and manage their team.

A dealer in class asked this question:

> *"Joe, if my sales force is only averaging 7 units per person, does that mean we're incompetent as managers?"*

The class answered, "Duh!" before I could respond, but yes....

> *The production of the sales force is a direct reflection of management's skills at hiring, training, coaching and managing.*

Don't just fire salespeople who aren't competent – it wouldn't be fair, because it isn't their fault if they haven't been trained or managed. You have to train and manage them first, to determine their competency.

You can't hold management accountable to be *competent* either, if they've never had the training it takes to hire, train, coach, track, set goals, motivate and manage a sales team effectively.

Make a list of the employees who are currently *not competent* in their positions. Then attend training *with them,* and you'll quickly determine whether they can stay or need to go.

Name   *What skills do they lack?*

_____   _____

_____   _____

_____   _____

_____   _____

_____   _____

If you need extra space – that's really bad – but add extra pages.

Remember 'competent' means, "Having the skills or ability to do (the job) properly."

#2 – *Resistance Fighters...*

You read the headlines or see movies with resistance fighters who fight for their cause, truth and justice ... or whatever. We're all proud of them because they're fighting for a *noble cause.*

Some dealerships have *resistance fighters* both in sales and in sales management, who fight just as hard, and it isn't for a noble cause. They simply do their best to prevent any type of positive change in the organization.

In good times, we develop bad habits and dealerships and managers everywhere overlook the incompetence and resistance from employees that keep them from improving and growing. In bad times, you can't keep your head in the sand and ignore the negative impact these types of employees have on your dealership. If you do, one day you'll look up and the transport is hauling away all of your inventory.

Dealers have salespeople who absolutely refuse to do their job. They do not give everyone a presentation, do not do their follow up, they do not prospect, do not follow the phone script you gave them, do not follow your procedures when they bring you a deal and they have no intention of changing. If you try to make them improve so they can sell more, half will threaten to quit. ("If you try to force me to earn more money, I quit.") Wow – is that just dumb or what?

There are some managers who also refuse to do their job.

As the dealer, you've told your managers to track everything so you'd know what's going on, some of your managers don't. You said to train daily so salespeople could get better, they don't. You said to make sure salespeople do their job with every customer so you could sell more, your managers don't. You said you wanted managers to get out from behind the desk and get involved in every deal so you didn't miss any, your managers don't. You said to verify every appointment so more would show up, your managers don't. Go try to make them do their job so you can all sell more cars and make more money, and some of them will threaten to quit, too.

Time out: If you're the dealer, don't get ready to fire any of your salespeople or managers. You can't, or at least you shouldn't, because *you* probably haven't done what you're supposed to do, either.

Recovery and Growth

Dealers are supposed to be the leaders and set clear goals for their organization, so everyone knows the plan. Most dealers don't – how about you? Dealers are supposed to make sure everyone has the initial training and the continuing education they need to do their job successfully, especially as the market changes. Do you make sure everyone is trained? Dealers are supposed to make sure their managers train, track, coach and motivate the salespeople so they'll sell more – are you requiring this or buying into their excuses? Dealers are supposed to make sure that negative, incompetent employees get the boot instead of protecting them – are you firing or protecting them?

Most important, as the dealer, if you don't require your managers to do their job, it's guaranteed they won't require your salespeople to do theirs.

Resistance is usually a lack of know-how. So always train them first, Plan A, and then go to Plan B if that doesn't work.

If you want to recover, everyone from the dealer down will have to stop resisting and get on board to improve. First, you all have to get to class to learn how to do your jobs and work together as a team to make sure the job gets done, instead of pleading insanity on why you can't, won't, or don't make it happen.

I try not to use 'have to' very often and I do realize I said 'you have to' several times in that last paragraph. Sorry though, we're way past *you should, you need to,* or *you ought to.* Too many dealerships are down to survival at this point, and if you plan to actually pull it off, the correct words are 'you have to' do your job.

It's real important to realize the old saying, "If you keep doing what you've been doing, you'll keep getting what you've been getting," isn't valid anymore. That has been changed to...

If you keep doing what you've been doing,
you will very likely go broke in today's market.

Make a list of the resistance fighters in your dealership, include their title and a date you'll send them to class, or send them packing so they can go destroy some other dealership, instead of yours.

Name	Title	Date
_____	_____	____ / ____ / ____
_____	_____	____ / ____ / ____

If you'll train this group, almost every one of them will jump on board!

#3 – *Destructive Employees...*

Too many dealers have a salesperson or manager who does their best to disrupt anything positive, or anything that would help the company grow. Hopefully, you don't have this problem, but some of you *do* have these destructive employees in sales or in management.

Some of these employees have *some personal chip on their shoulder (for who knows what reason)*, and their goal is to destroy attitudes and everyone's success – including yours, by default. Maybe you've seen that gleam in their eye and that little smirk, when they know they've turned somebody's head, or cost someone a deal.

Whether they're low achievers or high achievers doesn't matter, some will mess up everything they can, whenever they can. Worse, some of these employees have been with you such a long time, that you may call them loyal employees. (Unfortunately, some may even be related to you.)

You may brag about how long they've been with you, they might even get special treatment, and maybe you give them advantages that only a good employee should have.

> *But destructive employees are not good employees.*
> *You may be loyal to them, but they sure aren't loyal to you.*

As the dealer, this is critical – because if your dealership goes broke, you lose everything and all of your good employees lose their jobs, too. And that's what some of these negative employees want to see happen. They don't care what happens to you or your people. Their goal is to just turn heads and cost you sales. And if they win, they'll just find themselves another job.

You may also have some employees with such an exaggerated view of their ability to sell or manage, they just think you're plain stupid when you present your goal or a new plan – if it wasn't their idea, they'll do their best to make sure your plan doesn't succeed.

The worst offenders usually stay under the radar. After you talk, they smile, nod and say, "Yes, Boss!" and walk out the door with the intention of undermining you. These people run off your brightest and best people and will put you out of business, one day at a time.

> *Train and manage your underachievers to make them better.*
> *Push your most resistant group hard to either do their job or quit.*
> *The destructive employee won't change – so cut your losses fast.*

Last Thought On This...

I really do believe 95% of the dealers, managers and salespeople in this business have a great heart, solid gold intentions and want to do a good job for the dealership, for you, the customer and themselves.

If you're the dealer or if you're a manager, it's your job to *spot those other 5%'ers and get rid of them, as quickly as possible.* You can't pass the buck on handling this either, because it's your responsibility to put a competent and effective team together.

The porter, a tech or the receptionist who really does care about the customer, the dealership and who tries hard to do their best, can't do anything about disloyal, disgruntled employees who do a bad job for you and your customers. Only you can.

Plus, when it comes to generating the revenue dealerships need to avoid more cuts, even though the porter, a tech or the receptionist does their best and tries as hard as they can – they still can't do enough to improve sales or generate enough revenue to protect their own or anybody else's job in your dealership.

Your managers in sales and service, and your salespeople on the drive and up front, have the ability to improve profits right now, today. Service writers can become salespeople instead of just clerks who write orders. They can increase revenue today, but they won't without training, coaching and daily sales management.

Salespeople up front can improve their unit sales 30%–50% and their gross profit 40% virtually overnight, too. But the same is true there as well; it has to start with the dealer and the managers to train, coach and manage them every day, too.

Recovery and growth has to be a team adventure. If only one person improves, it helps, but just a little. When everyone works together to improve – *that's when the magic happens in sales.*

If every salesperson, every manager and the dealer decide to work together as a team – making money will never be an issue in an automobile dealership, in any market condition.

RECAP OF THESE TWO CHAPTERS ON EMPLOYEES

*If you enter a sail boat race and want to win, you
either have to pull in your anchors, or you have to cut the rope.
You can't win with even one anchor out, much less several.*

1. It's always less expensive to *reel in* your anchors than it is to
    replace them.   ❏ **True**   ❏ **False**

    List your anchors below (or in your notebook)...

    _____   _____
    _____   _____
    _____   _____

    If you need more space, you're in trouble.

2. If you try to reel in the anchors in your dealership through training
    and counseling and they won't budge, you're going to have to cut
    the line, or lose the race.   ❏ **True**   ❏ **False**

3. Firing is tough, but if you've tried your best, if your anchors refuse to
    budge, that's *their* decision, not yours.   ❏ **True**   ❏ **False**

4. Some anchors also pick up *sludge* that will eat away at your
    boat, and they not only slow you down, they'll sink your ship
    if you don't act fast, especially today.   ❏ **True**   ❏ **False**

5. I know the ship stuff seems corny, but it's easier to talk about
    anchors, sludge and sinking ships than it is to talk about your
    favorite negative old timer or a relative.   ❏ **True**   ❏ **False**

Use Your Ad Money To Save An Anchor

Most anchors in sales and management can be saved *with effort.*
Besides, it'll run you over $50,000 to replace a salesperson and twice
that to replace a manager. Even $50,000 is cheaper than what they
cost you now, though, if they refuse to come around.

Big Tip: Use some more of that ad money to get them to class. But
here's the catch, especially with anchors – *you have to sit next to them
in class.* Why? So they know that you know, that they know, that you
know *exactly* what they have to start doing differently to keep their job.

After class you have to be unrelenting in your effort to improve or
replace them, and if you back off, so will they. Again, drop the guilt.
If they refuse to change, then it's their decision to leave, not yours.

32

Track Your Way To
More Sales

We were on a conference call yesterday with our trainers. We were talking about how we can help dealers grow and improve right now in today's market, when they need it most.

Everything we've talked about in this book is critical to your success; you *have to* have strong Leadership, especially today. You *have to* Manage your salespeople's activities and Coach them every day, not just when it's convenient – and you *have to* make sure your salespeople do their job with every prospect and customer they have.

Training and Tracking are the two most important things you *have to* do to recover and grow. Picking the most important of the two sometimes feels like that "which came first, the chicken or the egg" question. This one is easier though, because to know what to train on, you *have to* track everything first.

If your dealership uses our tracking in JVTN®, you can call me or one of our trainers, we can look at your tracking online and within minutes, we can tell you exactly where you should focus your training to get immediate results.

Let's put the fun back in tracking!

Tracking to Train

There is no question training is critical, especially daily training, and that's why we pioneered online training. JVTN® is a total training and management platform, and it has all of the training, role playing and power drills you'll need on any important topic in sales. You can search on topics to train on the spot as soon as you notice a problem, it includes a video 'vault' for your own internal videos of your walk arounds, etc., a forms vault for your forms or procedure manuals, its own internal email program for everyone – and so much more.

Because JVTN® is a training platform, one of the critical tools it has is the most complete *training focused tracking* in the car business. *You need to know exactly where you are to target your training.*

The training, testing, role playing and reporting in JVTN® are critical to developing skills and to managing your salespeople. Having said that...

There is nothing more important to your success than tracking.

How could tracking trump training? How could tracking take precedence over skills, product knowledge or even who you hire? It's simple, because *tracking is your only pipeline; your only source of information on exactly what you're doing now, how you're doing now, and exactly what you need to change or improve to grow.*

In 20 groups, I ask dealers to pull out their financial statements so we can figure out how to grow. Everyone holds theirs up and is ready to go. Then I correct myself with, "I'm sorry, there's nothing in your financial statement that can help you grow – I meant did you bring your tracking sheets so we can figure out how to grow?"

Your financial statement only tells you what happened, your tracking sheets (if you do them accurately) tell you *why* it happened. Your financial statement is a history book, and it's about yesterday's results. Tracking is a living file that keeps you informed of everything that's happening to you *right now, today* in your dealership.

You need to know exactly how many *opportunities (ups, calls, leads)* you had yesterday, exactly what *type* of opportunity you had (walk-in, repeat, referral, etc.), exactly what *activities* (presentation, demo, write up) took place and the exact *results* you got from those opportunities and activities (units, gross, by salesperson, manager, etc.)

Why is tracking so important?

Every Fortune 500 company tracks everything they do and their annual goals and projections are based on their most recent quarterly averages. (Those quarterly averages are the same 'Current Averages' we've taught for 30+ years). It's simple: you track, find your most recent 90-day average to find your base, and then you set your goals based on *that number,* not goals based on last month or a 12 month average that's out of date.

Every professional team in any sport also tracks every putt, block, shot, run, walk, goal or swing and they use that information to *target their training* to prepare for every event and to improve the performance of every person on the team.

The most profitable dealerships and dealer groups track everything they do, for the same reasons.

Everyone reading this is already aware of everything I just said about business and sports. But 80% of the managers reading this don't track because they don't understand how to, or why it's critical to their growth, or because they lack the Leadership and Management skills to make it happen – *or because they just don't want to.*

The value of tracking is indisputable, so you really either need to get on board with tracking, or stop pretending you're serious about growth!

Most Dealerships Track Everything <u>BUT</u> Sales

There *is* tracking in every dealership, just not in sales...

- Your Inventory is tracked
- Accounts Receivable tracks everything
- Accounts Payable tracks everything
- Finance tracks every product and gross
- Service tracks everything; the customer, what they bought, who did the work, how many hours it took and the total sale
- Parts tracks every item on the shelf and when it's sold

That's why the Fixed Ops Managers who move up front to Sales Management ask us in every class, "Why doesn't Sales have processes and why don't they track everything?"

Service Tracks Everything

Those 3 words make Service seem like the hero in this, but in real life, tracking in Service isn't optional. In Service *everything that happens is tracked by the process itself*. Every piece of information is entered into the computer without exception for the work flow, inventory control and payment process to function.

Every Repair Order is numbered and broken down by customer type. Every 1/10th hour is tracked by the Tech or the book, and every dollar is also broken down by parts and labor.

At the end of the day, everything is entered into the computer (*manually* by writers, managers and clerks). After everything is entered, running reports on productivity is simply a keystroke. If you have an efficient Service department, you'll notice your Service Manager is constantly poring through all those reports, so he or she can find the areas they can improve to increase production. *They use their tracking information to improve.*

Even if Service didn't *want* to track everything, *they have to* track for payroll, to resupply parts, for warranty claims, to monitor work they've done on each vehicle and to report to the manufacturer.

The Sales Department Pleads Insanity

Service knows exactly how many people were on the drive. Sales can't even come close to telling you exactly how many people were on the lot.

Service knows exactly *who* the customer is (CP/Warranty/Internal). Sales only knows they delivered 100 units to *somebody*.

Service knows the breakdown on productivity by type of customer and by the tech. For the most part, Sales only knows they brought in $250,000 in gross profit ($175,000 front / $75,000 F&I).

Sales doesn't know how many or which types of prospects (opportunities) actually came onto the lot. They don't know how many of those walk-in prospects, previous customers, referrals, be-backs, Service, phone or internet prospects were sold, or the gross on each group.

Service knows everything about each opportunity and sale. Sales knows almost nothing about their opportunities, and for the most part, they only know the totals on unit sales and gross.

Doesn't It Take Less Time To Track In Service?

Great question – let's check. First let's look at the volume of prospects in each department and then break that down to how many prospects each salesperson has to track.

A 100 unit store with a 20% closing ratio has 500 people on the lot each month. An average 100 unit store will also average about 25 customers per day on the drive or about 500 per month out there, too. So the total volume of prospects on the lot or on the drive is about the same, in most dealerships.

When we talk about it being easier to track in Service, while total volume is the same, the volume per salesperson is way different.

What do I mean?

Service has 2 writers and 1 manager while Sales has 10 salespeople and 3 managers. With 500 prospects in each department, that means each service writer has to track 250 customers while each salesperson only has to track 50 prospects. Once you add in all of the other manual entries that are required to maintain the flow from the drive to the cashier ... tracking in Service is way more time consuming than tracking is in Sales.

So What Is Different About Tracking In Sales?

Let's compare the two...

Service ... First – virtually every opportunity in Service becomes a sale, whether it's a Customer Pay or Warranty. So Service does *opportunity*, *activity* and *result* tracking on every single customer without exception. Again, it's part of the process.

The tracking process in Service generally goes like this...

- The writer manually creates a Repair Order and / or manually creates a customer screen.

- Then he or she enters the information into the new or current customer screen.

- They print the work order and they either work off of the print-out or from the computer while the vehicle is in the shop.

- Techs make notes on what they do on paper or online.

- Parts works off its own copy or screen and enters whatever parts they give out or order for that job.

- When the job is done, the writer, or clerk compiles the parts and labor breakdown, separates Warranty from Customer Pay, completes that paperwork, updates the computer and sends the customer and updated paperwork to the cashier for payment.

- The cashier completes the transaction, enters the final information into the customer screen, and then everything moves into the system for accounts payable, receivables, restocking, etc.

- The warranty clerk fills in the forms to bill the manufacturer.

Sales ... In Sales, every opportunity *doesn't* equal a sale like it does in Service, so we have to manually do *opportunity* and *activity* tracking. Remember, we started with 500 opportunities, sold 100 and had 400 prospects that we didn't deliver.

As for 'trouble' ... *activity* tracking on the 400 lost sales is simple. Salespeople using an 'up' card or the back of their business card write down the prospect's name, address, email and phone numbers.

They need to ✓ whether it was a ❑ fresh up, ❑ repeat customer, ❑ be-back, ❑ referral, ❑ Service lead or a ❑ phone or ❑ internet lead. You need to know that information so you can see where your *floor traffic* is really coming from each month, so you know *exactly* where to put your money and marketing efforts.

They also have to ✓ whether they gave a ❑ presentation, ❑ demonstration and ❑ wrote them up.

I know it's time consuming to ✓ a box, but you need this information so you can find your *average performance* in each area, by salesperson. When you do, you'll know exactly where to focus your training, coaching, daily management time and even your spiffs to push more effort into activities that generate your greatest returns.

In real life, the tracking you need is not difficult at all. And if your salespeople use our Planners and Daily Activity Logs, the ☑ (check boxes) and categories are already listed.

Note: One other critical area for you to track *accurately* is your *sales by each ad source*. If you will, management can target your marketing efforts and ad expense in exactly the right direction and save you a ton.

To complete their tracking, at the end of each day a salesperson using JVTN® would enter the prospect's information in the Tracking module, a short note on what to do next, and input their total numbers in the appropriate categories – then all of the math, averages and charting is done for them.

If they're using our Planners, they do the same thing on the lot; jot it down in the planner and right before they leave, simply enter their total in the Daily Activity Log on the manager's desk. Total time: 2 minutes per sold customer and 1 minute per unsold prospect.

But What About Management's Time?

Compiling the tracking information off of the Daily Activity Log for management with 10 salespeople is about as time consuming as adding up your front nine scores on the golf course. And if they're using JVTN®, salespeople enter their own information, so there's nothing for management to do except review the reports and then set goals and plans for improvement. (Or have the receptionist do it for you.)

But Is It Worth It To Track In Sales?

Let's look at a couple of different ways tracking helps you improve productivity, so you know *exactly* what everyone is doing, and so you can find ways to improve and increase production.

Let's look at advertising; it's an easy example of a critical area we should be tracking every month in sales, but aren't. Let's see how our *assumptions* compare to what really happens.

Here's how dealers were taught to determine their ad cost per sale...

$$\begin{array}{ll} \$30,000 & \text{Ad Budget} \\ \div \quad 100 & \text{Deliveries} \\ = \quad \$300 & \text{Per Unit} \end{array}$$

That isn't how service does the math. They spend $5,000 on an ad campaign and know their response rate, because the customer comes in with a coupon (assuming it's entered into the system). That gives Service the information they need on which ads actually work, so they can target their spending to just the ads that generate revenue.

Sales spends $30,000 on ads, doesn't effectively *source* the prospects, so sales has absolutely no idea which ads actually produce.

Sales is so aware of the problem everyone laughs about, "Only half of our advertising works – we're not sure which half." ... Wow - that's at least a $15,000 "ha-ha" every month if you're spending $30,000.

Actually if you really track, and if you use real math, it's a much more expensive joke than that. When you look at the real stats; only 8 to 12 sales actually track back to the $30,000 in advertising in a 100 unit store.

Yes, I know your ad *source* tracking shows more than just 8 to 12 units come from your advertising. But I thought you knew: Most managers just guess and give credit to an ad in the paper or on TV for a vehicle advertised in that source. No one really knows if the customer ever saw the vehicle advertised there, but these 'guesses' also help protect a manager's favorite ad source.

While the math is correct on the previous page, the *formula is wrong*. It's for convenience and *assumes all sales came from advertising.* That formula is not correct for finding *your advertising cost per ad unit sold.*

The real math looks more like this...

	100	Sold Units
–	30	Sales to Repeat / Referral / Be-Backs / Service, etc.
=	70	Possible sales from advertising
–	62	62% on average buy based on your location
=	8	Probable sales from your advertising

Total cost per advertised unit sold...

	$30,000	Ad Budget
÷	8	Sold Units From Advertising
=	$ 3,750	Actual Ad Cost Per Advertised Unit Sold

If managers in a 100 unit store actually tracked their sales from ads, they'd find their $30,000 ad budget generates 8 to 12 units per month *maximum*. That means your Ad Cost Per Vehicle Retailed is closer to $2,500, than the $300 to $500 everybody assumes. (Ouch!)

Recovery and Growth

***Did you ever wonder why doubling down
on your ad expenses doesn't end up doubling your sales?***

Technically, you probably do *double sales <u>from ads</u>* when you double
your ad budget. It's just that everybody is disappointed when they
only deliver another 10 to 12 extra units for the extra $30,000 they
spent on those big ads or that Gorilla on the roof.

To be clear...

I didn't say you shouldn't advertise. On the contrary, I think you
should, but spend your money only on what works. To know that,
you have to track every opportunity, activity, and result effectively.

Track Results (Units And Gross)...

The average Service RO is around $200 and the average sale is
around $2,500, including Finance.

Service takes considerable time to input a lot of information so
they can track everything, so they can try to improve productivity
on their $200 ROs by even 10%. In comparison, how much effort
does Sales Management go to in an attempt to improve productivity
on their (100) $2,500 sales? *Not much at all – everybody just works hard.*

Remember every person Service talks to is a *customer (buyer)*.
Every person a salesperson talks to is just an *opportunity (prospect)*.

78% of the *prospects on the lot* are buyers though (that's 8 out of 10). But
sales only delivers 20% (that's 2 of 10) which means they miss 6 of every 8
buyers they could have delivered. Yet most managers won't spend the two
minutes to track, so they know *where and how* to improve units and gross.

The math...

	500	Prospects	
−	100	Deliveries	
=	400	Unsold Prospects	
x	78%	Who *will* buy (90% of those within one week)	
=	312	Lost sales every month who buy down the street	
x	71%	Said you had a vehicle they would have bought	
Ouch! =	221	Lost sales on vehicles they wanted you had in stock	

What's A 20% Improvement Worth In Service Or Sales?

Example: The Service Manager uses the reports to increase $$$ per RO on CP tickets by 20%. That's another $40 on 300 or so tickets.

Average Customer Pay RO	$200	
Improve 20%	x 20%	
Additional Revenue Per RO	$40	
	x 300	ROs
	$12,000	Per Month In Sales
	$144,000	Per Year In Sales
Additional Gross at 60%	$ 86,400	Extra Gross Per Year

In Sales: You can increase units by 20% (20 extra units) and gross by 20% ($500 extra on every unit), by effectively tracking your sales opportunities, activities and results by customer type, and then *targeting your training* to focus on the specific areas that need improvement.

Those extra 20 units will bring in $50,000 in extra gross. The $500 extra gross per unit on 120 units will bring in another $60,000 gross. That's a $110,000 gross profit improvement for a 20% increase.

Extra Units at $2,500 Each	20	
	x $2,500	Current PVR
	$50,000	Additional Gross
Extra Gross Per Unit	$500	Per Unit
	x 120	Total Units
	$60,000	Additional Gross
Total Gross Improvement	$110,000	Extra Per Month
	$1,320,000	Extra Per Year

The value of tracking for 'targeted' training to improve 20% ...

   Service ... $ 144,000 *sales* per year x 60% = $ 86,400 in *gross*

   Sales ...... $1,320,000 *gross* per year x 60% = $792,000 in *net*

No question – Service is the backbone. But if you'll track to help sales flex its muscles – you're talking huge, immediate increases in net profit.

33

Potential – Problems – Solutions

The most frustrating part of writing this book is trying to squeeze enough information from our 12 days of live training workshops (each with a 150 page workbook), and over 30 training courses (each with its own workbook and leader's guide) plus hundreds of training modules on JVTN®, in addition to 161 pages from my book 'Earn Over $100,000 Selling Cars Every Year', and 131 pages from my book for salespeople, 'Get Everything You Want In Sales: Goal Setting', 160 pages from my book, 'Top 7 Revenue & Profit Sources', 450 pages in my book 'How To Sell A Car And Close The Sale Today', plus 145 pages of sales tips in '38 Hot Tips' into just a couple hundred pages to help you see...

• The incredible potential you have today

• The problems that cause you to miss so many sales

• The steps you can take to improve immediately

Note: I urge you to read this book again and again, especially the chapters you disagreed with the most. Why? Because those things we disagree on the most are the things *most opposite* of what you've been doing. And if you keep doing the same old things, and thinking the same old way, you just can't grow in today's new business climate.

Adversity brings problems, and problems present opportunities. But it's (only) through change that we have the ability to grow.

Therein lies the first problem. Everybody wants to do better, but nobody wants to change what they're doing, so they can grow.

Your Potential Is Incredible

We analyzed your potential in just 5 areas, not the dozens we go through in class. Because you sell a product everyone has to have, your true potential in the car business is almost unlimited. With 3 vehicles per family and with people trading every 4 years, (even if it's closer to 5 or 6 years in this market), the incredible opportunity and potential is simply in the math.

Assume they have 3 vehicles and only buy every 5 years – that's one every 1.7 years, so round it up to only one every 2 years for easier math. That means to sell 1,000 units per year, you just need 2,000 families you take care of so well they would never consider buying or servicing their vehicles anywhere else but at your dealership.

Want to improve sales every year? No big deal, *just spend as much time and money learning to add families* to your dealership as you do trying to generate floor traffic for the weekend and it's easy.

Not counting your current base, if you just *add 50 families per month (600 per year)* to your base, and make total retention your priority, in 5 years, you'll have 3,000 families who generate 1,500 units per year. And that doesn't include the ton of referrals you'll get from loyal customers.

We've done exactly that and have grown 60.4% per year since the day we started. Over 90% of our business is repeat and referral business, because we've always had those simple 3 goals we identified as your salespeople's job: *get* a customer, *sell* the product, *keep* the customer forever with a great product and great *after the sale* support.

It's no secret that most dealerships have never focused on properly servicing the customer to keep them for life. I really believe you have a greater opportunity to grow more right now than ever, because your competition never focused on total retention before either, and they sure aren't going to start now that they're cutting expenses and staff.

Most of your competitors have lost their winning attitude and have cut so many expenses and support staff that training and growing aren't even on their list anymore. They're only thinking survival, and that's like a football team only thinking defense. If you don't make smart offensive plays, too, you can't possibly win the game.

Put that 'kid in a candy store' image in your mind and smile real big when you think of the opportunity you have today in your market.

The Problems Are The Same

The problems we have today are simply the problems we've always had, they've just been *amplified* because of the troubled economy and from the ripples throughout every industry. But our problems aren't new and I don't think I've uncovered any hidden secrets from the past in here. You already knew this stuff.

My goal was to remind you of the problems and the new and dire consequences you may face in such a serious market if you don't act fast. When times are great, we all get a little sloppy. When times get tough, that party is over and it's time to keep 'the main thing, the main thing' so we can get back on track fast.

> *Your common problems are all, without exception...*
> *Training & Management Related Problems.*

There isn't one problem we've talked about in this book that can be solved until *someone* teaches *someone else* to either do something they haven't been doing, or teaches them how to do it right or how to do it better. That's *management* and *training.*

A bad employee is a management hiring problem. Either that or it's a process, training or daily management problem. Missing sales is a training problem – either with management who isn't trained to know where sales are missed, or missed because management doesn't know how to hire, train, coach or manage salespeople daily.

The Solution Is Always Training

Most problems are employee related and the solutions are training related. Learn to manage your people better and you'll get more done each day. Learn to sell, and you'll put more vehicles on the road. Learn to follow up, and you'll solve your floor traffic problem.

There was an article (either in USA Today or in the Wall Street Journal) that clearly stated...

> *"There is nothing in your business that you can spend money on that will provide a greater return than training your employees."*

A few years ago, I read about a Motorola study that found training produced a $30 to $1 return on investment, and they were talking about training any and all employees, not just salespeople.

Return on Investment

I just read a book that reminds you to treat your used car inventory as an investment and manage it daily to improve your return. Dealers lose hundreds of thousands every year mismanaging that asset, and they lose even more millions every year by mismanaging their sales force. Then they blow another half million each year on ads that don't work.

Just do the math – when you *invest* $2,390 for you and your GM to attend our leadership class and you go back and improve sales 20% and gross 20%... that's a $110,000 return *every month* in a 100 unit store, and a $1.3M return every year for a one-time $2,390 investment.

Is that a lot to spend on training? Maybe, if you just look at the cost. But when you look at the *return*, it's the best investment on the planet.

• If you put $2,390 in the bank, you'll have about $2,500 in 12 months.

• If you spend $2,390 one time on advertising, you'll get $4,780 ($2 to $1).

• If you invest $2,390 in our class one time for a 20% improvement, you get back $110,000 each month, $1,300,000 in the next 12 months. That's $46 to $1 your first month, and $544 to $1 for the year.

If I gave the bank teller $2,390 one time and they gave me back $3,561 *every day after that*, I'd be first in line every morning without fail.

I asked our salespeople to list the *excuses they got yesterday* for not attending classes or getting JVTN® so their dealers could get those kinds of returns. Here's what they heard...

- That's what I pay my managers to do
- My salespeople and managers won't use it
- I like your stuff and know it will help, but I learned on my own and they should too – and I'm not sending them
- I know I can attend the Dealer class free (as a JVTN® subscriber), but sales are off and I can't afford it *(What???)*
- I trained a salesperson one time and then he quit 3 months later and I'm never sending anybody else to a class again
- You don't get it, my market is different, it's tough here in ...
- I've got a new GM, let me check with him to see if that's what he wants to do (What if he doesn't want the $1.3M?)
- Let me know when you have a class closer to us *(Isn't the $1.3M in potential enough to take a 2 hour plane ride, and didn't he know he could buy his own plane for half of that?)*

- It's too slow right now and I can't afford to have anybody out of the store. *(Say what?)*
- Money's tight so let me see if my new guys work out first.
- All of our guys like what they saw and want JVTN®, but right now it's just too much money – we'll hold off.
- Timing is off right now, we're making some changes.
- We're cutting all expenses right now, including training.
- I know (Bill) increased his units by 10 per month after your class, but I want to see if that lasts before I send anyone else.
- Let me see if my guys want to do it – call me back.
- I need to talk to my managers first, I want their buy in.
- It's too close to the end of the month – call me next time.

And that's just from yesterday.

There is only one way out of a slump and that's 'Up' and there just aren't any other ways to *move up fast* that can even come close to the results and return on investment our training offers. Here is an example about the return potential on your JVTN® investment...

"How did we grow 120% from January 2008 to January 2009 in our current market? All of our salespeople train twice a week on JVTN®.

For the salespeople who don't want to train no problem, they can work, just not here. The sky is the limit when training the Joe Verde way! Thanks, Joe." Craig Brown, Sales Manager, Kamloops Ford

---

Not only is training the solution to practically every problem that holds you back, it's the investment that keeps on giving. You could certainly spend the same amount of money for JVTN® on an ad and sell a car or two, maybe three or five. But whether your return on advertising is $2,000 or $10,000, it's a <u>one-shot deal</u>.

You've spent millions on advertising over the years.
Just make a real, honest commitment to training for one year
and you'll make more money than you could have ever imagined.

34

Hot Dogs – Gorillas – Training

Cut expenses, just don't cost yourself even more sales!

We're seeing way too many dealerships who are gripped by fear and are cutting things that are making them money and cutting one of their only lifelines to improvement, and that's effective training.

We're talking to dealers we've worked with who had record years after getting everyone trained, who are now balking because they're saying, "I've got to cut expenses." I couldn't agree more, but you don't cut expenses in areas that make you money.

Reduce all expenses that give you no ROI in this market, but increase spending in the areas that do generate more than they cost!

In that Support meeting Thursday, our conversation also turned to a great JVTN® dealership. They are using our online sales training and the dealer and managers completely agree they're making at least a sale per person each month (15 units) because their salespeople are using the heck out of JVTN®.

The managers want the training, the salespeople use it daily and the dealer and managers said they're bringing in $30,000 to $40,000 per month in extra units and gross because they have it ($30 to $1 ROI).

What's The Problem?

The dealer went to his 20 Group and heard he should cut all of his expenses. So without thinking through the differences between his expenses and investments, he came back all wound up *with good intentions* and made a rule; no more spending. Period.

If it was a *discretionary expense*, good or bad, it had to stop because he said so. While almost all expenses have some *value*, some have tremendous ROI, like we've seen. Painting the building is an expense, protecting it from the weather adds value, but not revenue. You could probably put off painting the building for a year.

As a quick reminder on how the dictionary defines
'Expense' and 'Investment'

• *Expense: Something that costs money.*

Example: Paint the building / pave the lot / buy shelves in parts.

• *Investment: Money spent to make a profit.*

Example A: Running an ad on a specific vehicle to sell it. Typical ROI on advertising $1.^{50} return to $1 spent.

Example B: The dealer above, spending $995 per month to train, with a *proven* return of 15 units. ROI = $30,000 in gross profit on a $995 investment. That's a $30 return *monthly* for every $1 spent.

Did they really say cut all expenses?

First of all, I've spoken to over two hundred 20 Groups and other State, Local and Dealer Group meetings. While the focus at a 20 Group mostly revolves around financial statements and composites, and certainly on controlling expenses today, I've never heard a good moderator say stop 'all' spending.

Why? Because common sense says 'all' spending isn't bad.

Without question, expenses should be reviewed and most of the extra checks you write should be stopped until and unless you can *prove* their ROI. *(I'm not just talking about training. I'm saying don't cut anything that makes you more money than it's costing you.)* I'm watching dealers cut spending in other areas besides training that also make them money. Some of the expenses you have are good investments and if you stop those, you lose sales and gross.

For example...

A Gorilla On The Roof

If you have an inflatable Gorilla on the roof and you're selling cars because people are saying, "I didn't know you were here, but then I saw that stupid Gorilla on the roof..." ... keep the Gorilla.

Another example...

Hot Dogs & Ice Cream

If you're giving away free hot dogs on Saturdays and you know for a fact you sold 2 units last month with $5,000 in gross because of those FREE hot dogs, do not let anyone cut the $200 per week hot dog vendor from your expenses.

Why? Simple math...

> $5,000 Gross Profit from having free Hot Dogs
>
> – $ 800 to the Hot Dog vendor
>
> $4,200 Additional revenue you *would not* have had

Returns on investment are like the tip of the iceberg.

If you know for sure you made 2 deals because you heard a customer say, *"Golly gee, we didn't even plan to look at cars today, but as we were driving by, little Johnny saw the hot dog stand and wanted one, so we stopped and ended up buying a car,"* that also means you probably made twice as many more sales you didn't hear about.

If you can prove one sale, you got more!

Common Sense Trumps Pride

The problem in the case of the JVTN® dealer not renewing his subscription wasn't a lack of common sense or in the JVTN® ROI; the dealer freely admitted a great 30:1 return on his investment.

Unfortunately, this became an ego issue, not a financial decision.

He'd made a decision – which in real life, was overall good, just not good in all cases. After he'd told everybody there would be *no exceptions*, he just couldn't allow himself to admit he should have said, "Unless our ROI is greater than the cost."

So within seconds, his pride kicked in to defend why he was making such a bad decision, he got huffy, his managers were bewildered, and the conversation was over.

His decision was such a bummer, for lots of reasons...

- If money was tight enough to cut expenses, saving $1,000 to lose $30,000 means he'll be $29,005 worse every month than before.

- Giving up 15 units and $30,000 in gross each month means his dealership will take a 180 unit drop, and a $360,000 loss in gross profit in just the next 12 months. (That's a huge loss to save just $12,000.)

- His salespeople will sell 15 fewer units and earn $8,000 to $9,000 less each month as a group – and his managers will earn less, too.

- Attitudes will suffer and his salespeople's and manager's families will have less to spend on rent, food, clothes, school, etc.

- Worse: Every employee in the dealership and their families will be negatively impacted and some may be laid off because of his decision, which he originally made with good intentions.

We lost our favorite kind of subscriber. His managers and salespeople were always excited about learning more and improving, and I'm sorry we won't be there to support them anymore, *especially in this market.*

One More Tip: Don't cut your key support staff.

One of the other biggest mistakes in cutbacks dealers are making now is that they're cutting support staff like receptionists, porters and some are even laying off salespeople.

Don't fire the receptionist, make her a profit center, instead. Train her and give her a list of 'aged' service customers to call at night to schedule appointments this week. Give her the list of customers with special order parts on the shelf and have her call them, too, and generate even more appointments (revenue) in service this week.

When she's done with that, have her verify sales appointments, have her contact people who didn't buy or log your tracking in JVTN® or whatever system you use. You'll lose thousands in recruiting, training and sales by laying off key support people. Find something for them to do to generate enough revenue to pay for themselves.

Salespeople? I'm not sure why anyone would ever cut a salesperson, unless they were one of the 'bad guys' we talked about before. The only logical reason is that they were on a salary, or a guarantee higher than minimum wage. And I have no idea why you'd ever put a salesperson on a salary, unless you're trying to make them so comfortable they have no need to really dig in to generate sales.

Teach all of your salespeople to sell, manage them effectively, and then you can ditch their salary, because with training, they'll make good money. If you insist on a salary, make it a stair-step salary and put a minimum on sales they have to generate at each level to earn it and then teach them how to sell, how to prospect and how to follow up. Just make sure your managers train, coach and manage their activities.

What if they're on a salary and they can't sell? Not everyone is cut out for sales, but too many slip through the hiring process. Train them right away and wind down the salary over the next 90 days. If you train, coach and manage them effectively and they still can't make more than your salary was paying them – the people who shouldn't have been hired in the first place will leave on their own.

If a salesperson can't make a living on the unlimited opportunity in our business (even in this market), they're either untrained, or just not cut out to be in sales to begin with.

Or, it could be that they're just lazy and you've been supporting them for years, instead of making them do their job and sell.

Last thought on cutting expenses...

Fear causes us to make a lot of bad decisions especially when it comes to advertising, cutting expenses and making money. Cut hard, cut deep and stop everything that doesn't make you money. Don't stop anything that generates more revenue than it costs.

When we're in times like these, you really have to have...

- A calm heart and a clear head

- Well thought out goals and plans

- People on your team who will do the job

- The training on how to do the job

- And a leader at the top to make it happen

With those 5 things, you win. So take a deep breath, jot down a few notes and then let's get back to work saving the world.

RECAP OF THIS SECTION

Recovery Step One

1. Because we need sales to survive or grow, if we keep salespeople who refuse to do their job, we can't grow. ❑ True ❑ False

2. Because we need sales to survive or grow, if we keep managers who refuse to do their job, we can't grow. ❑ True ❑ False

3. Because we need sales to survive or grow, if I don't do my job as the dealer, we can't grow. ❑ True ❑ False

4. If we can save our salespeople and managers by training them, that's far less expensive than replacing them. ❑ True ❑ False

5. If we don't train everyone, especially our 'less than competent' people and resistant salespeople or managers, they will hold us back and could cause us to fail. ❑ True ❑ False

6. If we don't immediately solve our problem with any 'destroyers' we have in sales or management, we may fail. ❑ True ❑ False

7. By tracking accurately, we will know exactly where we're missing sales and can *target* our training to improve. ❑ True ❑ False

8. It is critical that the Dealer, the GM, the GSM and every manager is on board 100% with one goal. ❑ True ❑ False

9. As the Dealer, I am on board 100%. ❑ True ❑ False

10. The General Manager is on board 100%. ❑ True ❑ False

11. The GSM is on board 100%. ❑ True ❑ False

12. Every Sales Manager is on board 100%. ❑ True ❑ False

13. As the Dealer, if I have salespeople who are not on board or not capable of selling in this market, if I am aware and do nothing, I have to accept full responsibility if we fail. ❑ True ❑ False

14. As the Dealer, if every manager isn't on board 100%, we risk not succeeding. If I decide to keep them anyway, I have to accept full responsibility if we fail. ❑ True ❑ False

Wouldn't it be great if you could pass that 'buck' about now?
Don't worry – just do your job and everything will work out fine.

SECTION 8

Your Recovery
Step Two

This old saying is no longer in service:

~~Insanity is doing the same thing over~~
~~and over again, hoping for a different result.~~

Please make a note that it has been changed to:

Insanity is being in the worst market in decades,
doing nothing all day to improve, just hoping
you'll get lucky and sell something.

35

Thirteen Things
You Have To Do Right Now To Grow

Everything we've talked about up to this point was to get you ready to take action. We've talked about your market, the bad habits most dealers, managers and salespeople have developed, specific job descriptions and the specific skills your sales and management staff will need to grow in any market. We covered these areas, because you have to know where the weak spots are in your dealership.

Then we covered your incredible potential (even if you cut it in half a few times) and we went over basic survival strategies to help you see the opportunities and that there is a logical way UP to recovery or growth in your dealership.

Now it's time to go over exactly what you have to do *immediately* to recover quickly and set yourself up for continued growth.

Whether you're dying on the vine or if you just want to take sales to the next level – these steps aren't suggestions and they aren't options, *they are requirements if you want to increase your sales quickly.*

I'll assume you've already gone through the dealership and cut all of your non-essential expenses and that you've cleaned house on any excess staff and any non-productive, resistant or destructive employees in every department. If you haven't, do it now.

This section will be your step-by-step plan for recovery.
Your assignment is for you and your management team
to apply each step in the process – so slow down.

1. Find Your Vision

"Your imagination is your preview of life's coming attractions."

– Albert Einstein

Before you can figure out how to recover or grow, you have to determine exactly what that means to you.

The directions to discovering your vision are easy...

> Build a mud hut, start a camp fire ... (Just kidding, but the point is the same – you need quiet time to think.)

A. Get a pen and pad of paper (or blank Word® document).

B. Go sit in a quiet room – no kids, no TV, no distractions.

C. First ... Take a few deep breaths and relax. This is not a timed event – you need to relax so you can think.

D. Let your mind wander and without worrying about the order of things, just start jotting down notes on your potential, your problems, your processes, your people and your long term (and short term) goals. What *exactly* do you want to see happen in every area? By what date?

Questions are the answer! If you ask the right questions, you'll come up with the right answers.

Examples:

- What is keeping us from selling more cars now?

- How many units do we want to average one year from now?

- Which managers can I really count on?

- How much longer can we go at this rate?

- Which salespeople can I count on to produce? How many units can they sell for sure?

- Who really isn't on board with me right now?

When I'm stuck on something, I just start asking every question I can think of on that problem. Don't worry about the solutions at this point, we'll figure those out later. Just focus on the questions that come up as you start thinking about your situation and what you want to happen.

2. Set Your Goals

- *87% of the people do not set goals.*
- *10% of the people set goals, but not correctly.*
- *3% of the people set – and reach their goals.*
- *94% of written goals are achieved.*

Your visions aren't always crystal clear. They're more like that day dream of taking a cross country trip to go fishing with your family. You see yourself cruising down those winding back roads with the top down, the wind in your hair, listening to your favorite music. You stop, see the sights, you can smell the homemade apple pie from that cute little diner on the corner and you see yourself pulling into the perfect camp site right next to the stream on a beautiful day, ready to fish and relax.

That's the vision – real life is usually not so rosy. When you finally hit the road, you don't get the wind in your hair because you're driving a mini-van with 3 kids and the dog and they all want the air on. You can't hear your favorite song, because they're watching Princess Bride for the 9th time. Those stops end up being at the rest stops and are a lot more frequent, because you can't get everybody to cooperate at the same time. That homemade apple pie ends up coming from the Golden Arches and when you finally get to that peaceful stream, you can't even see it, because all the other families got there before you did because you stopped so many times – and it's raining.

The end result is what matters most and you accomplished that. Just realize most visions / goals / planning / execution don't usually go quite as planned. *That's why most people who try to reach a goal, give up.* ... "I tried" is a common phrase from people who lacked a total commitment. *To set and reach your goals...*

- Your goals have to be realistic and achievable.
- Your goals have to be written.
- You have to sell your goals to the other people who will have to be involved in accomplishing them.
- You have to take personal ownership of the goal.
- Your goals have to be reviewed daily.

  Tip: Along with your goals, write this on a card and read it a lot...

  If it is to be – it's up to me!

You'd normally start with a one-year goal.

Find your current average (100 units), multiply by 12 to forecast what you're on track to sell this year (1,200) ... add 40% for growth, so in the next 12 months your goal would be 1,680 units.

In class, we spend an hour plus on how to set and reach your long term goals. In tough times when dealerships are just trying to survive, it's harder to think about a one year goal if you're just trying to figure out how to keep the doors open another month.

If you're selling 100 units, averaging only $1,500 per unit (instead of the $2,500 we've been using) and are losing $50,000 per month, I agree, you have to act fast. So if you're just 'hanging in there' right now, let's look at the short term fix.

(The fix is faster if you'll get to our Dealer / Manager Team Leadership class with your GM and your other managers.)

Statistically, if you, your managers and salespeople come to class, you can *buy* your way out of the problem and become profitable within 30-45 days. That's about a $20,000 investment, but the results will happen fast – like taking a bullet train instead of a stage coach.

Of course we sell training, that's our business. But when all of this stuff in the market hit, we did exactly what you've done so far. We cut every expense possible and we laid off some of our staff.

We already trained every day, but when things got tighter, we really hunkered down and started training and cross training our 45 employees even more, *every day*. The *extra training* started months ago, and we're still training more every day, than at any time in the past.

Skills and attitude are our most critical tools in sales. You and your salespeople can all have a 'gung ho' attitude and you can all work bell-to-bell until you can't see straight. But if you all don't have the tools and skills you need, working longer and working harder will just wear you down physically and mentally – which puts you at even more risk of slipping further.

You <u>cannot</u> just *work* your way through tough times. If you just focus on *work*, even if it helped today, within weeks or months, at best, everyone is so worn down you lose even more production and you fall back further than where you were before.

Urgent Planning...

If you're selling 100 units with $150,000 in gross profit, and losing $50,000 every month ... you have to act fast. Question: How much longer can you keep going with your current loss? ___ months.

Let's assume you just wrote in <u>3</u> months. That means we have to turn everything around 3 months from now. If you're losing $50,000 per month, we actually have to figure out how to generate about $80,000 more in Gross Profit per month. Why? Because even if you don't spend any more on advertising, you'll still have about 40% going out in sales and management compensation.

So at $1,500 per unit, we have to generate 53 extra units per month, or raise the gross $800 per unit on 100 units, or a combination of both. In real life, if this is your dealership, you can't afford to 'buy' enough sales through advertising and you can't work people long enough and hard enough to get you there – so if we're being realistic, *training* and daily *sales activity* management are your only hope.

Great news...

There are several ways to generate more units and more gross. Let's look at them, in order of *your fastest returns...*

1) The Basics ... If you train your salespeople on the Basics, stop selling price and start selling cars, you can quickly increase units 20%–30%, and gross 30%–50%, too, especially if it's only $1,500 now. And you can do both almost immediately because when you improve in the Basics, you sell more units *because you're building more value.* When you build more value, people also pay you more.

Minimum Results: 20 more units + $500 more gross:

Now..............100 units x $1,500 = $150,000 ($50,000 loss)

In 30 days ....120 units x $2,000 = $240,000 (= $5K to $10K profit)

2) Unsold Follow Up ... If you're not doing much follow up now and if you only hit the statistical average, you will also pick up an extra 30 or 40 units and another $45,000 to $60,000.

(Combine 1 & 2 and you're very profitable, almost overnight.)

You can do this – you can eliminate your losses quickly and get back on track and making money right away.

3.   Write Your Plans

> *A goal without a written plan*
> *is just another highball.*

Example...

Goal: Improve units from a rolling 90 day average of 100 units per month today, to 120 units three months from now. You hit 120 in the last example, now you need to *average* 120.

Your Plan: Train your management on 'how to', and then...

- Establish effective processes and procedures
- Replace any dead weight and hire the right people
- Train your staff on a daily basis
- Track all opportunities, activities and results
- From tracking, set clear training and performance goals
- Keep the team motivated and excited
- Become Leaders, so you can recover and grow

Focus training, coaching and spiffs on the Basics and Closing

- Teach salespeople how to avoid price to build value
- Teach them to ask questions to control the sale
- 75% demos in 90 days, 65% in 60 days, 60% next month
- Managers touch the customer *early* on every deal
- Teach salespeople to start closing at the Landmark
- Create a 'Sold Line' for the Sold Line Close
- Teach salespeople how to use 12 Action Closes
- Practice a 'Silent Walk-Around' of their trade-in
- Get a final commitment without talking price
- Start the paperwork correctly and complete it all
- Desk starts the negotiation with the 1st Pass
- 2nd Pass for Gross and 3rd to Wrap It Up

When you track everything accurately, figuring out your training needs is easy. Then just bullet point your plans like I did (above) and start training.

4. Assemble Your Team

On every team, you have players and coaches.

In a few pages we'll get into training and coaching your team to reach your goals to recover and grow. From the chapters on problem employees and those that just aren't cutting it, you understand that you probably have some people who just can't be on your team if you have any hopes of recovering or growing.

You need *teamwork* ... so what's the definition of teamwork?

"Everybody working together toward a common goal."

That's the standard answer everybody comes up with in class. So to clarify; does everybody mean *some, most* or *all* of your people? Does working together mean everyone *cooperating* and everyone pitching in equally? Does a common goal mean they *have to know exactly what they're working to achieve?* Yes, of course.

The catch: Even if everyone in your dealership is a *team* player, it still won't work, unless the team has a *goal* and every person on the team is *qualified and has the ability to do their job effectively.*

Question: We all know you've been kind of lax when it comes to hiring *qualified* salespeople. Assume you're coaching a baseball team, you have a big game coming up soon, and you need a few more players. Instead of recruiting the right players, if you settle for a couple of laid off basketball players, a tennis player with a bum knee and one guy who really likes baseball, but has never played before, how far can you realistically expect to get in your big game coming up?

I suppose it's great you gave your cousin, the van driver and the kid at the hardware store a job in sales. But you won't get any farther in your recovery with the wrong players on your sales team than you would in that baseball game – and you may not even survive if you don't develop your managers and salespeople quickly.

Based on the definition, do you have teamwork?   ❏ Yes ❏ No

Do you have all of the right players on your team?   ❏ Yes ❏ No

Business decisions are tough – especially in tough times. This is serious, though – so get the right team together so you can win!

5. Track Every Opportunity – Every Activity – Every Result

You know the benefits, so stop defending why you don't do it, and just start tracking everything that happens. If you will, you can start improving your production in almost every area, just by targeting your training and efforts on your 'obvious' problems.

Tracking is more than knowing how many 'Ups' were on the lot, how many sales you made and how much gross hit the books. *Remember the 5 types of customers we covered?* The walk-in prospect closes at about 10%, while the repeat customer is seven (7) times easier to close ... and generates 40% more gross per unit.

Do you remember the advantage we talked about of knowing exactly how many of your 100 units each month come from walk-in traffic, versus the repeat, referral, outside prospects and even your own Service customers who buy each month? Exactly, so come up with a goal and a plan to increase your easiest and most profitable sales.

No doubt sales have dropped the last few months, but once sales have settled, the amount of walk-in and 'other' sales you generate will be somewhat consistent every month, based on the market.

You need extra sales and it's impractical to increase advertising enough to bring in extra traffic. So instead, set a clear daily *prospecting* goal, teach your salespeople to prospect and then manage and <u>track</u> their daily activities to make sure they're doing their prospecting. With just a small number of *extra daily contacts per salesperson*, you can easily *generate 10 extra sales* – that are not from walk-in traffic.

From your prospecting and follow up efforts...

Sell 10 *extra* units to repeat, referrals, etc. (only 2.25 per week)

x <u>$3,500</u> gross ($2,500 + 40% more because they're repeat, referrals or outside prospects who 'like' you)

= $35,000 additional gross profit (with 60% to net)

Again, the 70 sales to walk-ins and your 30 to 'other' customers will stay pretty consistent, *and with these new sales you're at 110*. Now just keep focusing on building your repeat, referral and prospecting sales and keep adding 5 or 10 *extra* units per month, and in six months you'll be up to 130 – 150 units with an extra $100,000 – $150,000 in gross per month.

Bonus: Save 50% on advertising! Track your *sources* accurately, target your ads and cut 50% from your 'walk-in' advertising budget.

6. Initial Training On 'Core' Selling and Management Skills

*Everyone needs their basic education on how to do their
job properly. You have to stop stalling – they need it <u>today</u>.*

You just can't get this initial training in your dealership and it would
take you months or years to create it yourself. That doesn't make sense
either, because you have hard working salespeople and managers with
great intentions, *who don't even know what they don't know.* Worse,
they're never going to learn it just going to work everyday – they can't.

We'll teach your managers and salespeople more in our two 2-day core
skills classes than good, hard working 20-year veteran dealers and
managers tell us they've learned anywhere else in their entire 20 years.

*No other training is as important as these two courses and
no other company offers these <u>complete</u> courses.*

1) Leadership: Dealers and managers weren't taught how to manage
salespeople to increase production. When the dealer and managers attend our Team Leadership course together, you'll develop the
core skills you need in management to increase sales a minimum of
20% within 30 days. If everyone on your staff is totally committed
to growth – a 50% to 100% increase in units and gross is a realistic
6-month goal. *Using a realistic 20% improvement in a 100 unit store...*
*2 days of your time and a one-time $5,000 - $7,000 investment,
will get you a 20% improvement, and that's about $110,000 <u>per month</u>.*

2) Sales: You're losing sales daily. Salespeople and managers are only
closing 20% of the 78% who will buy within a week. *Statistically,
that means you're losing about 1 sale per salesperson daily.* They just
haven't developed the core selling, closing and objection handling
skills it takes to sell most of the people, especially today.

If you develop your leadership and management skills and then if you
make a total commitment to train your managers and salespeople on
these core selling skills, you can expect another 20% improvement within
weeks. Total commitment is the key, and there just isn't any more time
for half-hearted efforts or token training.

*2 days of your time and a one-time $15,000 - $20,000 investment, will
get you <u>another</u> 20% improvement for another $100,000 or so <u>per month</u>.
Then you keep it all going with continuing education daily on JVTN® and by
your managers doing their daily training, coaching and management.*

7. Train Your Managers And Salespeople Daily

To Grow: Every shift – every day – has to start with training.

Steps to effective <u>daily</u> training in your dealership:

• *Training* ... Go through the online training chapter on JVTN®, or if you've created your own internal training, go through that.

• *Testing* ... After each training chapter, we have a *quiz*. If you do your own internal training, create your own quizzes.

• *Role Play* ... After testing, it's *Virtual Role Playing* to make sure they practice on a Virtual prospect instead of on your expensive, tough to find prospects. No JVTN® ... create your own role plays.

• *Practice – Drill – Rehearse* ... After testing and initial role play, we have several Online *Power Drills*.

If you aren't on JVTN®, just jot down a few thousand quiz questions like we did. Then go around the room and use the questions at random in *fast practice* sessions to develop skills and timing.

How long should a training meeting last? Not less than 20 minutes, not more than an hour. 50%–75% of the time should be spent in practice.

Note: Sales meetings *are not training meetings.* Talk about 'stuff' or 'grind' them in a different meeting. Training meetings are to teach your salespeople *how to* do something and to *practice* what they've learned, so they're *prepared* to talk to a prospect and make a sale.

Who should hold training in the dealership? Every manager should be involved in the training. If that doesn't happen, you'll never develop the skills or the teamwork you need to realize your full potential.

How often should you hold training daily? We kid about this with the question, but the answer isn't as simple as it seems.

One of the biggest problems we fix when managers come to our Train the Trainer workshop is that we teach them how to *slow down* training. We shake our heads in disbelief when a dealership on JVTN® tells us, "We've watched everything, what's new?"

Trust me, power-watching 300 or 400 videos as fast as you can has nothing to do with training people. It's train, test, practice, drill and rehearse to develop the skill.

216

Recovery and Growth

Here's an example of an *ineffective* one week training schedule on the first four steps of the Basics:

MON ..... Look, act, sound like a pro to make a good first impression

TUE ...... How to greet the prospect with an open end question and immediately gain control with an either / or question

WED ..... Bypassing Price on the lot

THU ...... Asking Open End questions to build rapport

FRI .... Asking Either / Or questions to Investigate

That seems like a good schedule, why isn't it effective? Two reasons...

1) That's way too much to cover if you're trying to develop skills. Learning to *effectively* use Open End, Either / Or and Yes Questions is a minimum of 2 weeks, especially if you only training 30-45 minutes per day. Add in 1st impression, greeting, bypassing price, rapport and investigating, and you have a full 4 to 6 week training outline.

It's all we can do to squeeze the outline above plus presenting, demonstrating, closing and handling objections into 16 hours of training *and a couple hours of homework,* in our 2-day course. Of those 16 hours, we spend 5 to 6 hours practicing what we've taught them.

Speed kills selling – speed also kills training – so slow down.

2) With a typical split schedule and normal days off, if you hold that 5-day training outlined above every morning at 8AM, *at best* a salesperson may hit two of the classes each week.

Why? Pull out your schedule and you'll see the problem. The salesperson on Monday morning is off Tuesday, in late Wednesday, in early Thursday and late Friday. So he or she only catches two 8AM training sessions that week; make a good first impression and how to build rapport. They will miss everything else.

Solution A. Slow down, speed skills. If you're using JVTN®, just follow directions. For example, How To Sell More Cars Every Month is 23 chapters with 2+ hours of training. Done correctly, it's OK to require everyone to watch it all the way through in 2 or 3 days to grasp the concept quickly. But to develop skills, go back through it chapter by chapter for 4 to 6 weeks in your training. Practice, Drill, Rehearse!

Solution B. Hold two classes daily. 8AM for the 8 - 3 shift ... and 2PM for the 3 - 9 shift. Your morning shift is covering the floor for PM training.

Track attendance so every person goes through every class you hold.

Remember Why You Train

Spring was in the air and the annual wood chopping contest was the final event of the County Fair. The crowds gathered, the excitement grew as the two finalists were about to begin their match. One was the reigning champion, the hometown favorite who had won year after year. The other was a new guy in his first wood chopping contest. All of the odds were on the bigger, and more experienced champion.

The challenge was to see who could chop the most wood in one hour. Both men readied their axes, the starter fired the shot and the contest began. Trees fell, chips flew and wood was piling up.

About 20 minutes into the contest the new guy asked the champ if it would be OK for him to take a short break. The champion laughed and was all for him taking a 'time out', thinking 'what an idiot', while he just kept chopping and chopping.

After another 20 minutes or so, the new guy asked the champ if he'd mind if he took another short break. Again, completely sure of his win, the reigning champ said, "Take as long as you want."

The one-minute warning came as both men chopped as fast as possible, the final bell rang and the champ held his axe high in the air with no doubt in his mind he'd won, especially with the new guy taking breaks throughout the contest.

The judges counted the wood, handed their scorecards to the ring master who grabbed the microphone and said, "Ladies and Gentlemen, the judges have reached a unanimous decision. The winner of the 44th annual wood chopping contest is … the new guy!"

The crowds quietly cheered as they looked on in amazement and the champion was shocked. As the announcer interviewed the new guy he asked, "I'm sure everyone in the audience and our 12-time champ has the same question. How in the world did you win, especially since you took two breaks?"

The new guy said …

"I wasn't actually taking a break, I was sharpening my axe."

8. Coach Your Salespeople

Does a tennis coach show you *how to* hold the racket and swing the way they said you should? Sure. How about golf, baseball, or soccer; does the coach show the players how to do it better?

Pinch yourself; you aren't their boss, you're their coach, and it's time to be a good one so your team can start winning more often.

Success comes from effective coaching. In our new 2-day classes for salespeople, we spend 5 to 6 hours in each course *practicing* what we teach. In the "How To Sell A Car And Close The Sale Today" class, we role play how to ask questions, bypass price, how to close the sale, and how to overcome objections. In our "How To Close and Negotiate" for salespeople and in our "Negotiating & Desking" workshops for managers, same thing – it's practice, practice and more practice.

In our 2-Day "Train the Trainer" workshop, it's almost all practice for the attendees because we're teaching managers to become trainers (coaches) back in the dealership. Most are surprised we aren't up front for 2 days telling them what to do. Our goal is to teach them to develop their salespeople's skills through effective coaching and sales training back in the dealership.

There are 3 stages to skill development...

- *Recognize* the information is valid and will work for you
- *Duplicate* the skill, technique or method
- *Master* that skill or method through continued practice

If you're using JVTN® for your daily training, classes should last at least 30 and preferably 45 minutes. Five minutes for you to explain what we'll be covering (FAB), 10 to 12 minutes for us to cover it online (*recognize*) and test them, 15 to 20 minutes of role playing and practice (*duplicating*) and 5 minutes to talk about what they learned and how they'll use it. Then more practice every day, to *master* the skill.

Tip: So you have more time to practice in your meetings, if you have JVTN®, assign the chapter 2 or 3 days *before* the meeting. Then you can do an around the room discussion on what salespeople got out of the virtual session for 5 or 10 minutes, and spend the rest of your meeting role playing the skill you want them to develop.

Great teams have great coaches. Just go for it, they really need you now!

9. Manage Their Daily Activities

You don't manage results – you manage activities.

One of the worst things we were all taught, or that we learned through experience, is that we're supposed to manage *sales*.

While the goal is more sales on the board each day, you can't manage *sales*, you can only manage the *activities* that create more sales.

We have the longest running online survey in the car business. It's been up for over 5 years and one of the questions for salespeople is, "How many hours do you actually work each day?" After thousands of responses, the answer is always the same as what we hear in all of our classes – about 3 hours of a 9 hour shift.

As a manager, most of us spend our days complaining about what salespeople *don't* or *won't* do, instead of tracking to find out what they should be doing. If we tracked, we'd spend our day training and coaching to make sure they *can* do it, then manage their daily activities to make sure *they are doing it.*

Until you manage their activities – what you see is all you get.

How long does a 5-minute prospecting call take? Exactly, about 5 minutes. So if salespeople are wasting 6 hours of a 9 hour shift each day, they have time to make five, 5-minute calls, right? (25 minutes.)

OK, so if you taught them to prospect correctly, role played with them so they were confident, and then *managed* their prospecting *activities* each day ... with 10 salespeople, they'd be making 50 extra calls per day, 250 per week and over 1,000 calls per month.

Is it safe to say that by training them and then managing that *activity*, that you'd sell some extra units from those 1,000 calls? Of course. Is there any extra cost involved? Not a penny.

Now take them to Service and teach them to prospect there, too. You have 500 people on the drive every month, 30% have a family member who'll trade in 90 days (150), so get them to meet a total of just 10 people each day in Service and they'll find 3 buyers there accidentally.

How about more demos, more follow up calls, more mail outs and more responses to web leads? All of those activities = more sales.

Our job as managers is to make our employees better than they would have ever been on their own. Take pride in that responsibility!

10. Plan This Month, This Week and Tomorrow

*Today you'll either be proactive, or reactive.
One helps you grow, the other just wears you down.*

You know how your job works; you come in early, you work through the fire drills all day, you're the last man (or woman) standing to lock up, and tomorrow you'll do it all over again.

The fire drills are just a part of business, but that doesn't mean you can't start controlling your day by planning your month, week and day, and then following your plan (or at least most of it, each day), so you start moving everything forward.

Goal setting and planning are critical, so come to class. This is important and there is too much I have to leave out in this book.

1) Identify your *results* goals for the month.

Example: Write out how many units or how much gross you want.

2) Break your monthly *results* goals down by week.

Take each monthly *results* goal, then break it down by week.

Example: You deliver 100 now – your unit goal this month is 120.

You know that if you get about the same floor traffic, and if you just keep giving the same number of presentations, demonstrations and write-ups you do now, you'll hit 100 (+ / – a couple) each month.

You want *20 extra units* this month though, so you need to generate an extra 5 units every week.

You normally sell 25 units from Monday through Saturday. This week, you want to add an extra 5 units. Don't call the paper to run another ad, that's a crap-shoot at best. Instead, use *activity goals* to generate 5 more units.

3) Set your daily *activity* goals to achieve your results goals.

Your *results* goal is 5 more units per week. You'll reach that goal by managing *sales activities*. So what activities can you manage?

• *Manage Your Appointments:*

Working backwards, we know when an appointment shows on the lot, it will close at about 50%, depending on the type of prospect.

That means...

    A. *To sell one unit*, we need *two appointments that show.*

    B. With a 60% show ratio, to get 2 appointments that will show, *we'll need to average 3.5 confirmed appointments each day.*

    C. If we want 5 extra sales this week, then the math says we need 17 confirmed appointments on the board (about 3 per day).

    Tip: Go for 20, just in case.

• *Or Manage Write Ups:* We'll assume you deliver 50% of your write ups. If you're selling 100 units now, then your salespeople are putting about 200 people on paper each month.

Two ways to sell more with write ups...

    A. To sell 5 more units each week, you'll need to see 10 more write ups per week.

    This one is easy to pull off ... just cheat. Start paying **BIG** write up spiffs in the $25 to $50 range. BUT – and this is a big but; *do not pay for the write ups you already get.*

    What do I mean? Back to 'tracking' ... if you track and know that Bill usually writes up 20 people to sell his 10 units, you'd be throwing away money if you just paid Bill $50 for *every* write up. If you paid for his *current* write ups, he'd make an extra $1,000 without doing anything different. You want *more.*

    Using his *current 90 day average,* pay Bill $50 for every write up *above* his current average. If he averages 20 now, at 22, he makes $100 bucks and if he writes 30, he'll make $500 in spiffs. The good news: if you have to pay him $500, you'll sell 5 more units, just from Bill writing up 10 more deals this month.

    Tip: Set very clear guidelines for what counts as a write up; commitment, down payment, completed forms, etc. *And don't let any manager make any exception.*

    Just by setting this rule, you'll sell more units right off the bat without spending any extra money, because they'll all start doing a better job with commitments and paperwork.

    B. Teach salespeople to stay off price, stop pre-qualifying, close at least 5 times and handle objections. *(Yes, we have that class, too.)*

11. Write your training plan for tomorrow.

Daily training, like goal setting, starts with a long term plan. If you're having a tough time right now, the 'Basics' is always the subject that offers the fastest return on your training time and money. What we cover in a two day class is a minimum of 30-45 days of training, if you're going to do it in the dealership.

Why so much longer when you do it?

Our 2-day classes are all 16 hours of class time plus 2 or 3 hours of homework at the end of day 1 and homework assignments for the next 90 days. If you train for 1 hour per day in the dealership, then it takes you 16 days to cover just the 16 hours we spend in class.

But, when you figure the schedule changes, days off, weekends, etc., to make sure *every salesperson* gets every training session, it'll easily take you 30 days and most likely 45 days, even if you're actually training for one full hour each time you hold the meeting.

Plus, skill development comes from practice (role playing). With the extra distractions in-house, if you aren't practicing twice as long as you're teaching in your meetings, you aren't developing their skills.

With JVTN®, planning your training is easier. There are dozens of complete training courses plus hundreds of individual topics. Four of the courses target the 'core skills' every salesperson needs right now in today's market. There are workbooks, quizzes and power drills to teach them *everything they need to say and do*, to sell more:

The "core four" courses on JVTN®...

1. *How To Sell More Cars Every Month*

   This course defines "Joe's New Basics" for converting more of your phone, internet and walk-in customers into deliveries.

   • Warm Up • Building Value • Closing The Sale

2. *Ask The Right Questions And Close More Sales*

   Clarifies 3 types of questions that control your success in sales.

3. *How To Handle "PRICE" in Every Situation*

   This course covers how to manage price and work with it correctly on the lot, when you're closing and when negotiating.

4. *Skills You Need To Sell A Car To Your Next Customer*

   This training course describes the other skills every salesperson needs today to sell more cars.

For a long term training plan...

Ideally, you want to plan your training out for a quarter, or at least a month. Pick one of those 4 courses and plan on spending a minimum of 4 weeks on it, so you're actually developing their skills. The training courses are listed in the order I'd recommend that you hold them.

But if phones are the problem, why the Basics first?

For a couple of reasons...

• Phone skills are just the same control, questioning, objection handling, bypassing price and closing skills salespeople use on the lot. The phone is just a tool they use – it's their 'core' skills that determine what will happen on the phone and whether the call ends with an appointment that shows. You close on an appointment on the phone with the same types of questions you use to close the sale on the lot.

To have good phone skills, you need good selling skills.

• Developing phone skills to put more people on the lot won't help that much if your salespeople don't follow the Basics, can't control the sale, skip steps, focus everything on price and don't know how to negotiate once they're there. First they need 'core' selling skills.

I can't tell you how many disappointed dealers have asked me, "I sent my guys to one of those phone training classes. They're putting people on the lot, but we aren't selling more units – why?"

Develop 'core' skills first, then phone skills are easy.

What about other things they need to know?

Let's say you're in the middle of one of our JVTN® courses on closing the sale, you pull up your tracking charts and realize 'demo ratios' have slipped and are way down. Logically that's costing you sales and you need a quick tune up on demos.

If you know you want to focus on 'demos', just use the *search* function in JVTN® to pull up all of the chapters in the system on 'demos' that you can use for a quick meeting, and take your pick.

Plan your training in advance, hold training daily, keep it interesting, informative, valuable, make it fun and have them practice everything you teach. You'll recover quickly, start making money, you'll eliminate turnover in your sales department and grow, year after year.

12. Hold Yourself Accountable

For over 200 pages, we've been talking about...

• Why sales have fallen (other than the market)
• The bad habits salespeople and managers have developed
• The types of training and the skills every person needs
• The vision, goals, planning and execution that has to happen
• The daily training, coaching and activity management required
  daily to get results quickly and maintain those results

Most important in everything we've covered, is to believe that you can do anything you want in sales, even in this market.

Even more important is to realize that if you don't personally step up to make it happen, it probably won't happen. If you can't make yourself do it, that's such a shame for you and all of the employees in your dealership who depend on you.

If you're the dealer, this starts with you and trickles down. Without the discipline and personal accountability to make sure your managers are properly trained and managed effectively (by you or the GM) and then to hold each of your managers accountable for production ... not much will change – it can't.

If you're the manager, same thing. If you don't have the discipline and personal accountability to train your salespeople properly, coach them in every area, manage their daily activities, and hold each of your salespeople accountable – again, nothing changes.

If you're a salesperson reading this – you're going to need that same discipline and personal accountability as well. Sorry, but saying, "My dealership doesn't train me," doesn't get you off the hook, either. This is your career and everyone would be very foolish to use that as a lifetime excuse for not developing your own skills and income.

Everyone just needs to remember that you can't wait for someone else to come along and save you, today or next year.

It sure helps if you have teamwork. But even then, you still need to assume your step in the process is the make it or break it step, so one more time; write this on a card, carry it with you and read it often...

If it is to be – it's up to me!

13. Get Out Of Their Way – Make It Easy For Them To Grow

We've had a booth at the NADA Annual Convention every year for the last 25+ years. Every year dozens of people who work for the various other vendors there come up to us to say "thanks" for teaching them so much about selling and managing people.

When we ask why they got out of the retail car business if we taught them so much – the answers are all the same...

I couldn't find a good dealership to work at.

We're still letting the brightest and the best slip through our fingers in sales and management with ineffective processes, procedures, not enough good training and just plain dumb stuff we do in dealerships.

When you have a good salesperson, instead of figuring out how to *control* everything they do – do the opposite and figure out how to let them grow. You put a *control* system in place to get average results from below average salespeople – not to develop winners.

When you have a race horse, you have to trust them a little and loosen the reins and let them *run at their speed*, instead of the speed of the (average) group. I said *loosen*, not drop the reins completely.

Almost everything that affects the sales department, in almost every dealership, is set up to run with average and below average salespeople. Almost none of the systems, processes, pay, scheduling or management styles are set up to develop high achievers, or to keep them.

Go back and read about that dealer who *eliminated the barriers* in his dealership so his 15-car guy could finally get to 40 units.

Can you imagine the true value of having 25, 35 and 40-car guys on your selling team? Here's one key point; if you had just those 3 salespeople, they'd sell the same 100 units that the 10 to 12 you have now are producing. You'd have all repeat business, no advertising, high gross, easier management and super customer loyalty.

Making these changes we've talked about in here are your first steps to developing your management staff and creating the environment to build that kind of winning sales team.

Almost all of us were taught to play defense, yet it's offense that runs with the ball and scores the points. You've been playing defense, now it's time to build a strong offensive team too. Hire them, train them, coach them, manage them – and you'll win BIG!

RECAP OF THIS SECTION

Recovery Step Two

1. I have a clear vision of where my dealership is headed. ❏ **True** ❏ **False**

2. I have set clear 1 year goals for sales and gross profit, broken each into 6 month, 3 month and next month goals. ❏ **True** ❏ **False**

3. I have taken each goal and written a clear plan of action on exactly what we have to do to hit each one. ❏ **True** ❏ **False**

4. I have assembled my team and "everybody is working together toward our common goal". ❏ **True** ❏ **False**

5. I have set up an effective tracking process in our dealership to track everything that was covered in this book. ❏ **True** ❏ **False**

6. I have sent *myself*, *every* manager and salesperson to their *core training classes* with JVG®, or we're signed up now to attend. ❏ **True** ❏ **False**

7. I have implemented *effective daily* training for salespeople *and* managers using JVTN® and will mandate usage. ❏ **True** ❏ **False**

8. I have implemented an effective *daily coaching* process with management to *coach* each salesperson daily. ❏ **True** ❏ **False**

9. I have implemented a *daily activity management process* so that our managers *manage* our salespeople's activities. ❏ **True** ❏ **False**

10. I have set my *results* and *activity* goals for this month, and have created clear plans for everyone to follow. ❏ **True** ❏ **False**

11. I have written, or my GM or GSM has written, a clear training plan for the month, and for tomorrow. ❏ **True** ❏ **False**

12. I realize I have to be responsible to make sure every manager and salesperson does their job *every day*. ❏ **True** ❏ **False**

13. All managers are meeting at least 3 times per week to cover our action plans, and we have listed and are eliminating everything that holds our salespeople back from improving and growing. ❏ **True** ❏ **False**

14. I realize that leadership means the dealer and all managers have to set the example on everything we implement. ❏ **True** ❏ **False**

   ❏ We will attend classes with SP   ❏ We will be first to practice

   ❏ We will be first to log onto JVTN® ❏ We will complete 8 chapters/wk

   ❏ We will look, act, sound like and become professional managers.

   Can't you just feel the positive control you can have – exciting, isn't it?

36

There Is One Other 'Real Important'
Thing You May Have Overlooked

Because we all spend so much more time at work than at home, your employees in your dealerships become your extended families. *At least that's true in small dealerships.*

But from the corporate office of a dealership group, it becomes far less personal because you don't know the receptionists, the techs or the porters in your dealerships, or even most of the salespeople and managers you depend on for your own success. In real life, too many people who work for your group are just names and numbers on that list some of you are looking at right now, to see who to cut next.

We're talking to dealers and dealer groups who say they don't need training because they've cut expenses to the bone, and are making money off of lower sales. Some have even told us they're making more money at half the number of units they were selling before.

But there's something real important you may have overlooked.

While the dealership may not need to sell more units or make money, your salespeople and managers do. Salespeople's income has been cut in half or more. They desperately need our training and your daily management so they can learn to sell these extra units. They need the money to feed their families, and pay the rent. The same is true for most managers. Even if the dealership is hitting home runs on profits right now, your employees aren't.

Recovery and Growth

What is our training worth to your employees?

Just look at the potential we've talked about. If your salespeople are on 25% commission, if you teach them how to pick up that $7.5 million, they'll earn almost $2 million more in commission this year.

If you didn't buy into the $7.5M in potential in your dealership, and cut it in half a couple of times, that's OK – the extra $2 million in gross will still mean every salesperson will earn $50,000 *more this year*. So if you or your dealerships don't need to sell more – do it for your employees.

But wait a minute. Isn't one of the primary goals in your dealership or group, to make more money? If you've cut expenses enough to make a profit off lower sales, if you pick up that $2M *per store*, you're talking millions and millions in additional net profit for your group.

Remember that 'good gross' we talked about? If you improve your sales by 20%, 30% or 40%, every extra dollar you bring in now is almost pure profit, and heads straight to the bottom line.

Those increases are just standard results with our training, but when we try to talk to CEOs, or dealers in groups to help them improve, we run into a wall with the standard *'we have our own in house training'*.

Creating your own training could be great if it's working, but...

If you'll take two minutes to do some basic math, you'll be shocked at the outcome. Just grab the report for this year that shows total retail sales, then divide that by the total retail salespeople you have.

You won't find a 10 or 12 unit average per salesperson per month like with salespeople we train. What you'll find is closer to the 5, 6 or 7 unit average per person that we're seeing in most of your dealerships today. The dealerships who embrace our training sell 50% more per salesperson than the salespeople in your dealerships are selling.

Worse, when a manager is hired into your group, who used us successfully at another dealership, they're told immediately they can only use your in-house training now and can't use our training to improve.

One General Manager managed to keep us under the radar and got us into a group store a couple of months ago.

Unfortunately, he had a record month and picked up an extra $100,000 in gross the first month we did our training in his dealership.

How could having a record month be unfortunate?

Because his extra hundred grand in gross rang the bells at corporate, and they wanted to know why the store had such a good month. When corporate found out he'd used our training to increase sales, they made the dealership stop the training immediately, *because corporate policy says 'no outside trainers'.*

Wow, you'd think in today's market, they'd want to do just the opposite and invest $1,000 in every dealership, so they could have a record month in every store. It's even more puzzling because their return on investment was $100 to $1. It's even more puzzling because his group has sold or closed stores, and made front page news for their losses this year.

*As a dealership, or dealer group, here are the
bottom line results you can expect with our training.*

1) 10% increase in units and gross with JVTN® only. When you install our Online Virtual Training in every dealership in your group, even though some dealers, managers or salespeople won't all use it correctly, your units and gross for the entire group will go up more than 10%.

That puts your cost at about *2% of your extra gross.* Even better, if you *mandated* my recommendations for minimum usage on JVTN® like you guys mandate everything else – you will double your improvement to 20%. Mandating usage by managers and salespeople drops the cost to just 1%, because we don't charge you more for your extra sales.

Which is better: 30% or 1% in expense to buy another sale?

Right now, just in direct advertising and direct marketing expenses, you're spending about 30% of your gross per unit to make a sale.

JVTN® will bring in those extra 10-20% more units and the extra gross for *only 1% to 2% of your additional gross profit.* Plus, we'll do something advertising can't – we'll cut your turnover *in half* almost overnight, which means even more profit hits the bottom line.

2) Want to double that 10% to 20% return to 20% to 40%?

Add our two initial training workshops for your managers and sales-people to your JVTN® training, and your return doubles. That means your total investment using our training effectively, will only cost *5% or so of the extra gross for the first couple of months during the initial training*, and then your costs drop back to 2% or 3% with JVTN®.

Recovery and Growth

Isn't profit and growth your responsibility to investors?

As a private or public dealer group, you have the responsibility to each of your investors and partners to protect their interests and to increase the value of their stock or other investments.

An individual dealer can blow off a guaranteed 10%-20% increase if he wants to for no reason, because it only affects him. But logically, blowing off that kind of growth can't be an option in a private or public group when your GMs, partners and stockholders are involved financially.

Please Note: There are fewer buyers to go around these days!

We hold 10 to 12 classes each month across North America. Other dealers, managers and salespeople in *your* market are attending them, and over *a million* training chapters will be taken on JVTN® this year.

You need to consider those numbers, because you're either attending our management and sales classes, and are online training with us every day – or – you're competing with the dealerships in your market who are increasing their market share as we speak.

Sell more units = higher stock value (fast)!

Add us as your training partner, and we'll take great pride in helping you move up that top 100 dealer group list year after year. Not only will our training and your sales improvements raise your value faster than anything else you do, our training will develop more teamwork in your group than anything you've ever done – and did I mention *you will just about double your net profit overnight?*

We've been the number one training company in this business for over 25 years for one reason – we get results by teaching your salespeople and managers a proven, repeatable process that will improve your units, gross and profit immediately. That's why half of the top 500 dealers, and half of the top 100 internet dealers rely on our sales, management and leadership training as one of their critical steps to growth.

If *you* want to earn more in today's market, *keep passing your input on our training up the line until you get the attention from corporate.* It's important to *you*, because whether you're the CEO, a partner, stockholder, GM, manager or salesperson in one of your dealerships, *our training will improve your personal income*, without exception; and I'm pretty sure that's why we all go to work each day.

Call us today so we can help you increase the value of your corporation, and help you sell more units, have more fun and make more money!

37

CONSISTENCY

Your Next Step
Is Critical

"From 45 to 70 In One Month!"

"After attending Joe's 2-Day Management Workshop we came back rejuvenated, ready to motivate our sales staff and sell some cars.

We started getting more involved with our one on one's, tracking, goal setting, and utilizing JVTN® with each salesperson. We went from selling 45 units in March, to 70 in April '09!

This class was exactly what we needed and it's great to be reminded of these key aspects of sales and management that we so easily lose sight of, so Thanks, Joe!" JP Doiron, Sales Manager, Norden Autohaus (Audi / VW), Edmonton

---

About Joe Verde Training

I want to congratulate you for hanging in there in this tough market, and I also want to thank you for giving me the chance to help you reach your goals through the information in here.

We both know that if you apply the common sense things we've talked about, you can recover and grow. I'm sure you also realize by now that you can do it quickly, even in this market.

If you've hung in there and read this far, whether your goal is to survive these tough times or have your best year ever – by now you understand the importance of taking action, instead of just working long and hard and hoping for the best until things turn around.

One of the other most important things I hope you realize from this book is that consistency in everything you do is the deal breaker for growth in any market condition. If you're wishy washy on what you do, how you do it and how often you do it, good luck growing or sustaining any real level of success.

Grow → *Stabilize* → *Grow More* → *Stabilize* → *Grow More*

Growth is a step-by-step process. You work hard and grow, then you stabilize at your new level by being consistent in everything that got you there. Then you just repeat that process over and over again.

Logically, getting everyone trained initially and then daily is critical to recovery and growth. But it's the *consistency* of training with the dealer, all managers and all salespeople that pulls everything together.

Example...

Let's say you decide to only send your salespeople to our selling and negotiation classes. We'll teach them to stay off price, find hot buttons, build value and get a dozen firm 'non-price' commitments. Then we'll show them how to start every deal at the top with an easy 3-Pass, customer friendly negotiation process that will maximize gross on every deal with a value-based, budget-focused negotiation.

But if your managers didn't come to class, they're still selling and working deals the 'old' way. They treat selling as a numbers game; advertise big with low price specials to fill the lot, pre-qualify everyone fast, land them on a car, get a quick price commitment, peel 'em off the ceiling with the first pencil to set up the negotiation, and try to grind out a deal.

You now have two opposing philosophies, not the teamwork you need.

It's the same with everything you do...

• When you want a team of professionals in sales who deliver 15 to 20 units per person every month, you'll send them to class so we can teach them how to sell and how to get to that level. The catch: Your management staff also has to attend that same course or they won't even understand what salespeople at that level need to do each day.

For consistency in the process, your managers *also* have to attend the management course so they can learn how to hire, train, coach and then manage salespeople of that level, or they can't possibly staff the sales force properly, or keep salespeople at that level once we get them there.

• Once you get JVTN® into your dealership for training every day; because they're the coaches, managers also have to use the management training, and go through the sales modules, too, or they can't possibly coach your salespeople as they develop their new skills.

If you really want to recover or grow, your plan has to involve...

The Dealer – Every Manager – Every Salesperson

From the dealer's vision, to management's hiring and training, to a salesperson's presentation and closing, you must have consistency. That's why we're the highest rated training company in the car business.

Our training is consistent from top to bottom. We have the only complete training for every process, for every person, and for every responsibility in sales and management.

Even though that's true, here's a comment I hear too often from dealers and managers who don't use us, but think they understand our training. Last week, a 30 year veteran General Manager who had to be coerced and shackled (OK, not shackled) into attending our Dealer / Manager Leadership class, told me at the end of class...

"I've had your (training) stuff in my office for years and never looked at it even once. When somebody said, 'I see you use Joe Verde's training,' I always said, 'No way, I don't like it, somebody else left it here.'

But I am completely blown away by your class – it is nothing close to what I thought. We're doing so many things wrong and have so much potential – we're the dealership sitting on that gold mine you talk about, and I wish I had come to class years ago." Lexus GM

I hear that way too often after class about our training. This GM wasn't even sure why, but he just didn't think he'd like our training.

The focus of our training...

Our focus is on *education* and common sense processes to sell more units and maximize the gross profit on every unit you deliver.

• *If you have a team / team leader system,* or if your process is to have salespeople take a number for the next 'up' ... our training will not interfere with your program.

When you send your salespeople to our classes, we'll simply teach them what to say and what to do with your next prospect, *so you can deliver more units at higher gross profits.*

We'll also teach your managers how to hire, train, coach and manage more effectively within your system – no matter what system you use.

• *If you have a straight sell system, or if you're a high-line store,* that's fine, too. Even the wealthiest people *(especially the wealthiest people!)* want to deal with a salesperson who not only knows the product, but who understands how to sell on a professional level.

We know 'pros' always like working with other pros.

• *Used car lots / buy here – pay here* ... Of course there's a difference between the person you're selling an $80,000 new vehicle to for cash and someone who can barely afford a $2,000 used car on credit.

The core principles don't change, though.

We had a sales manager from Fletcher Jones Mercedes–Benz in one of our Team Leadership Workshops in Orange County who was sitting next to a manager from the smallest used car lot in Los Angeles. Training, coaching and managing people isn't about the product you sell or the size of your dealership. It's about training, coaching and managing your people.

• *RVs, Motorcycles, Motorsports, Marine, Mobility, etc.* ... Same thing. The steps of selling don't change whether you're talking to a potential RV buyer, or talking to someone about a new boat, motorsport or motorcycle.

Training, coaching and managing a boat, motorcycle or RV salesperson and their day is not much different than managing someone who sells cars.

Top 500 Dealers | Top 100 Internet Dealers

We work with half of the Top 500 dealers in the US, some of the largest dealer groups in North America and over half of the top 100 internet dealers. Having said that, we also work with another 3,500 or so dealers every year of every size and type of product.

Best Practices in sales and sales management would be the most accurate description of what we teach dealers, managers and salespeople.

You read my short story – I didn't learn how to sell my first five years in the car business and was stuck at 8 units per month all five years. Then I used the two years I had my accessory business to get my home schooling from about 100 books, tapes and seminars on how to sell, how to close sales, how to set goals, how to build a business and how to manage and lead people.

From everything I learned about selling in different industries (real estate and insurance), I found that regardless of what product they were selling, 93% of the information was the same. It was always the Basics, Closing, Objections, Follow Up, Prospecting, etc. on the sales side, and it was always Train, Coach, Manage and Lead on the management side. It just wasn't in 'car talk', so it was hard to figure out.

From what I learned, I developed my own best practices and processes in sales for automobile sales and applied my new skills when I got back into the car business. *In less than 7 months, I had sold more, and earned more than I had my first five years combined.*

When I started holding training classes in 1985, the processes I had developed became my course materials. The principles of buying and selling haven't changed in thousands of years, and won't be changing soon. The processes I developed then are virtually unchanged in our courses today, except for updates that reflect market changes.

While the core principles don't change – the internet's influence, the economy and customer's new concerns and objections do change, so we continually adapt and adjust our courses for today's changing market.

I just rewrote every sales course and added our new management course on negotiation and desking. All of our courses are the most relevant and most effective for selling and managing in today's market.

Recovery and Growth

How do we train?

In Live Workshops, In Your Dealership & Online

A. We hold workshops across the U.S. and Canada

Sales Workshops (For Dealers, Managers & Salespeople)

- How To Sell A Car And Close The Sale Today
- Closing And Negotiating With Today's Buyer
- Business Development Workshop
  (Phone & Internet Lead Management – Prospecting – Follow Up)

Management Workshops (For Dealers & All Managers)

- Team Leadership: Manage Salespeople To Double Your Net
- Desking Deals For Maximum Gross Profit
- Train The Trainer (Coaching, Training & One-On-Ones)

These are our 6 core workshops – they are packed with tons of information, extremely effective and affordable for every dealership.

B. Closed workshops, for larger dealerships or dealer groups.

We can bring our classes to you. You'll save time, travel expenses and we can spend extra time focusing on the situations *you* face to improve your unit sales, gross profit, retention and especially teamwork.

C. Custom training packages.

Whether you want a half-day or a five-year training plan, we can create a custom package just for your dealership or group to address your specific goals to improve your units, gross and retention.

D. In-Dealership Consulting, Coaching, Analysis

We'll do our homework first. When we come in, we'll meet with the dealer and the managers first, then hold training to kick-start the program. We'll spend the rest of the time focused on targeted training and coaching in one-on-ones with management and salespeople and end with a needs analysis and completion report for the dealer.

→ **Train Now – Pay Later.** Did you know you can *train now and increase your sales and gross profit right away*, and pay monthly to even out your expenses? Call our Director of Sales for more information.

E. JVTN® Kick-Off Meetings

These are half-day meetings to kick off your new online training process in your dealership. We'll start with a dealer and then management meetings, followed by a full court press in a general meeting to get everyone up to speed on the power and benefits of using our Virtual Training Platform for every person, in every department.

Recommended: These can be extended to a full day and can also be set up as quarterly coaching / consulting meetings specifically on improving usage and results. (The cost can be added to your monthly statement.)

F. The Joe Verde Virtual Training Network® ... JVTN®

We pioneered online training in this business and our Virtual Training Platform is the glue that holds all of your training *and* management efforts together, and helps you see the continuous improvements, month after month, that we've talked about.

No matter what position you hold at the dealership, our live class-room instruction is always best for your *initial training*. The secret to exceptional results using our system is for the Dealer and GM to attend our Dealer / Manager Team Leadership Workshop right away.

In this workshop we cover the critical information most dealers and managers never got on "Sales Management" that will help to grow your dealership and improve your sales process in today's changing market.

After that, our online training modules are your *continuing education* and your most important skill development resource.

Can you just use Virtual Training instead of live classes?

Yes – but! Nothing can ever replace the intensive back and forth interaction in our live workshops with our trainers, *but having said that* we have a ton of dealerships who are knocking 'em dead in this market with only JVTN®.

What's on the Joe Verde Virtual Training Network®?

This is such a huge question because there are so many sales training modules and so many *other* features in our system that make training and managing your salespeople more effective. Plus, everything about JVTN® can also be customized for any type of dealer group.

JVTN® Online Training and Platform Features

JVTN® Online Training...

• 30+ courses and always growing, with workbooks & leader's guides.

• 250+ quick & easy sales meetings 'on demand'.

• Departments: Primary ... Sales & Sales Management
Plus ... Service & Finance

JVTN® Feature Highlights...

Testing.....Every training chapter has a fairly easy quiz to reinforce what your salespeople have learned.

Certification.....Available on all major courses. 50 to 100 in depth questions to make sure your salespeople paid attention and understand the skills or processes.

Reporting.....Accountability: Management can view the course and score for every chapter that every person takes.

Tracking.....The tracking you need to target the specific skills and activities that the group, and / or each individual salesperson needs to improve.

Practice.....Virtual role-play sessions to beef up retention.

Power Drills.....Timed, power practice sessions.

Watch Dog.....Assign the # of chapters you want users to train on each week, and the system will notify you by text message or email if your goal isn't met.

File Vault.....Add your dealership forms, policies and procedures here, and print on demand.

Video Vault.....Create short company videos for company policies, goals, monthly meetings, etc.

Dealer Groups....With Super Access you can pull live training reports for any dealership or team to help you keep your training 'activities' in line with your goals.

~~The End~~

This is not the end – it's just the opposite.
It's the beginning of your new life in this business as a
Management Driven Dealership!

Congratulations on your decision to take
the bull by the horns and turn the worst market
in decades into your best years ever.

Have a great year!

Manufacturers...

To state the obvious...
You need to sell more units!

What would a 20% – 30% increase in sales
today mean to your company right now?

I know a ton of you guys from meeting you over the years, and you do a lot of great things – but some of you have the habit of being so focused on product and marketing, that you miss the obvious: *your dealers and their salespeople need to learn how to SELL more units.*

You spend $5,000 to $10,000 per vehicle (billions) generating traffic and making sales easier for your dealers. But your prospects are leaving empty-handed, because the final outcome of all of your money and efforts is left up to the *only point of contact* your prospect will meet at the dealership – *and that's most often a below average salesperson.*

That means the average untrained salesperson in your dealerships, *not your lack of the perfect product for the times,* is killing your unit sales, profits – and your stock value, when you can least afford it.

Why is it you'll spend $10,000 to market and incentivize a vehicle to put a prospect on the lot to buy it – but don't spend $30 to $40 per vehicle *so we can teach those managers and salespeople to sell it* to your next prospect – and to improve your sales 20% to 30%?

It's time for you to get involved. Your dealers do want to sell more, but in real life, not enough of them will pull the trigger on training *on their own at the same time,* to get you those extra units you need *today.*

Do what most dealers do – steal the $40 bucks from the $10,000 per unit you're spending now. You'll still have $9,960 to blow on stuff that can't possibly improve sales 20%-30%, like a well trained sales and management team can do overnight.

Let's get special classes set up around the country for your dealers, managers and salespeople right away, and get all of your dealerships online with JVTN® for their daily training. If you'll do this, we'll put you back on track overnight with a 20% - 30% increase in retail units.

I'd wish you luck, but if you use us – you won't need it.

Bring A Special
Joe Verde Training Program To Your Next
Dealer Group – 20 Group – ADA – Industry Conference*

Dealers of every size, with every product line, lose sales every day.

You and I know your dealers well, though – and we know most of them won't take that critical first step on their own to attend a course like this to learn the common sense solutions to selling more units and making more money.

That means they need your help...

If you believe the message in this book can help your dealers, now you can bring Joe or one of our trainers right to your next meeting and we'll present a special training session...

"How To Have Your Best Year Ever"

This information is so critical for every dealership today, that we would encourage you to have your dealers bring their General Managers to this meeting, too. This will be the hardest hitting, most in-depth look at their salespeople, their management staff and the critical mistakes they're making in today's market that hold them back from greater success.

This will be the most talked about and most beneficial meeting you've ever attended. Even more important, your dealers will start seeing immediate improvements as they begin implementing the dozens of solutions we'll give them in this special session.

Speaking dates are very limited, so call us today to schedule for your next event.

Call NOW 1-888-835-5187 • 1-949-489-3780

* Special offers are subject to change at any time, without notice.

New Dealer & Manager Training Course

Free 30 Day Access To This Online Course*

"Fast Start To Recovery & Growth"

To complement this book, I've taped a complete dealer and management online training course with 24 chapters on recovery and growth. This book and the online course will make great management meetings to pull your team together, so you can quickly get everyone on the same page and headed in the same direction, toward the same goal.

*I want you, and any dealer you know, to have a copy of this book and access to the online course for 30 days at no charge for two reasons...**

1) We have grown since 1985 to become the largest and most recommended automotive training company in the business. In our years of service to this industry, we've met at least half a million dealers, managers and salespeople, and that means it's very likely that we've met you, too.

   We've grown every year because of the contacts, friendships, referrals and training partnerships we've developed with so many of you who are reading this now. So please accept a free book and utilize this online training course to help you and your dealership grow, as our 'thank you' for helping us grow.*

2) Of course we also hope to pick up new business, and I hope this will be the foundation for a long-term relationship down the road.

You'll certainly improve faster with our workshops and JVTN®, but even if you choose not to train now – you will definitely increase sales and profits from the information in this online course.

* There is no catch to this offer, so set up your management meetings, and let's get you on track selling more cars, having more fun and making more money. Go to JoeVerde.com/RG to get a free book. Log in to JoeVerde.com/RGvideo for your password to access this free online course.

Everyone here at our company wishes you our best in the coming months and years. Please call us if we can help you in any way.

* Free Access to this online course is for a limited time only.

$7,171,988 Million Reasons Why You Should Train On JVTN®

$7,171,988 is the realistic *improvement potential* I covered in my book, "Top 7 Revenue & Profit Sources In Your Dealership" that *a 100 unit dealership has available to them, right now, today.* Lack of traffic never has been the problem, and buying more traffic isn't the solution to making more sales. Your managers and salespeople just need more of the selling skills we teach in class and on Joe Verde's Training Network® (JVTN®).

Follow my directions in setting up and using JVTN® as your daily training source, and you'll be shocked at the differences from day one.

Selling more and increasing your gross profit will be immediate, and you'll win hands down against the competition, year after year.

Selling More Requires Better Skills & Processes

We aren't the razzle-dazzle guys and we don't do sound-bites in our workshops or online.

We clearly explain critical processes you need, like: Selling, closing, negotiating, follow up, handling calls & leads, and a dozen+ others. Then we teach and help your salespeople and managers develop the skills it takes to master each specific process.

Accountability ... Testing • Reporting • Certification

All of our online courses include workbooks you can download, quizzes for every chapter, a Leader's Guide for your managers to follow and a final course Certification Test.

JVTN® gives you 'live' reports on every chapter (% in progress, pass / fail) for each salesperson, team, or by dealership for dealer groups. Access your reports anytime, from any location.

"I've made sure JVTN® has your back in every critical area to guarantee your success with our training. Start today and see results tomorrow."

Start Training Now – Call Today (888) 835-5187

JOE VERDE WORKSHOPS

"From green pea to dealer with your training."

"I was lucky to start selling in a dealership that believed in the value of training. They sent me to a Joe Verde Sales Workshop, and it gave me the tools to succeed...I attended more workshops to keep me on track and to further my professional skills. In 2014, after getting my 2nd location as a dealer, I looked back at those goals and I had achieved them all...Thanks Joe, for giving me the tools to accomplish all of my dreams."

– Joey Prevost, Dealer
MacCarthy Motors Terrace, Ltd., B.C.

"I went from 7.5 units to 21 units!"

"Last year I sold 88 cars and averaged about 7.5 units. In your class, I learned how to slow down the sale, be a better listener and ask the right questions to build more value.

The Results: 2 months ago I sold 13 units and last month I was the Top Salesperson with 21 units and great gross!"

– Paul Poltz, Salesperson
Goss Dodge Chrysler, VT

SALES WORKSHOPS

- **How To Sell A Car & Close The Sale For All Salespeople & Managers**
  Only send people to this class you want to improve 20-30% overnight

- **How To Negotiate & Close For More Gross Profit For Salespeople**
  Advanced Closing, Objection and Negotiation skills for everyone

- **Turn Your Leads Into Appointments That Show For Sales & BDC Staff**
  See how to turn your phone and internet leads into deliveries now

MANAGEMENT WORKSHOPS

- **Team Leadership For Dealers & All Managers**
  The critical class managers never got on "Retail Sales Management"

- **Negotiating & Desking For All Managers Who Work Deals**
  Develop a "1-Price" Mentality – STICKER... See how it's done in this class

- **Train The "Sales" Trainer At Your Dealership – For Managers Only**
  You know that when you train, everyone improves. Get to class and see how easy it is!

Get to class now so you can double sales and increase your profit!

For More Info • Call Now (888) 835-5187

Beware of the imposter who will
walk into your dealership and promise they
can teach you everything I've just covered.

Don't waste your time or money.
If they could, they would have written this book.